By The Same Author

*Grand Openings Can Be Murder*

*70% Dark Intentions*

*Out of Temper*

*A Shot in the 80 Percent Dark*

*Free Chocolate*

*Pure Chocolate*

*Fake Chocolate*

*Story Like a Journalist*

*There Are Herbs in My Chocolate*

AMBER ROYER

# *A STUDY IN CHOCOLATE*

GOLDEN TIP
PRESS

GOLDEN TIP PRESS

A Golden Tip Press paperback original 2023



Cover by Jon Bravo

Distributed in the United States by Ingram, Tennessee



ISBN 978-1-952854-16-3

Ebook ISBN 978-1-952854-17-0

Printed in the United States of America

In memory of Yuki, the sweetest bunny and the model for Knightley in these books.

# Chapter One
## *Saturday*

"This house has always creeped me out," my best friend Autumn says as she takes the key out of the ignition of her car. She unbuckles her seatbelt. "I don't know how you talked me into coming here."

I understand the creep factor. The house we're parked outside of sometimes gets called the murder house – though the murder was about a hundred years in the past. It's perfectly fine now. I've toured it. There's no bloodstains or anything.

I tell Autumn, "You felt bad for me. I had to take a plus one on the super-mysterious afternoon tea invite. And assuming this is a networking opportunity – which is what it seems – you didn't want to see me roll up in front of this place in my catering van."

The catering van is my only mode of transportation. I had bought it with a good chunk of my settlement money, after my late husband's accident. It had been the beginning of a new dream, opening my own bean to bar craft chocolate company on the island where I'd grown up. I haven't done a lot of actual catering gigs yet, but the van comes in handy for festivals, transporting beans from storage to the shop and delivering large orders. As with any small business, I can't ignore viable networking even if it's in a weird location.

Autumn and I both turn our heads to look up at the massive house. Wobble House used to be on Galveston Island's historic homes tours, alongside Ashton Villa, Bishop's Palace, and Moody Mansion. But Wobble House had recently changed hands and had been abruptly shut for tours. I'm friends with a real estate agent, and she just can't stop talking about the unusual terms of the deal. No one has been allowed to see the inside since. Or to meet the new occupant.

It was odd, getting invited to tea via a formal invitation card slipped into the shop's mailbox, with no postmark or host's name. I almost hadn't come.

I tell Autumn, "I'm nervous. I'm glad you've got my back here."

Autumn is already getting out of the car. I don't think she heard me. Autumn comes around to my side of the car as I get out.

We've both dressed up for the party. She's a little on the curvy side, and has chosen a dress that flatters, a maroon A-line tea-length one, with a matching maroon cloth band constraining her afro – and a matching manicure on her nails, which have been decorated with lines of tiny gold dots.

I'm wearing a black dress with a pattern of bright pink gerbera daisies swirled across the bottom. My brown hair is in a messy updo, which feels a bit like overkill now, but had seemed perfect for a fancy afternoon tea when I had been getting ready at my aunt's hotel. I have enough foundation on to cover the scattering of freckles that cross my paler cheeks.

Autumn and I are both wearing our "comfortable" heels. We had each bought identical pairs, after trying them on during a shopping trip to plan for Autumn's upcoming honeymoon.

I reach back into the car and pick up the neatly wrapped loaf of banana bread and the box of truffles that I'd brought along as a host – or hostess – gift. The invitation hadn't mentioned bringing anything, but I always hate to show up at parties empty handed. Call it Texas hospitality.

As we start walking up the sidewalk towards Wobble House, a screen door slams somewhere behind me. I turn, and there's an old white guy in a bathrobe and pajama pants standing on the porch of the much smaller Victorian-style house across the street. That's the way the historic part of Galveston looks – a hodgepodge of architectural styles and different sized houses jammed in together.

The guy sees me looking and waves us over.

I exchange glances with Autumn. She shrugs. I shrug. We can take a few minutes to talk to the guy. So we carefully head across the street.

He has only a fringe of gray hair, and what's there is sticking out at odd angles like he just woke up from a nap. He gestures at the murder house and asks, "You ladies know who bought that place?"

"Not exactly," I say. "But hopefully we're going to find out."

"If you do, then tell me." He shakes his head at the building and grimaces. "I've seen people coming and going over there, but only at night. I think something shady has been going on."

Autumn and I exchange another look. We don't know this guy, or what his perceptions are like. This could be a warning we should heed – or he could be completely over-reacting.

Autumn forces a smile. "Don't you just love historic homes? There's something about the architecture, the sense that there's something permanent in the world – despite the fact that, on this island, very little is permanent, with the weather and the waves."

The guy nods. "That's what I've always liked about them too. I used to be proud of living across the street from one of a handful of structures that made it through the 1900 hurricane."

"You struck me as a history guy," Autumn says. She reaches into her purse for a card. "Autumn Ellis. I sell historic jewelry pieces on Etsy."

"Silas Bere. Retired." Surprisingly, he produces a wallet from the pocket of his bath robe and hands Autumn a card of his own. The guy starts to say something else, but another car pulling up behind Autumn's distracts him. Silas says, "People have been showing up over there for the past hour."

Gently Drifting – a painter I had met when I'd taken a commission to make a massive chocolate sculpture from a local art museum – gets out of the driver's side of an old green Toyota SUV. Gently is actually his name – as well as an apt description of his attitude towards life. He has a strong jaw and strategically messy brown hair, along with a nose that looks like it may have been broken at least once. All of which counterpoint his timid personality. Today he's wearing a black turtleneck and gray slacks, though he's generally more of a jeans and band tee guy.

He immediately moves to the SUV's back door and removes a cloth cat carrier from the car. Which makes sense. Gently is never far from his emotional support cat, Ruffles. Gently's girlfriend Violet gets out of the other side of the SUV. Violet has short fluorescent pink hair, and she's wearing incongruous pearl drop earrings. Her delicate Asian features come from Korean and Japanese roots. She has on tons of eye liner, and hot pink shadow, but it is applied with a skilled hand and comes across as edgy and intense, rather than tacky.

They must be here for the party, since they're both dressed more formally than I've ever seen them. Violet's crimson dress even has long draped sleeves, covering the tree I know is tattooed on her forearm.

Gently spots us and waves.

"That seems to be our cue," I tell Silas.

We make our way off his porch and over to the artists.

I ask, "Did you two get an invitation to tea?"

Violet scrunches up her nose and says, "Gently got an invite. I'm his plus one."

Gently asks, "Do you know what any of this is supposed to be about?"

I glance over at Wobble House again. The architecture is somehow just slightly off, the massive gray stones and delicate pink trim a poor match for each other. The house itself has always been structurally sound. It just got reworked a few times too many before it became a historic landmark. A cloud goes by overhead, casting everything into shadow. The house suddenly looks ominous, rather than cheerfully wacky. But maybe that's just Silas's influence. What's really going on?

I say, "I guess we'll never know if we don't go inside."

So together, the four of us walk up the sidewalk, go through the wrought iron gate, and make our way up to the massive door. The door is closed, and there aren't signs welcoming us in.

Gently rings the bell, then recoils at the massive gong sound that echoes back at us. Startled, he clutches the cat carrier to his chest. There's a questioning meow from inside the cloth.

The door opens, and a dour-faced blonde woman enters the shop. She's dressed in a white button-up shirt and black skirt. She ticks mine and Gently's names off of a list, then points us toward a long hallway. I know from having taken the tour that at the end of the hallway is a massive room once used for dances. The woman gives us a painfully fake smile and says, "Please make your way to the ballroom."

As we start down the hall, Gently says, "A bunch of people, invited to a mysterious house, with formal staff and no sign of the host. Did you ever see the movie, *Clue*? I think it opened just like this."

"Don't say that," Autumn says. "Do you know how many murder investigations Felicity has been involved in?"

"Four," I say, before anyone else can comment, and again for emphasis, "Only four."

Autumn says, "*Only* four? People were calling you a murder magnet after two."

None of those investigations had been intentional. I am a craft chocolate maker. I can't help it if I keep winding up in the right place to solve murders.

"Maybe it's more like *Murder by Death*," Violet says, as she peers at the vintage patterned wallpaper and wainscotting.

"You know, the Peter Sellers movie? Nobody actually died in that one."

"Let's hope so," Gently says. "My therapist is getting tired of hearing about the murder I witnessed. It set me back by years."

I feel a pang of sympathy for the guy. His anxiety dates back before I met him. I never did find out what trauma he'd had to deal with, but it must have been awful to have left him with such serious anxiety issues. And seeing one of his friends killed two months ago couldn't have helped.

"I've never seen *Murder by Death*," I say. All three of the others look at me incredulously. I clear my throat and say, "What? Not all of us are old movie buffs. I read a lot, though. And I did see *Clue*. I like how they had all the different endings." I sound defensive, though I'm not exactly sure why. I know I tend to care too much about what people think. And Autumn is writing mysteries again – after a long hiatus from the literary world, working out issues of her own – so I guess I feel like I should have more interest in the things she obviously likes. Unable to completely stop talking, I say, "That scene from *Clue* is a little like the opening of Agatha Christie's *And Then There Were None*."

Autumn shudders. "Don't you think you've had enough Agatha Christie in your life?"

Autumn is referring to the copy of *Murder on the Orient Express* that I had won in a raffle on board a cruise ship a few months ago. Someone had tried to steal it out of my cabin – in the middle of my attempts to solve the murder of a writer that had happened shortly after the start of the cruise.

"What are you talking about?" Gently asks.

I say, "Nothing good seems to happen when I have an expensive book edition just handed to me. One of them has shown up sometimes during the course of each investigation I've gotten drawn into."

Violet tries to stifle a laugh. Then she says, "That's a bit superstitious, isn't it?"

I am not by nature a superstitious person. And I feel weird that my brain keeps trying to make that connection. "Okay, honestly, I know it has just been a coincidence."

"You probably just started looking for books as self-fulfilling clues," Violet points out.

"But better safe than sorry," Autumn says. "Let's just enjoy this party and leave the talk of mystery novels for some other time."

Gently says, "Aren't you writing mysteries again? Shouldn't you *want* to talk about it?"

Autumn sighs, "Yes, and I'll tell you all about it, when we're no longer in this weird house. Even when I toured it in high school, it made me uncomfortable."

"That's intentional, on the architect's part," Violet says. "There's design elements intentionally at play."

Before she can tell us what those design elements are, we reach the ballroom and all fall silent as a couple dozen people all turn to look at us. They're seated at round tables placed strategically around the room. We're twenty minutes early. I know it. So why does it feel like we are late?

A pale, skinny guy with shaggy dark hair stands up from one of the tables. He's in his late thirties and wearing a full suit with a purple tie. Mitch has a narrow nose and blue-gray eyes. His smile is awkward and gap-toothed, but in a charming way. "Come in," he says, with a soft British accent. "Join the party. I'm Mitch Eberhard. And I wanted to introduce myself to the community."

There aren't enough seats for all four of us to sit together. My friend Sonya, who owns a local yarn shop, is waving me over to her table, which has two spots. Autumn and I sit between her and a retired couple whose names are Ben and Pru. I know this because they come into the chocolate shop every Monday morning for a "day date" with a coffee and a craft chocolate treat. Pru is black, with a pouf of graying hair and she also has gapped teeth. She has several moles arching prettily across one cheek. Ben is a thin white guy with a ruddy complexion, and thick hair that has grayed to almost white. Pru's dress is green, with gold polka dots – and Ben is wearing a tie made of the same fabric. They're holding hands under the table, which is adorable.

Gently and Violet wind up at the same table as Mitch. They seem happy enough over there, engaging in conversation with our host, who seems a little dorky – not at all the mysterious or dangerous person the next-door neighbor had led us to expect.

Mitch says something to Gently, and Gently takes Ruffles out of his carrier and settles the cat on his lap, despite having to reach over the large black and white animal to reach the trays of chicken salad tea sandwiches in the middle of the table. Even from here, I can hear Ruffles' hopeful meow.

I stifle a laugh and take a sandwich from the tray on my own table. I take a bite. It is light, with pecans and grapes and a hint of lavender. It's hard to work with lavender. Too much, and the food you're flavoring starts to taste like soap. But these are perfect. Whoever is catering this tea has a good hand with flavors.

Gently seems to know that lavender is toxic to cats, so he just pats the big tuxedo cat in an apologetic manner for denying him the treat.

Mitch says something to Gently, and then scratches the cat's chin. The two of them get up from the table. Gently looks happy as he follows Mitch out of the room. Maybe they're going to get Ruffles a treat.

Sonya leans towards me. She's a bottle-redhead with Romanian features. She stage whispers, "Can you believe Mitch Eberhardt moved to Galveston?"

"Yeah, I can't believe it," I say, trying to understand her excitement. But honestly, I'm puzzled. "Who's Mitch Eberhardt?"

Sonya laughs. "Only one of the most eccentric art collectors ever to wander out of London and show up in New Jersey. And apparently, he's heard enough good things about the art scene here to move across the Atlantic."

Sonya's preferred art medium may be yarn, but it's not her only interest. She'd recently helped me out with the oversized chocolate sculpture, and I'd learned she'd minored in art.

"Cool," I say, with enthusiasm I can't bring myself to feel. Doing that sculpture, I'd discovered an artistic side I hadn't realized I'd had. But just because I'd realized that creating can be fun doesn't mean that I am ready to start collecting it. Or that I can understand someone sinking all of their money into such a hobby, when there are so many places money allows you to travel to, with real experiences and memories, that you can capture in pictures you take yourself.

A server in a white long-sleeved shirt puts a tray of mini pupusas on the table. Pupusas are thick cornmeal cakes, presumably stuffed with meat and/or cheese. These have little smears of red sauce on top, and perfect tiny stacks of cabbage slaw perched atop that. I take one and pop it in my mouth as a single bite. It's crispy on the outside and soft on the inside, and the filling is once again perfectly spiced. It reminds me of a flavor profile I've tasted somewhere before. But I can't quite place where.

No one else at our table seems to recognize where the food might be from, and the conversation drifts to other topics – how cold Galveston's weather is for January, where Ben and Pru plan to go on their next vacation. Apparently they take a once-in-a-lifetime trip about once a year. They're retired – but they must have retired quite comfortably.

We have that love of travel in common. One reason I fell in love with craft chocolate is the chance to travel with purpose, visiting origin to work directly with farmers to procure the best beans for the chocolate I want to make – at prices that will actually help the farms. I've met some amazing people, who are passionate about their work, and about the land in their care. I have another trip planned – and some of my friends are planning to go. It won't be until Autumn returns from her honeymoon, but

I still can't help but share some of the exciting details with Ben and Pru.

Pru says, "Brazil is a lovely country. Ben and I used to go diving there. Not since Ben slipped a disk in his back a few years ago. But I miss it."

Mitch and Gently come back into the ballroom. Gently's face is red. He's clutching onto Ruffles for dear life, and Ruffles has his claws in Gently's long-sleeve shirt. Whatever had happened between the two of them hadn't gone well. Maybe Ruffles had been a picky eater, knowing that chicken was on the table, both literally and metaphorically.

Pru gestures to the box on the table in front of me and asks, "What are those lovely truffles?"

Though how she knows they're lovely, I can't guess. After all, the box is opaque, with an outline of my bunny Knightley stamped on it, above the words Greetings and Felicitations, the name of my shop. My usual gift boxes are pale pink and gray, but I had some red ones left over from the limited-edition cherry cordials we'd offered last month, so I'd used one of those. This is a gift, so it is tied shut with bright pink ribbon, making a jaunty bow near Knightley's lop ear.

I try to focus on Pru – a regular customer who's asked me a question – instead of what is going on halfway across the room. Though it is hard not to worry about Gently and his debilitating anxiety. He does not do well with confrontation, so on one level it is surprising that he doesn't just leave.

I make eye contact with Pru and say, "They're infused with limoncello and a reduced infusion of Earl Gray tea. I thought it would be the perfect gift for a tea enthusiast."

Pru looks intrigued. "I've never had anything like that. I'd love to try one."

If they weren't a gift for our host, I'd open the box right now and let her have a sample. I am rather proud of how the truffles came out. I'd dipped them in white chocolate and added little candied lemon balm leaves to the top.

I tell Pru, “Come by the shop the next time you and Ben do your date day. I’ll make sure to have a batch ready for you to sample.”

“You’d do that just for us?” Pru asks.

I say, “If I’m making them, I’m going to make a lot of them. So it will be a limited time item, just like what Carmen does with the baked goods, and I sometimes do with special chocolates.”

Pru nods. “I remember that sea salt bar you did in honor of Clive the Octopus. It was divine. I still have one, squirreled away for a special occasion.”

I feel heat in my cheeks. It may be silly that I’m blushing from the compliment, but I take pride in my work, and having my successes recognized is always a lift. Besides, it’s nice thinking about Clive. That quirky Octopus had been instrumental in helping me solve a murder, once.

## Chapter Two

Mitch gets up from his table and comes over towards ours. Sonya smiles and starts to stand to greet him, but before she can he says, “Felicity Koerber, as I live and breathe. I apologize for taking so long to make it over here to talk to you. The duties of a host, you know? I am ecstatic you accepted my invitation. I had started to worry you wouldn’t come.”

Sonya settles back in her seat, trying mostly successfully to hide her look of disappointment. I’m just blinking at the odd way that Mitch had spoken. Was that part of his persona for the party, or really the way he talks?

I paste a smile on my face. “How could I not? Your invitation was so . . .” I search for the right word. “Mysterious.”

Mitch’s smile gets even wider, so I guess it was a good word choice. He says, “I’ve always thought it best to cultivate a memorable reputation, right from the start, in a new place.”

“You’ve certainly done that,” I say, gesturing towards Sonya. “My friend Sonya tells me that-”

Mitch holds up a hand, interrupting me with, “I had hoped to speak with you privately regarding a chocolate-themed project.”

I glance at Sonya, who looks crestfallen at being first ignored, then slighted. But she makes a tiny gesture with her chin that I should listen to Mitch’s proposal. After all, he could be interested in a chocolate sculpture, which has become a new facet of my business.

Still feeling guilty, despite the slighted party's prompting, I stand up and hold out the banana bread and box of truffles. I tell Mitch, "I brought you a box of my bean to truffles, and a loaf of my pastry chef's newest creation, banoffee banana bread. It's a riff on banoffee pie, with cacao nibs instead of nuts."

"I don't do gluten," Mitch says dismissively. But he takes the box of truffles out of my hand.

"We'll take it if he doesn't want it," Pru volunteers.

Not sure what else to do, I hand the loaf to her. She immediately opens it, and as the cellophane is removed, the smell of toffee and graham crackers hits my nostrils. Carmen, my pastry chef, is a bit of a genius. She ground the graham crackers to crumbs and mixed them with the recipe's flour and added some dulce de leche and toffee bits, giving humble banana bread a completely different flavor profile. Mitch has no idea what he's missing.

Mitch grimaces down at the loaf. "Let me show you my private gallery, and we can talk about the project."

I cast a look back at Sonya and Autumn, but I get the idea that they're not invited for this private tour. And I'm a bit nervous about following this man I just met into this maze of a house. There are rumors of hidden passageways, and booby traps.

I go with him, my heels clacking loudly on the terrazzo tile as we leave the area of the house that had been on the public tour and enter a wing in the back that may have once been servants' quarters. It has now been turned into several rooms of luxury-lit gallery space. The air in here feels colder – probably from a different system controlling temperature and humidity than the rest of the house. This building is still on the historic register, so the remodel may well have broken some of the rules about keeping a structure in historic condition, but the tile looks like it is repurposed, from the same period as this part of the architecture, and the house was remodeled so many times over the years that maybe it doesn't matter.

The paintings on the walls are in a number of different styles too, from different periods. Mitch gives me a little while to look around.

Mitch says, "I'm absolutely in love with this house. Every day I discover some new little detail in the architecture or some bit of furnishing that has been tucked away in a closet. And you would not believe some of the things that were uncovered during the remodel." He waggles his eyebrows. "Potentially scandalous things."

"Oh?" I ask, but Mitch doesn't seem inclined to elaborate. He gestures for me to return my attention to the art.

Finally, when I've seen everything, Mitch asks, "Who's your favorite painter?"

I look around at the paintings on the wall in the gallery. "Of the ones here?" I ask, flustered. I've never really chosen a favorite artist. I mean, I like art, and I know when I like a painting, but I've never felt like I know enough to choose a favorite.

"Of all time." Mitch grins at me, and I feel like the question is a challenge. And this may well be some kind of job audition for the shop. Too bad I'm here instead of Tracie, the resident art expert – and chocolate sculptor – at my shop.

I blurt out the first thing that pops into my head. "Monet. All those water lilies."

Mitch looks at me skeptically. "I don't think so. It's okay. You can have a favorite who isn't necessarily popular. So, who is it?"

I feel heat coming into my face. "I don't know."

He looks shocked. "You don't know?"

I change the subject. "What was it you wanted to talk to me about?"

"I wanted to offer to paint you." He throws up his hands, like it's a hopeless idea now that I'm not as into art as he thought. "In chocolate. I thought it would be both flattering and profitable for you. Don't worry. It wouldn't be anything risqué."

I blink. Is that something I should be worried about? I feel a hint of a blush in my face. “Is there money in painting with chocolate?”

“Not as much as dealing in famous paintings,” Mitch admits. I realize he’s lost the affected way of speaking he’d shown earlier. “But a hand-painted piece, done using a thin chocolate slab for a canvas, can go for close to a grand. Especially if the subject is interesting, and you have to admit, you do have a rather unique following.”

The following he’s talking about is in the true crime circuit. Which isn’t a group of fans I’ve intentionally tried to encourage. I want to lead a normal life, to stop having murders drop into it, but I don’t seem to have much control over that. After the last case I’d gotten caught up in, a local blogger had called me a mega murder magnet. And then he’d started a podcast dedicated to all my cases. I feel the heat in my cheeks intensify. I say, “That whole murder-magnet death-dare thing wasn’t the reputation I actually wanted for my chocolate shop. I got into the craft chocolate business because I wanted to make people happy.”

“Well, you’ve certainly made the true crime people happy.” Mitch laughs at his own joke. It’s not really funny. People come to my shop because of their curiosity about the murders I’ve help solve. They buy chocolate – and often, they come back. I hope that is because they’ve realized I make excellent chocolate, that there’s more to my shop than some tacky gimmick.

“Can we not talk about that?” I ask.

“That may be difficult,” he says. “Because it’s part of my proposal.”

“I don’t follow,” I say.

“I thought the chocolate paintings would be an excuse for you to come to the house, for us to be seen together. Because what I really need is a private detective.”

For a moment, I’m not sure if I’ve heard him correctly. Every time I’ve helped solve a case, it is because someone I care about has been involved. It's been a bit overwhelming, even if I have to admit I have enjoyed the puzzle aspect of it. And here is a perfect stranger trying to hire me to get involved in something that is obviously none of my business. I say as gently as I can, "I'm sorry. I'm *not* a private detective."

He says, "Maybe not a licensed one. But I don't need to hire you officially. Let's just say you can keep all the profit from the paintings, and we can call it even. I've sold a couple already, as commissions."

"I'm sorry, but I can't-"

Mitch holds up a hand, stopping me mid-sentence. Does he realize how annoying that is? And the gesture seems to be a habit with him. "At least hear me out. Then you can say no. I had to hang this one over the empty space. The canvas that was there was missing."

He moves over to the wall and removes a giant painting. Behind it, the word *Revenge* has been scrawled on the wall with red paint. The lettering looks like calligraphy, and there's the image of an ornate knife painted underneath the word. There's something vaguely familiar about this scene, though it is difficult to place why.

Mitch sighs. "Whoever did this was in my house. And they left this, in the pocket of my smoking jacket."

Mitch withdraws a small plastic bag from his suit jacket. It's a long piece of red thread, with a small silver charm tied onto one end. The charm is shaped as a knife going into an anatomically correct heart. It's rather macabre, and I have a visceral response to it in the pit of my stomach.

"You should call the police," I say, rubbing at the sudden goosebumps that have appeared on my arms. It's not the air conditioning.

Mitch scoffs. "And what exactly are they going to do? Trace the paint? I looked up the charm, and they are sold in bulk on the internet. I believe my life is in danger. I need someone who can be nearby, to catch things I might miss, to figure out who hates me enough to want to kill me."

"I'm sorry, but that's not anything like what I've done in the past. I do have a friend who used to do private security. Maybe he can help." I dig in my purse and pull out one of Logan's cards. I always carry a few on me. After all, he and I are business partners, since he invested heavily in Greetings and Felicitations when I had a crisis. It's always good to cross-support his business too. And Logan and I have flirted with being more than just business partners – though that's gotten complicated, since my ex showed back up in my life and is trying to get a second chance.

Mitch takes the card, and I swear he flinches when he reads the qualifications. So what if Logan is a puddle jump pilot now? He used to be a bodyguard, and before that he was a cop. Mitch says, "I'd much rather work with you."

"I'm sorry," I say. "But I don't have any more ideas on how to follow up on this graffiti than the police would."

"At least consider posing for the paintings. I promise to make it fun."

I have such a hard time telling people flat out no. So I say, "I'll think about it."

Mitch doesn't look exactly happy. But he at least seems willing to accept my response. He says, "If you come back next week, I should be able to show you an example."

"Maybe," I say, reluctant to commit to anything that would bring me deeper into Mitch's world. I force a smile as I head into the hallway leading back to the ballroom, ready to enjoy my tea and try not to feel uneasy about that stabbed-heart charm.

Mitch follows along behind me, brooding.

I can't help but ask, "If you don't do gluten, why are there so many gluten-rich items at your party? Sandwiches, pupusas, cookies and cakes – it doesn't sound like you can eat any of it."

Mitch grimaces. "I haven't been able to eat anything but fruit and chicken salad in a lettuce leaf all night."

His gluten sensitivity must be serious. I've never heard of it being fatal, but it can be a major inconvenience. Someone is going to have to scrub this kitchen down after the party.

"That sounds frustrating," I say.

He grunts in agreement. "The caterer I originally hired had worked out an entire gluten free menu. But she and most of her staff came down with food poisoning this morning, and neither she nor I trusted the food that had already been prepared. My sister's hairdresser recommended this guy who sometimes does pop-ups. He also does catering, and he had done the hairdresser's baby shower. She made the call. Supposedly, there's another chef in there working on something I can eat without it being cross-contaminated."

"Oh?" I say, honestly curious. There's only one person I know who does pop-up dinners on the island. He got in trouble not so long ago for holding events without the proper permits, but I understand that since then he has mended his ways. I ask, "Is there any way I could meet the chef? I want to compliment the pupusas."

"Anything that might get you on my side," Mitch says, and we make a detour to the kitchen.

Both the tile and the cabinets in the kitchen look the same as when this structure was open to the public. But the appliances have been upgraded, and a gorgeously embossed louvred tin panel has been added to the pantry door, probably to avoid humidity building up inside. And there, looking at home at the six-burner range, is Enrique. He's dressed in professional chef whites. Enrique had been doing those unlicensed pop-up dinners to help fund his college education in food science and hydroponics. Only in his mid-twenties, he's already a gifted chef, so whatever he does after he graduates is going to be spectacular – as long as his minor criminal record doesn't hold him back.

He sees me in the doorway and turns away from stirring more of the red sauce. He has deep-set dark eyes and thickly bowed lips, with a hint of stubble across his jaw. He breaks into a smile. "Felicity! I didn't know you were coming, but sí, we can always use another pair of hands – despite how you're dressed. This is Yoli and that's Iris." He points in turn to each. Yoli is short and on the curvy side, with cat-wing eyeliner and a penciled-on beauty mark. She has multiple small earrings running up both ears. Iris is tall, and seems to be all angles, from her sharp nose to the thin wrists poking out from a slightly-too-short chef's jacket. She has long, curly brown hair. Enrique says, "Maybe one of them has a spare pair of chef's whites. This Mitch guy is particular."

"What makes you think I came to cook?" I protest. I'm obviously dressed as a guest for the party.

"I just assumed, considering . . ." Enrique gestures to a door that may or may not lead to a separate kitchen for gluten free cooking. The door opens, and Carmen – my shop's pastry chef – comes through with a covered tray. She sees me, and her cheeks – with their dramatic high cheekbones – go crimson. "Felicity!" she squeaks. "What are you doing here?"

Carmen, as usual, has her dark hair up in a ponytail. She's wearing chef whites too, which is a bit jarring, since she usually cooks in casual, athletically style clothes – paired with cute aprons, a look which encapsulates both sides of her personality.

I've never discussed Carmen working outside of Greetings and Felicitations. I honestly don't mind her helping out a friend. I do wish she'd told me, though, so I wouldn't have been out of the loop when I'd talked about the gluten free stuff with Mitch. I look back, and Mitch has disappeared from the hallway.

Carmen says, "I'm sorry if you feel like this is a conflict of interest."

I wave a hand, dismissing her concern. "No worries. I'm sure Mitch is going to love the gluten free items you made for him. Look at this as free advertising for him to get more through Greetings and Felicitations."

"You mean advertising I'm paying her for," Enrique says. "She's not just here out of the goodness of her heart, you know."

"Neither are you," I point out. The catering fees for this kind of party would be high, even after he paid everyone helping out. I turn back to Carmen and say, "Why did you let me take the loaf of banana bread, if you know this party was supposed to be gluten free?"

Carmen blushes again, even deeper. She says, "You said it was going to be mysterious and dramatic. I thought you were going to the party at the Opera House – which is also today. I tried to call to let you know Tracie was coming in to cover the counter, so I could be here, but your phone was off."

I take my phone out of my handbag. I usually carry it in my pocket, but the line of the tea dress didn't allow for that. Apparently, my phone's battery is dead. Which is odd, since I keep close tabs on it, to make sure I don't get stranded. "I'm sorry," I say. "I must have missed it."

Carmen looks skeptically at the dark screen. She knows I make sure to stay in communication. She says, "I didn't leave a message. I figured better to just get on the road and talk to you about it later."

"It's fine, really. I'll charge my phone when I get back in the car with Autumn," I say.

Iris says, "You mean Autumn Ellis. The famous mystery writer. It's so cool that you two are friends. Is it true you solved four murders, when the police couldn't?"

I look at her warily. Iris is older than the other cooks – who are in their twenties – as well as me at thirty-two. She's pushing forty, and small lines around her mouth are emphasized by the way she puckers her red-lipsticked lips, waiting for my answer. First impression: she's probably a gossip, looking for tidbits to share. Getting access to this mysterious house – with a rumored historic murder – must be a goldmine for her. I don't want to say anything bad about the police, especially since my long-ago ex-boyfriend – who still wants to know if we have a spark, now that we've met again – is a homicide cop.

I say cautiously, "I'm sure the police would have solved the cases without me. I was just in the wrong place at the wrong time, which gave me access to information the police didn't have."

"Four times?" Iris asks, skeptically. "You sure you're not just smarter than those guys?"

Enrique snorts a laugh.

I give him side eye. I don't want to take credit for things I hadn't done on my own. But I also don't like the slight to my intelligence. Of course, I can't really blame the guy for questioning my deductive methods. I had tried to chase him once, and he had twisted his ankle. It wasn't bad – and as a former physical therapist, I had helped him keep the injury from getting worse – but it could easily have cost him his football scholarship, which is helping fund his education.

Enrique tells Iris, "Felicity's smart, but so are a lot of people. It's more that she's lucky. Even if she wanders down the wrong path at the start, she always stumbles onto one thread that unravels to the truth."

Carmen says, "It's not luck. It's persistence. And she's getting better. Solving mysteries is just like surfing – you're going to wipe out a lot when you first start, until you get in the practice."

Ignoring the way they're talking about me like I'm not there, I tell Iris, "I'm not going to lie. I enjoy the puzzle aspect of the cases I've gotten involved in. But I'd like to start leaving murder to the police."

Now Carmen laughs. She agrees with Arlo – my cop ex – who thinks I ought to get licensed as a private investigator. But that's not something I'm prepared to do.

Yoli says something to Carmen in Spanish. I don't catch all of it, but it ends with, "Consigue su autógrafo por favor."

I feel my own cheeks go hot, probably more bright pink than Carmen's crimson. I say, "I still can't get used to people asking for my autograph."

Carmen gestures to the doorway with the tray. "She wasn't asking for your autograph. She was asking for Autumn's. I already told her that her favorite writer was here."

I think back over what Yoli had said, and I realize one of the words had been *escritora*. I've been learning Spanish for a while now, but I'm still far from fluent.

I say, "You knew Autumn was coming, but she didn't mention me?"

Carmen says, "She called wanting to change some design elements for her wedding cake. She asked if she needed to come in, so I told her not to panic, because there's plenty of time until her wedding. Almost four weeks."

Yoli says, "But you will ask Miss Ellis for me? Por favor."

"I'll tell her it's for a fan," I say. Now that she's writing again, Autumn's backlist is getting interest. Her new book is bound to be popular. Autumn won't let me read her work-in progress, though. She said that some elements in the new book echo a few minor elements of things that had happened during the course of those four cases I'd helped with. She wants to make sure I feel like she's done them justice – once she has the manuscript polished. I gesture at Carmen. "Yoli, you might want her autograph too. After all, Carmen has written one of my favorite cookbooks."

## Chapter Three

I always love walking into my own shop. I usually go in through the back door, into the spacious kitchen. The kitchen has become Carmen's domain – where she tests recipes and makes refined pan dulce and other treats. She works for me, but she basically does her own thing. Everything she makes here includes some form of my chocolate, from nibs to cocoa powder.

Sometimes I do need to work in the kitchen, making ganaches for truffles and doing a few experiments of my own, but my main workspace is off of the kitchen, in the two rooms where I roast cacao nibs and process them into chocolate. I quickly check in on the melangers, which are grinding away, smoothing out my nibs into chocolate. The processing room has a sink, and cabinets, which hold most of what I need. When we moved into the space, it had formerly been a French restaurant. I had never painted over the blue and yellow sunflower mural on the wall, and now the cheerful flowers just feel like part of my workday. There's a space in the mural where the shop's electrical box was painted around. It's covered by a white metal panel. A door leads from the processing room back into the bean room, and a door there leads into the hallway, which at least muffles the noise of the grinding from the customers.

The customers are making their own noise, chatting and moving chairs and throwing things in the trash in the front of the shop. It's a space that I decorated to be comfortable, in gray and pink, with a shabby chic vibe, so that people would stick around for a while. So any time the shop is loud with laughter – that's a noise that makes me happy.

It's maybe an hour before our posted closing time. I don't know of any groups that have planned meet-ups here today, and it's a bit late in the day for us to have a rush – we do most of our business when people come in for a coffee before work, or a mid-morning pick me up of a couple of truffles and whatever treat Carmen has baked. I take a lot of corporate orders, from people wanting to treat their clients, or to offer guests or customers unique local perks. Other than that, there's a lot of folks on dates, groups of friends exploring the island, and people buying gifts. And then there are the true crime aficionados, of course. But for some reason, they tend to show up earlier in the day, too.

I hear Carmen laugh. I'm surprised she got back to the shop before I did. I'd changed clothes after the tea and then gone with Autumn to look at stationary for her wedding invitations – she and Drake are having a hard time choosing between pearl gray satin finish and dove gray matte finish. But we hadn't been gone that long. Autumn had dropped me off here and then headed to meet her future mother-in-law to negotiate last minute additions to the guest list. Autumn had wanted a small-ish wedding – after all, they have been planning the whole thing in just a couple of months – but Drake's an only child, and his mother keeps pointing out that she only gets to do this once. Autumn may be independently wealthy, but she doesn't want to blow a big chunk of her inheritance on the wedding – and neither does Drake.

So that's one meeting I'm glad to not have to sit in on.

I go through into the front of the shop. We have a space near the counter set up for drip coffee, but there's also a full coffee and horchata bar – which of course also boasts the richest drinking chocolate in town. There are displays and shelves for my different chocolate bars, and our in-house snacking nibs and cacao powder. I also make gift sets. The truffles are available pre-boxed, or as individual selections at the counter, where they share space with whatever Carmen has baked. There are four trays of brownies on one of the wooden tables, near the coffee station. The tables take up a large part of the space, and a few of them are up near the big windows looking out onto the Strand, perfect for people-watching, especially when the cruise ships disembark just down the way. There's a couple sitting at one of the other tables, nibbling from a shared chocolate bar. I can't see the label to know which one. But they look happy. Which makes me happy.

There are about a dozen other customers, chatting quietly, or have out laptops and are studying or playing games.

On the other side of the room, there's a bookshelf and reading nook, behind the hallway leading to the bathroom and my office. There's plastic sheeting covering part of the hallway, with a makeshift door leading through into the space next door.

In front of that, there's a locked flat display case, displaying what have come to be known as my "murder books" – the books Autumn had been joking about. I'd happened to find a book that inspired me about each of the murders I had helped solve. In at least one case, the book had provided actual physical evidence I'd used to uncover the identity of a killer. I'd initially bought a small case to show off the three volumes of *Sense and Sensibility*. The glassed-in case is disturbingly large now, and the books are spread out enough that other volumes could fit, with a little rearranging. Not that that's going to happen. There may have been a blip in my life where I've stumbled on a surreal number of dead bodies. But I am hoping – sincerely hoping – that I've moved past that. I know I've said that before, only to get caught up in another case. But I mean it. Maybe if I let one go, and just let the authorities handle things, the universe will stop throwing puzzles at me to solve. If it even happens again.

Carmen and those she'd been working with are gathered around the locked case. Miles and Tracie, my two baristas / shop assistants, are sitting on the sofa with small plates in their hands. Tracie is small-framed, all angles and elbows, with gobs of curly brown hair. Miles is built from playing college football and has a tight fade haircut.

Tracie is blindfolded with a cloth napkin. Miles has his eyes closed. I guess he still has too much residual trauma from having been attacked by a killer – in an attempt to rescue me – to be willing to be blindfolded.

Carmen's boyfriend, Paul, is standing nearby with a pad of paper, and Paul's son Luke is holding a sheet of stickers, using them decorate his dad's shoe. Paul may have neck tattoos and a notch out of one of his blonde eyebrows, but there's something sweet about him and his four-year-old hanging out together.

From the sound of the conversation, the cooks are conducting some kind of taste test.

I walk over to them and say, "I feel like I've walked in on a session from Hell's Kitchen. I give up. Which one of my employees has the best palate?"

"That would be me," Carmen says. "But I can't judge what I baked."

Luke hops up and wraps me in a pint-sized hug. "Aunt Felicity!" Kids in Paul's family call all the adults they are close to Aunt or Uncle. Paul and Carmen are getting more serious about their relationship, which means I've been seeing more of Paul and Luke. And over one chocolate dipped marshmallow a couple of weeks ago, I got upgraded to Aunt. It is a title I take with a great deal of affection – especially since I was never able to have kids of my own. Luke says, "Winners get stickers." He peels one off the sheet. It's a cartoon dog wearing a super hero cape. He hands it to me.

I take the sticker and put it on my blouse. "I guess that makes me a winner then."

"There can be only one," Enrique says. "You see, we got to talking about how hard it is to make gluten free food taste good. And we all have our tricks for making the best gluten free brownies. I do mine with a base of black beans. Carmen prefers chestnuts. Yoli swears by a pre-made gluten free flour mix. And Iris goes for coconut oil and almond flour. So we decided to test them against each other, and to send a tray of the winning brownies tomorrow to Mitch as a thank you."

With his eyes still closed, Miles says, "I want to get this finished real quick, before the conversation gets side-tracked again. I give the third one seven out of ten points."

Paul writes it down. He asks, "What about you, Tracie?"

Tracie says, "I still like the second one best. But this one is pretty good. So maybe a seven point five."

Then Paul hands each of them a cup of water to palate cleanse.

Carmen says, "If you want to try them, the brownie trays are still on the table."

"I don't mind if I do," I say, making my way over the table. I cut off a tiny sliver of each and put them on a plate. By taste, I can tell which brownie is made with coconut oil and almond flour. It's good – but a bit crumbly. One of the other brownies is dry and slightly gritty. The remaining two are rich and fudgy, but one of them has hints of cardamom and there's toasted pistachio on top. Which is totally Carmen's baking style. The other has chocolate chunks and walnuts mixed in.

I walk back over to the group. "I say it's a tie between the pistachios and the walnuts."

"Too late," Enrique says. "Our judges have voted, and the walnuts won."

"He means he won," Luke clarifies.

Enrique shows off his sticker. It's a superhero cat wearing a black cape.

"By a quarter of a star," Carmen points out.

"I don't care," Iris says. "I got a picture of Carmen with the murder books. Felicity, can I get a picture of you and Carmen together?"

Suddenly, my smile feels forced. I ask, "Are you that into true crime?"

She nods. "I'm a loyal listener to Ash Diaz's podcast. Even if there are only three episodes, so far. It's one of my favorites. I got hooked on the stories from Dateline and never looked back. I travel a lot, so podcasts make good companions on cars and planes."

Carmen gestures for me to come over and pose with her. "I've been amusing them with the stories of how I've helped out with your investigations. Including how at one point, we lured out a bad guy, who turned out not to be a bad guy but to be a private detective, after Logan tackled him."

"A would-be private detective," I point out. But still, that story makes me smile. So I pose for the pictures with Carmen. We've been through a lot together, in the time since I'd hired her. I'm sure she never imagined her name would show up in Ash's true crime podcast, when she took an entry-level job as an assistant here after being harassed into leaving her previous job as a restaurant pastry chef.

"I'm glad you all got to enjoy the shop," I say, "but I have to get some cacao beans roasted and winnowed, so they'll be ready to go in the melangers tomorrow, once the current batch of chocolate comes out."

Enrique says, "I brought you a few things. Let me give them to you before you get caught up in your work."

I follow him into my own kitchen, where he's made himself at home, to judge by the can opener and the bowl with the batter-coated whisk and the line of spilled oatmeal heading away from his bag on the counter. He unzips the oversized refrigerator bag, which has a fabric panel inserted behind a clear plastic cover. The image on the fabric is clearly Enrique, done in embroidered needlework, wearing chef's whites, with the words *Yes Chef!* in red above his head. The whole thing is super cute.

He zips the bag open and starts taking out containers of leftover chicken salad and pupusas and cream of celery soup. He says, "Mitch ordered way too much, and then refused to keep the leftovers. It's more than I can eat before it goes bad, so I thought I'd share."

"Thank you! I'll make sure and get your containers back soon." I start transferring the containers from the counter to the fridge. But a colorful sticky note randomly stuck to the side of the fridge catches my eye.

I pluck it from its spot. It's in Traci's handwriting – complete with hearts over the I's. It says, *International Flower Society Dinner – 6,000 pecan pie truffles – tomorrow night, will pay extra. Moody Gardens!!!*

I take the note out to where the others are still chatting. I have a whole line of truffles based on Cajun desserts. The pecan pie is one of my more popular flavors. I also have a bourbon pecan truffle that is rolled in cocoa powder instead of dipped, but the request is for the more labor-intensive ones.

Tracie sees me coming, and holds out her hands. She says, "I was going to tell you after everyone went home. I tried to call you, but your phone kept going to voicemail. So I told the organizer yes. You've been teaching me how to make ganache, so I at least got a start on it."

Everyone else looks confused – having no context for what she's talking about – but I can see why she said yes. Doing a job for Moody Gardens would be huge for my little craft chocolate business. It could lead to additional jobs with them, maybe even referrals, too.

I hold out the note. "I think we had maybe two dozen of these truffles in stock. How many did you make today?"

"A couple hundred?" Traci says. "We were busy and it was just me and Miles here."

Miles says, "We can get some more done tonight."

Carmen says, "I'll stay to help. Paul?"

Paul puts a hand on his kid's head and ruffles his hair. "Sure. I've got a couple of coloring books for Luke. He'll be fine for an hour or so, then I've got to get him home. If he goes back to his mom tomorrow tired, she'll make it hard for me next time."

It's taken me a long time to really trust Paul – as he freely admits he used to be a criminal – but his willingness to help Carmen has shone through on more than one occasion. And he's trying hard to be a good dad, despite difficult circumstances.

The odds of five people getting 6,000 truffles done tonight is slim. We're going to need all hands on deck tomorrow, to get it finished. But it's not an impossible project.

"Okay," I say. "See how far you can get. I still need to get the beans roasted, and then I promised to make a special order of the tea truffles for that cute retired couple, for next time they come in. So I'll be here too. Let me know if y'all need anything."

Enrique and the two cooks make their excuses and leave before they get roped into helping out. I head to the bean room and start pouring beans into the electronic sorter, which will remove any rocks or other impurities.

I hear Carmen and Miles talking to customers as people order one more horchata to go, or ask what baked goods will be available in the morning, and the door opening and closing as people leave. I assume Tracie is already making another batch of ganache.

Chocolate roasting has to be precise, as the heat brings out different flavor notes at certain time and temperature combinations than at others. The beans I'm working with are from a new collective I'm working with in Ecuador. I want to bring out the nutty and earthy aspects, and I've done a couple of test batches in a small countertop roaster to get an idea of where I'm going with this larger. The trick is to get the beans out of the roaster just shortly before they reach the peak of the notes I want to emphasize.

Which is why, when Arlo walks in, I have to ignore him. Mostly. Even if he's waving a gift bag at me. Arlo's Cuban, with thick dark hair and warm brown eyes, and he fills out his suit extremely well. I'd dated him back in high school, when becoming a cop hadn't even been on his radar. We'd had an awkward breakup, then recently reconnected – after I'd started a tentative relationship with someone else.

I get the beans where I want them, test them, and then transfer them to the cooling tray. The smell of chocolate is thick in the air.

"That never gets old," Arlo says. "The moment when you release the roasted beans, and it smells like we're submerged in chocolate."

Over the past couple of weeks, Arlo has come in numerous times, wanting to talk. I've promised him that I'm not going to draw out choosing between him and Logan. I just need a little time to sort out what my future needs to look like. I think Arlo wants to use the time while I'm sorting my feelings and motivations to get to know me all over again, in a more grown-up way. It's sweet, really.

Now that I've gotten the beans to a stopping point, I turn my attention to him. I arch an eyebrow and ask, "What's in the bag?"

"Open it," he says, holding the bag out to me.

I take it, and pull several sheets of tissue paper off the top, revealing a plush cat holding a plush cupcake.

Arlo says, "You seem to have everything you need, so I thought I'd get you something frivolous. And, I don't know, it reminded me of you."

"Thanks?" I say. I don't mean for it to come out as a question, but I'm not sure what about this comic-looking cat reminds Arlo of me. Maybe he just means he thinks I'd like it. And it is cute.

Arlo steps closer, and I can tell he wants to kiss me. I've kissed Arlo a couple of times – though I keep telling him I shouldn't, that I haven't made any promises to either him or Logan. But when he leans in, I can't help but kiss him back, at least briefly. And the kiss brings me back to where the two of us were kids, falling in love for the first time, familiar and warm. I don't know if what we have is real – or if I'm trying to recapture the past. Which is part of what has been taking me so long to figure out.

I pull back, and point at his lips, where he's now wearing a thin layer of my lipstick. He wipes it away – mostly – with the back of his hand. He says, "I keep saying I'm going to stop doing that."

"Yeah," I say. "Me too."

The door opens and closes loudly at the front of the shop. "Felicity," a voice calls. "Are you back there?" It's Ash, the local blogger who seems to think I'm local news. He's the one with the true crime podcast Iris had said she's addicted to. But his blog still covers more general news – which is really mostly gossip, opinion pieces and personality profiles. He started out as a major annoyance in my life, but over time, he's mellowed and we've become friends.

"In the bean room," I say loudly.

Ash comes through. He's got his phone in his hand, and he gestures at me with it. He says, "How could you have gone inside Wobble House and not taken me as your plus one? You know how I feel about architecture. And I could have gotten exclusive photos about the event for the blog."

I wipe at the edge of my lip, to tidy any smudged lipstick. Then I ask, "How did you figure out so quick that I'd been there?"

He says, "I follow Autumn on social media. Hashtag plus one. Seriously, after all the advertising I'd done for you, that should have been me."

I guess where there's social media, no event goes unrecorded.

## Chapter Four
## *Sunday*

The next morning, I'm right back at the shop, behind the counter running the coffee and horchata bar. It's just me and Carmen covering everything.

Miles is running late this morning, and Tracie is over at the workspace inside the expansion, working on some 3-D printed chocolate elephants for a wedding order. When the expansion is over, that work station will be part of the tour, behind glass partitions where people will be able to get in close to the printers at work and watch the devices layering down chocolate.

Tracie is all excited, despite the need to clean the cubical first to remove construction dust, because she worked out how to tint white chocolate bright pink and yellow to separately print tiny flowers, which she will use edible glue to attach all over the elephant sculptures, for textural decoration that would be impossible to create by printing each sculpture as one piece. The wedding is in Houston, and we were contacted by a wedding planner who is the cousin of Syed, one of the artists who had helped out with the sculpture for the art museum. If all goes well, the project could lead to a number of additional referrals among the Indian wedding planning community.

I ordered a couple of elephant-shaped polycarbonate molds so that when the batch of nibs that will be going into the melangers today is finished, I can shape some of that chocolate into solid pieces that will go into little sparkly mesh bags as complimentary gifts for the wedding party.

There has been a steady stream of customers. At this hour, most of them are here for their morning coffee – with or without a chocolate treat on the side. For the customers currently at the counter, I put ice into four plastic cups, then fill the cups half way with horchata – a sweetened spiced rice-based beverage. I top that off with cold brew coffee, pop on some lids and hand them to the four sleepy-looking girls. One of them puts her dirty horchata on the counter and leans in low to photograph the color gradient, which shifts as the dark coffee starts to sink into the off-white horchata. I give her my Instagram account for her to "at" us, and see her hashtag *#dairyfree #ricemilk* and *#govegan*.

On a business-survival level, it's a relief to see that people are still making room for treats, even with dietary restrictions and a level of health consciousness. After all, both chocolate and coffee can be good for you, in their pure forms. It's all the sugar and cream and other additions that make them something that needs to be limited. At Greetings and Felicitations, we are happy to decrease sugar in our drinks – which are less sweet than at most places, anyway, since we make our own syrups and sauces – and we have both an unsweetened 100% Cacao bar, and a bar sweetened with low-glycemic monk fruit. It's not my favorite bar, but it does serve a purpose, allowing people who otherwise couldn't to enjoy high-quality chocolate.

A woman comes into the shop, trailing two kids, and they head for the book nook. I don't have time to hand-sell books, since I'm still getting these customers sorted, and one of the girls wants to impulse buy one of my multi-bar collections.

But then there's a *whooshing* noise and a clatter that gets my full attention. One of the kids lets out a whoop and pulls several more books off the shelf and tosses them into a pile onto the floor. The other kid sticks out her tongue at the first one and grabs several more books, throwing them on top.

I quickly give the customer her change for the chocolate bar set, and then basically leave them standing, sorting their straws, while I quickly move around from behind the counter.

"We don't really have any children's books," I say, rushing over to book nook. The shelves contain a hodgepodge of travel books and classics that I've collected and curated personally. The whole setup is there to give shoppers more than just a few chocolate bars and truffles to look at, encouraging them to spend more time in the shop, as well as providing extra revenue, as we do sell a surprising number of books.

There have been children I haven't minded perusing the shelves. Well behaved children who like to look at the pictures in travel books or read the easier adventure books – not like the ones who are currently still pulling all the books off one of the shelves and throwing them into the growing pile on the floor.

The kids' mom looks up from perusing a book of her own. "Ryan, Shayleen, you two stop it."

The kids each throw one more book onto the pile, then reluctantly slink away.

The mom shrugs and says, "You know. Kids will be kids. Especially when they know they're at the beach."

"I don't think the location makes any difference," I say tersely. After all, she's responsible for any property damage her kids do while out in public.

Now the kids are on the other side of the store, and they have a chocolate bar open. It's 90% dark, which is too bitter for a lot of adults. So it's not surprising when Ryan says plaintively, "Mommy, this chocolate tastes bad."

What is surprising is when Shayleen spits out a big piece of it onto the floor.

"I'm going to have to ask you to leave," I tell the mom.

She looks at me like I'm crazy.

I like to think of myself as a nice person. And I am usually very patient with customers. But I can't see this situation having a positive outcome.

The mom says, "You can't say that to me. "

I ask, "Are you going to clean up where your kids spit on my floor?"

She looks puzzled. After a minute she asks, "Why? It's your chocolate and your floor. And obviously, you make horrible chocolate."

I feel my hands clenching into fists. I force them to relax. There are other customers here, and I don't want to make a scene. "In that case, it shouldn't be a problem for you to check out the other candy store down the street. Maybe they will have something more suited for your children's taste."

The lady isn't happy about it, but she leaves. And as soon as she's gone, I realize that one of my free-standing chocolate displays is completely empty. Did the lady distract me so that her kids could shoplift? I sigh. It's just going to be one of those days.

There's construction noise starting up from the space next door, where Logan and a couple of guys he hired are transforming what used to be a souvenir shop into an interactive space where customers can watch us making chocolate.

Tracie comes back through the plastic partition. She says, "I have a tarp up over the cubicle, to keep the dust away from the 3-D printers. I'll go check on it in a bit. In the meantime, it looks like my truffle reinforcements are here." Tracie gestures to the four girls, who are still at the counter, sipping their dirty horchatas. I had told Tracie we would need all the help we could get, and she knows I've paid temp help before. She says, "These girls are taking one of my classes over at Pottery and Paint. They asked to be notified when I had something different to offer, so when I said free experience learning to make ganache and roll truffles in a real chocolate factory, they jumped on the opportunity."

You have to admire Tracie – she turned a need for help into a work-cation and Instagramming opportunity. It doesn't even sound like the volunteers are expecting to get paid.

"You should have said something," I tell the girls. "I'd have given you the horchata on the house. Next round is on me, okay?"

Carmen comes out of the kitchen, wiping her hands on a dishtowel. She surveys the mess of books on the floor. "Everything okay out here?"

"Absolutely," I say overly brightly. "Tracie was just about to start her truffle making live experience."

Carmen raises an eyebrow, but just says, "Great. I don't mind tidying up out here so she can do that." She takes her dishtowel and heads for the blop of chocolate on the floor.

I hear noise in the back, heavy objects moving. I guess Miles has shown up.

The girls are still drinking their dirty horchata and chatting excitedly. I take a moment to ask Tracie, "Do you know anything about chocolate painting?"

Tracie says, "I've seen examples of it, while researching technique for the chocolate sculptures. You basically have the color pallet of a sepia-toned photograph to work with, unless you add in tinted white chocolate. I haven't seen it done, but I think it would be fun to add little pops of color. Why? Do we have a commission?"

"No, I've been asked to sit for a portrait, by Mitch Eberhardt. And I have to admit, I'm intrigued." Because, even though I'm not qualified to help Mitch with his security needs, it's flattering that he wants to paint me. Nobody's ever asked me to do anything like that before.

But before I can even think of taking on something that glamorous, I have to take care of the very unglamorous crime that just took place in my shop. I glance at the customers. There's a lot of people here, enjoying coffee or horchata with either my chocolate or Carmen's chocolate baked goods. And most of them are looking curiously this way. I don't want to mention the shoplifting in front of them. It isn't something that happens often, not in a shop this small. I should report it, though, even though there's not likely much anyone can do. I tell Carmen, "I'm going in the kitchen. I need to make a phone call."

"Okay." Carmen puts her dirty dishtowel into the bin under the counter, where we collect linens that need to be washed, then moves towards the untidy pile of books.

I go into the kitchen to make my phone call. But when I take my phone out of my pocket, it's dead again. Which makes no sense. It was at 100% when I took it off the charger this morning, just a few hours ago. Maybe there's something wrong with the battery. That would explain why it had been dead yesterday, too.

I can see into the chocolate processing room, where Miles is busy filling one of the melangers with the beans I roasted last night. It had been a huge leap of trust to let someone else to complete steps in the chocolate making process. I'd started this business intending to process each chocolate from choosing beans through finishing bars, all by myself. Each step has something satisfying to it. The roasting of cacao beans releases satisfying scents and requires split-second timing. The transformation the beans undergo in the melanger from nutty chunks of bean to silky chocolate is almost magical. And shaping the finished chocolate into bars never gets old. The machines are loud, so Miles doesn't even look up as I make my way over to the outlet where I keep my spare phone charger plugged in.

The shop is getting bigger, and taking on more corporate orders, and now that we're annexing the space next door, I'm going to have to make my peace with letting some elements of control go. After all, it's going to be impossible for me to take care of everything.

This giant truffle order is just one more example of a time when I've had to call in extra help to get a big order done on time. And I've found that delegating to someone responsible, who can keep track of the temporary workers, has taken stress off me at critical moments. I'm learning how to let go and stop micromanaging everything. I'm not there yet. It's a process. But I'm making progress.

I'm starting to understand that my need to control things down to the tiniest detail at Greetings and Felicitations had been a response to the uncertainty in my life that followed having my husband die from an unexpected accident. Everything about my life had changed, without my consent.

It had been especially hard for me when I'd taken on Logan as a business partner – for many complex reasons. Not the least of which is that Logan and I have had a near-romance, and if I wind up choosing Arlo instead of him, Logan and I are still going to be working together. I'd given myself until Autumn's wedding – which is coming up sooner than I am ready for – to make a decision about my love life.

So when Logan had proposed taking on the annex – and even fronting the cash, since my funds are still tied up in the hotel my aunt is flipping – I'd been hesitant. And I think that had hurt his feelings – yet another thing that feels out of my control.

I think a lot of my hang-ups still come from my husband's death. That upheaval, that sense of somewhat illogical guilt that if I had only made a different choice that day, hadn't distracted Kevin with my talk of vacation plans, he might have avoided the accident. Honestly, that's probably the root of my inability to choose between Arlo and Logan. What if I make the wrong choice and one of them is miserable for the rest of his life? Or what if I am? I don't like having that kind of power. Or that much responsibility.

I know it doesn't make any sense, that the correlations aren't exact. Accidents happen, and we all internalize things that aren't really our fault. But knowing that and believing it enough to trust myself are two different things.

But I'd rather not think of the past today. Today, I want to think about family. After all, my parents are coming for lunch. I don't get to see them as often as I'd like, and I need them to see everything going smoothly here, so I can make a good impression. After all, I'm planning to ask my dad to design a "chocolate feature" for the space immediately in front of the windows in the expansion. He's a respected architect and if he puts his name on part of the expansion it would open up a new clientele. I'm not expecting anything as large or dramatic as the multi-tiered chocolate fountain at the Bellagio Hotel in Las Vegas – certified in the Guinness Book as the largest chocolate fountain in the world – or the 30-foot-tall stream of chocolate cascading from a golden whisk onto a giant truffle at the Lindt chocolate museum in Switzerland, which may be even bigger than the Bellagio's exhibit. But I do want something that is a visual draw, from both inside and outside the building, and that ties into whatever we wind up doing with the classroom space.

I plug my phone into a spare charger, then I use the shop's landline to make the shoplifting report. I turn to go back out front. Miles finally notices me. He waves, "Hey, Mrs. Koerber!"

I wave back. "Hey!"

I'm still proud of the *Mrs.* part of my name. I had had a happy marriage before my husband's untimely death. This life – moving back to my hometown, quitting my thriving physical therapy practice to open a retail business – isn't the one I had imagined. But there are parts of it that are more rewarding than I could ever have imagined.

Miles asks, "You okay?"

Miles is a sensitive kid – just in college, and a football player – who picks up on things with a great deal of empathy.

"I'm fine," I say. "I was just thinking about how lucky I am to be surrounded by so many supportive people."

"That's random," Miles says.

Carmen comes through from the front of the shop. She's holding a thin book with a grubby-looking cover. Carmen asks, "When did we get this?"

Miles notices another customer coming in out front, so he heads out there to take over the counter.

I take the book from Carmen. It isn't familiar. All the books we stock in the store are priced with easy-to-remove stickers to keep the covers from getting damaged. This book isn't priced. I take a closer look at it, confusion fighting with dread. The cover is an orangey-brick red. It's a bit faded, but still clear enough to read. *A Study in Scarlet*. Underneath the title, there's a picture of a certain iconic detective, and below that the name A. Conan Doyle. The book looks really old. There's no way I could have gotten a rare – if battered – copy of the first book Doyle wrote featuring Sherlock Holmes and not have realized it.

A chill goes down my spine. Bad things seem to happen when rare books come into my life in unexpected ways. And the only thing I can imagine here is that someone specifically placed this book on my shop's shelf – like shoplifting, but in reverse. Why would someone want me to have a book about revenge and murder? I flip through the pages, and a black bookmark falls to the floor. I pick it up. There's a quote cross-stitched on it with red thread: "There's the scarlet thread of murder running through the colourless skein of life, and our duty is to unravel it, and isolate it, and expose every inch of it."

The words are a quote from the book I'm holding in my shaking hands. It's been a long time since I read Doyle – it had been during a reading kick in high school that had started with Poe, after we'd been assigned a couple of Poe stories in English class. Poe's "Murders in the Rue Morgue" was supposed to have been the first modern detective story, and had been a huge influence on Doyle when he started writing Sherlock Holmes. There's even a discussion of the character in *A Study in Scarlet*, but Holmes dismisses Dupin as something of a hack.

I try to remember the plot of *A Study in Scarlet* – at least the first half, where most of the detective-ing happens – and I realize that this is why I'd thought the word *revenge* written on a wall was familiar. That's what the police find at the murder scene that is the heart of *A Study in Scarlet*. Though in the book, Holmes had to translate the word from the German. And the victim hadn't tried to hide it from prying eyes by putting up a very large painting over it.

A heavy coldness settles into my stomach. That threat to Mitch – this book basically falling into my hands. This can't be a coincidence.

I study the bookmark. It looks hand cross-stitched. I flip it over to see if the threads go all the way through, and they do, with the messy knots where the threads got tied off. On the back, there's a message, done in silver ink, in script that looks calligraphic.

The front had been a quote about the need to find justice, and Holmes's drive to make that happen. And written on the back, I've been addressed directly, with a message that reads, "Are you up for the challenge, Mrs. Koerber? The game is indeed afoot."

Suddenly, the book in my hands is trembling, and I drop the bookmark again. Carmen picks it up for me. "This is bad," she says.

"I know," I say, trying to put together all of the implications. Whoever did this – how could they know I would notice a book that had been slipped onto the shelf? It could take a long time for me to decide to inventory the books, or for someone to bring it to the counter to try and buy it.

But having this show up in a pile of books that would have to be reorganized from the floor – that pretty much guaranteed that someone would notice it.

I rush out into the front of the shop. I ask the customers, "That lady who was in here with her kids. It's important. Does anyone know who she is?"

One woman says, "Yeah. That's Eunice Brewer. She's a waitress over at the Prime Circle. You should watch out for those kids of hers. They've stolen stuff from my store, more than once."

The Prime Circle is a high-end steak restaurant, over on the Seawall side of the island. It's hard to reconcile Eunice's rudeness with the upscale atmosphere of the place where she works. And if her kids behave outrageously regularly – maybe it was just a coincidence that they pulled the threatening book off the shelf.

I hope so. Because this book is creeping me out, and I don't like to think about kids having anything to do with the kind of person who would have made that bookmark. I look at the book, still in my hand. I love books, and reading. So how come I keep seeing them as harbingers of bad things in my life? But I can't ignore the message on that bookmark.

I go back into the kitchen and put the book down on the counter next to my phone charger. Hopefully my phone is charged enough to snap a few pics and make a call to Arlo. I know Mitch didn't want to get the police involved, but now this is involving me, despite my protests, and I want backup.

I leave the phone plugged in, so it can continue to charge, but I punch at the power button. Nothing happens.

It takes a few minutes of me intermittently pushing the power button, but finally my phone decides it has enough battery to turn on. When it does, it shows that I have a missed call from an unfamiliar number. Almost all of the calls I get from unknown numbers are junk, but having a small business, I can't ignore potential clients, even if the chance that it actually is one is slim. So I click on this voice message automatically, even though I turned the phone on to make an urgent call.

The message sounds weird, like the voice has been muffled, and at the same time sorted through a digital device. I can't tell if it's male or female, old or young. In the message, the altered voice says, "The game is afoot, Mrs. Koerber. I'll give you an hour head start. But Mitch is home alone right now. And I can only wait so long."

There's a sudden pounding as I hear my own heartbeat in my ears. If this message was left in earnest, Mitch's life is in danger . . . if it's not already too late. I call Mitch, scrambling for the card he gave me and then having trouble punching in the numbers because my hands are trembling again. There's no answer.

Dread washes through me, making everything seem gooily divided from reality as I call Arlo. When he picks up, I say, "There's something I need to tell you."

There's silence on the other end of the line. After a moment, he asks, "Do you mean about us?"

"No," I say, as gently as I can. "Not yet."

He sighs into the phone, in a way that makes me think he's relieved. I don't like the idea of Arlo bracing himself for the possibility that I'm going to hurt him. Yet he sounds upbeat when he asks, "Okay, then what's up? I thought it was bad news. You sounded serious."

"I am." I explain about how Mitch had tried to hire me for security, and about the book and the threatening bookmark. While I'm talking, Logan comes in, his shoes and jeans covered with dust from the construction area. He moves to the oversized fridge and grabs a bottle of water. Logan is tall, with a strong chiseled jaw, piercing green eyes and tousled dark hair. He's originally from Minnesota, but now he's tanned from spending time along the beach. He usually wears a pilot's jacket, over jeans and a tee, but he's ditched it today, since he's working hard on the remodel. The tight tee over his well-muscled arms makes him look exceptionally hot.

His face takes on a note of concern as I try to describe what the voice on the message had sounded like to Arlo.

I wrap up my explanation with, "I think Mitch might be in danger. And that call came in early this morning, only I didn't notice because my phone was off. It's been way more than an hour."

So Mitch may well already be dead.

I don't say that part out loud, because if I do, then that makes the danger real. And I don't want it to be, since I'm about to head over to Mitch's place, which isn't that far from my shop. There's no real choice, not after what the voice had said. The person threatening Mitch might be waiting to see if I show up, giving me time to get the message. I could be the only thread he has tying him to a chance to live.

Arlo specifically tells me, "You just stay put. Don't worry. I'll head over there personally to check on him."

I answer noncommittally. I really am close by. And it feels like my responsibility, after turning Mitch down yesterday afternoon when he'd asked for help.

When I hang up the phone, I turn to Logan. He's already getting his keys and shrugging on his jacket. "Come on," he says, "showing up in my car is going to be a bit less ostentatious than if you take your catering van."

"True," I say. I hesitate, "Maybe Mitch is fine, and whoever is playing this literary game isn't serious."

Logan doesn't say anything in response. But he looks plenty troubled.

And my heart feels heavy, while my anxious arms feel light. He puts a guiding hand on my back as we head out of the door.

When we pull up to the mansion, everything looks much the same as it did yesterday – with the exception of Silas's house, where there's a big bouquet of blue balloons in the front yard, and a bunch of cars in the driveway and lining that corner of the intersection. Behind us across the street from Wobble House sat an old-fashioned white carriage pulled up near the curb, with a brilliantly white horse placidly watching traffic. The horse has a distinctive marking on one side of its face, mottled heather gray and black starting under its eye and trailing towards its nose. I like horses, but I've never taken one of those carriage rides. They're for tourists, mostly, and I grew up on the Island.

The horse doesn't look alarmed, and from the sound of things, the party at Silas's house is in full swing. Surely that means that nothing bad has happened here. I hold onto that, steadying myself as I get out of Logan's car.

We go up to the front door of the mansion, the same grand entryway where I'd been received last night.

I knock on the door, then after a moment, I realize it's such a big house that if Mitch isn't standing in the foyer, he'd never hear a knock. So I ring the bell. I'm still startled when the resulting sound is a loud gong, even though I'd heard the same gong last night. I bring a hand to my chest. "My goodness!"

After a minute or so, I ring – gong – again. Anxiety swells inside me as we stand there in the lovely afternoon, with no response from inside the house. From across the street, there's a *whuffling* noise and the jingle of tack as the carriage moves out onto the street. I'd been so focused on Mitch's door, I hadn't even noticed it picking up a passenger.

I gesture at the door. "I have a bad feeling about this. I think we should try to go inside."

Logan looks at me warily. "Maybe you should wait out here."

I shake my head. Logan's background is in private security, among other things. And because of my aversion to violence, he often tries to protect me. That aspect of our relationship is influenced by the fact that I'd once hired him as a bodyguard. I tell him, "This time, the person on the phone has made this personal. It was my decision to come here. I need to take responsibility, if Arlo arrests us for breaking and entering."

"It's *because* it's personal that I want you to be extra cautious." But from the look on his face, I can tell Logan realizes it is pointless to tell me to wait here while he clears the house. He sighs. "They can't arrest you for breaking in if you have a probable need to render aid." Logan tries the handle, and the door swings open. "And it looks like we're not breaking, just entering, anyway."

But an unlocked door in a place like this is never a good start.

I step through into the foyer. There's no sign here that anything has been disturbed. I start to lead Logan through to the gallery space Mitch had showed me last night, but I notice some unusual marks on the floor in one of the side hallways. I turn and walk down the hallway to examine them, and find they are sooty pawprints, most likely from a cat, leading away from a door that is standing slightly ajar.

Logan asks, "Does Eberhardt have a cat?"

I follow the prints towards the door, and whisper back, "I don't think so. The only cat I've seen here belongs to Gently."

Maybe this is where Mitch and Gently went last night. I pull open the door, despite Logan's grumbled protest, revealing a cozy study lined floor to ceiling with books. On one wall there's an oversized fireplace – likely the source of the soot that had gotten on the cat's paws. At first, nothing seems amiss, but then I notice a ball of sooty red yarn that has been pulled into the fireplace, with kitty paw prints and smears in the soot around it. The other end of the yarn strings out across the room, towards a desk. The box of truffles that I'd given Mitch is flipped over on the desk's surface, and the truffles themselves have rolled across the surface, implying a struggle. Only – these aren't the truffles I'd put in the box. These are dipped in dark chocolate, with scarlet swirls on them. Weird. Who would change out the truffles in a chocolate box?

I follow that crimson strand of yarn until it disappears, then I gasp as I see a slippered foot on the floor, poking out from behind the desk.

I rush over, despite Logan calling that I should wait. Somehow, I'm not surprised at what I find. The desk chair has been knocked over, and sprawled between it and the desk, there's Mitch, wearing his smoking jacket. He's been stabbed with a pair of knitting needles, one of which still has a piece of knitting attached, a long narrow strip like a red banner trailing artistically onto his chest, this knitted piece made of one knotted long red thread, echoing the quote from *A Study in Scarlet*.

I pull back in revulsion, as a chill goes down my spine. Before I switched careers to become a chocolate maker, I was a physical therapist, but it doesn't take medical training to take one look at Mitch and realize it is far too late to render aid.

"That thing with the yarn and the needles looks too perfect for a struggle," I tell Logan, struggling to keep my voice even. This isn't the first dead body I've discovered, but it's always shocking. Plus, as eccentric as he had been, I had liked Mitch. There's not much blood – which implies the actual murder happened somewhere else. "You can tell the box of truffles was flipped on purpose, and artistically arranged. And the truffles traded out for different ones. I gave Mitch that box, and the truffles I made were dipped in white chocolate. I don't even make one with red swirls. I think this scene was staged."

Logan nods. "I agree. But I think the cat was getting in the way. Part of the knitting looks unraveled, so that's why the killer picked up the cat and dumped it into the hall."

That makes sense. Otherwise, how are there so many sooty pawprints near the fireplace, and none crossing the room?

I can't help but picture Gently's face last night, how upset he had looked coming back from his chat with Mitch. Only – Gently would never hurt anyone. He's too much of a pacifist. And if he had accidentally hurt Mitch, he would never have tossed Ruffles – who is a registered emotional support animal – out of the room while dealing with such an anxiety-inducing situation.

"There's so much soot and ash," I say, "But it doesn't look right for a fire. And it smells like plastic and celery. Was somebody burning a bag of celery?"

Logan says absently, "Nylon smells like that when it burns. Maybe somebody burned whatever they wrapped Mitch in to move him." Looking more focused, Logan asks, "Does your friend Sonya have any connection to this guy?"

He's studying the knitting needles. How he has the steady nerve to just logically observe while there's a dead body in the room is beyond me. I feel the adrenaline-induced need to do something – even though I've called the police already, so there's nothing really to be done. I usually gather and prepare food to help steady others in times of crisis, but this isn't even my place, so I can't just go into the kitchen and assemble snacks for the soon-to-arrive cops.

I try to calm that need-for-purpose instinct, become less antsy, overcome my revulsion to study the knitting needles as closely as Logan is. And I realize they're engraved with the initials S. P. Which are, indeed, the same as my friend Sonya Popescue.

"Don't suggest that to Arlo," I tell Logan. "Sonya knew *of* Mitch, and respected his reputation in the art world, but when she tried to introduce herself last night, he basically ignored her – despite having invited her to his party."

"Good," Logan says. "Because I did know this guy – though he wasn't calling himself Eberhardt at the time – and Mitch Fontaine wasn't the kind of person someone like Sonya would want to be mixed up with."

"You're sure it's the same guy?" I ask.

Logan looks glum. "I helped get him arrested eight years ago in Paris. It's the same guy."

I blink, puzzled, looking at Mitch's still face with deep curiosity. It's such an uncomfortable feeling, this need to know more about him, riding on the back of the shock if his death. Finally, I ask the immediate question, "If you knew him in Europe, then what on Earth is he doing here? He just randomly moves to Galveston, Texas? That seems like a huge coincidence."

"It does, doesn't it." Logan looks thoughtfully over at Mitch. I avoid following his gaze. "But he didn't bother to tell me he was in town."

I hear sirens outside. Arlo had taken my distress call seriously. I'm glad he has arrived so quickly.

"Come on," Logan says. "It's better if we meet them by the front door and lead them back here."

"There's one thing we know about whoever did this," I say as I follow him out of the room.

"What's that?" Logan asks.

"They really like their puns." I gesture back at the study. "The whole scarlet thread thing, and the reference to a *Study in Scarlet*. They killed the guy then moved him into the study, when it would have been more meaningful to stage the scene in his private art gallery. It had to be because they wanted to taint this study with scarlet. So, literally, they're labeling this murder in the study."

"Like in Clue," Logan says. "Miss Scarlet, in the study with the knitting needles."

## Chapter Five

It takes a while to tell Arlo everything that happened.

But when I am finally allowed to leave, I go on my own to visit Eunice at work at the Prime Circle. I am going to have a hard enough time getting her to talk to me. If I bring a cop, that's guaranteed to spook her. And Logan might not be a cop anymore, but he still looks like one.

I'll just share any info I get with Arlo – along with the fact that Eunice had been at my shop, which I forgot to tell him earlier.

When I park my catering van in the parking lot at the restaurant, there are only a couple of vehicles, all of which are parked in the row farthest away from the building. Staff, obviously, getting things ready for the restaurant to open for lunch. It's still early, but I go up to the glass door anyway and knock.

There's a woman in there sanitizing menus at the host stand. She looks up, frowning. She makes her way over to the door and says, loudly enough to be heard through the glass, "We're closed."

I bring my hands together in a pleading gesture, and shout back, "I need to talk."

I can see the woman sigh, though I can't hear her. She flips the lock on the door and opens it enough to talk to me. "What's so urgent?"

I say, "I need to talk to Eunice Brewer. She'll know what it is about."

The woman rolls her eyes and turns away from the door.

Behind her I recognize Doug Nichols, who I haven't seen since high school. He was my lab partner in Chemistry, and I was the reason he got an A in the class.

I wave and he comes over. "Felicity Marchetti, is that you?"

"It's Koerber now, but yes." We chat for a few minutes. He never left the island. Bought this place a couple of years ago when it came up for sale. When I ask to talk to Eunice, he doesn't ask why. He just uses the sound system at the host stand to ask her to come to the front of house. The woman I initially talked to has disappeared somewhere in the building.

Eunice looks confused as she makes her way through the tables, a half-rolled napkin full of silverware in one hand. "You wanted to see me?" she asks. But then she spots me and gives Doug a look as if to say, *Am I in trouble*?

I feel like I have to push here. Eunice is the only suspect I have so far in Mitch's murder. And if it is her – the killer who called me out is going to want a decisive accusation. It seems unclear why she would have given me a puzzle this easy to solve, but I don't want to mess this up. If she does confess, I don't know what I plan to do after that, but I'll tackle that bridge if I come to it.

But if she's not the killer – I just hate that I'm doing this in front of her boss. I try to draw her away to talk, but she's not having it.

"Look," Eunice says, backing away from me a little, "I don't know anything about any missing chocolate."

"Who said you did?" I say softly.

"What?" A look of confusion crosses her face.

"I don't care about the chocolate," I say. Of course, that's not completely true. I add, "Not much anyway. What's important now is the book. Did you leave it for me? Did you bring it to the shop after I didn't answer my phone, after you killed Mitch Eberhardt?"

"What?" Eunice says again, in a completely different tone of voice. She looks to Doug for any clue to what I'm talking about. "I didn't kill anybody. Who's Mitch Eberhardt?"

So much for an instant confession and congratulating me for how smart I am.

"But you do know something about the book," I prompt, willing for the moment to take her at her word.

Eunice looks to Doug before she answers. "I might."

"Someone was murdered?" Doug asks. He looks overwhelmed by this idea.

I explain about finding Mitch dead in his study, and about being called out by the killer. About the threatening bookmark placed in the book. I'm still not completely convinced that said killer wasn't Eunice. But if she'd intended to challenge me, surely her reaction now should be different, gloating, asking where my evidence is – something.

She says carefully, "It's hard to raise two kids on a waitress's income. So sometimes on my day off, or before work like today, I run errands through a service. I was asked to deliver that book to you, specifically like I did. That's all. I didn't know anyone was going to die over it."

"Okay. I'm sorry I accused you." I really am, because now she looks like she's about to start crying. I've tried to learn to be more tactful, over the course of multiple investigations. I've nearly lost friendships over circumstantial accusations, and it's almost always unnecessary. "Please. I need to know who hired you. Maybe it will help make sense of it all."

Eunice takes a phone out of the pocket of her small half-apron and shows me an app. She says, "I had a request through the Hustle Help app this morning to pick up the book from the lost and found at the Tremont House. The message said there would be an envelope inside it containing a tip for five hundred bucks tucked inside the back of the book. And that I'd get another five hundred added to my pay after the task was complete."

"The message told you to have your kids trash the bookshelf in my shop, and then shoplift," I say skeptically.

She replies, "It said to draw your attention to the book without handing it to you directly. I just used my imagination. The instructions then said to wait around somewhere outside until I could make sure you'd seen the book."

I shudder at the thought of Eunice staring in surreptitiously while I'd been having that conversation with the customers. If she's not the killer, then it was harmless observation. But still, nobody likes the idea of being watched.

"And then what did you do?" Doug prompts.

Eunice says, "I marked the task complete, and I got paid as promised. Then I dropped the kids off at my mom's – she home schools them while I'm at work – and headed here." Eunice looks me straight in the eye and adds, "That's all I did. You believe me, right? You're not going to get me into trouble with the police."

I hesitate. "Well, I already reported the shoplifting. It's required, if I'm going to claim the missing inventory on my insurance. I'm willing to tell the police that the missing chocolate was just a misunderstanding, if you show the assignment details in that app of yours to the homicide detective handling Mitch's case. We can even meet him at my shop, so you won't have to go all the way to the police station."

Eunice looks questioningly at Doug.

He says, "Try to make it back before the lunch rush."

"So I still have a job?" Eunice asks. "Even after the stuff about Felicity's chocolate?"

Doug says, "I have four kids myself. I can understand the temptation. Just – don't do it again. And definitely don't do it here."

Doug always was a really nice guy. I'm glad his life seems to have worked out.

Eunice follows me over to my shop, and by the time we arrive, Arlo is already there. He takes her over to a table in the corner to take her statement, and after about ten minutes she leaves.

By that time, Logan and I are sitting at a table near the windows trying to process the shock of everything that has happened this morning, though there's so much to do, both of us should really be working.

Logan seems to be thinking the same thing. He says, "I've got all the partitions up, so you can see the line people are going to follow along the tour. I've painted swatches on part of the half wall, so we can pick between the different shades of gray from the paint chips." He waves a dismissive hand. "I hate those things. There's never enough there to really get an idea of what the space will look like completed."

It's always odd to talk about mundane things after a death.

"I'll put on a filter mask later and come have a look." I haven't seen much of the annex, since everyone seems so concerned about crossing construction dust with any potential residual asthma symptoms I still have after the experimental treatments I'd undergone. I lean closer to him and say, "I just – look, thank you for all the work you're putting into this. I know we're business partners and all, but this place was my vision, and it means a lot to me that you respect that."

Logan looks embarrassed. He starts to say something, but before he can, Arlo comes over and sits down with us.

Arlo says, "It's pretty clear that Eunice didn't do it. She and her kids made a memorable impression at the McDonalds on the other side of the island about the same time we're estimating Mitch was being killed."

We are going with the idea that he probably died an hour after the phone call, just like the voice on my phone threatened. However, it obviously took a long time to set up that murder scene – including moving Mitch from wherever he was actually attacked. So in theory, the killer might not have left until shortly before I arrived. The person could even have been nearby, waiting for me to arrive. So, Eunice's alibi probably holds up.

I ask, "What kind of person uses an errand service as part of their elaborate murder plan?"

"A literary one, apparently," Logan says.

"Says the guy who rarely reads," Arlo points out.

"I read. We've established this." Logan waves his phone at Arlo. "I've even started listening to fiction on audiobooks. It's been helping pass the time while working on the expansion."

This is news to me. "What are you reading?"

"I'd rather not say," Logan says. He doesn't elaborate.

Arlo laughs, then his expression turns serious when he turns to look at me. "You said there was something about the crime scene you wanted to discuss."

I nod, and take out my phone, ready to show him the information I had looked up. I say, "I found a shop in Houston that sells truffles with the same style of red swirl as the ones that got swapped out for mine." The screen lights up for about half a second, then goes dark. I let out a frustrated grumbly noise. "Okay, my phone is dead again. Just look up Trufflocity. It's their red velvet cake truffles. Which are more like cake pops without sticks than actual truffles. It doesn't make sense. Do you think the killer took off with my truffles, because they're better than the cake crumble ones?"

Arlo says, "Then why not just take the box with your truffles in it? I think the killer left your box simply because it was red."

"Presumably, Mitch ate the truffles you gave him," Logan says. "Or the killer ate them, while staging the scene."

I shudder. "So you think we're looking for a suspect pool of interior designers?"

"Or an artist, or someone known for having a good eye for fashion," Arlo says. He shows me his phone where he has up the website for Trufflocity. "Don't worry – I'll send somebody over to see if there's a record of anyone buying a quantity of these red velvet things in the last few days. It's probable that someone planning to set up a murder scene would have paid with cash."

It's a somber thought. Whoever killed Mitch might not have left enough clues to get caught. I could have this unasked-for guilt of not having helped Mitch weighing on my conscience forever.

Arlo says, "One odd thing. Several people should have been at the house this morning – including the housekeeper and the personal assistant, but Mitch made a phone call to the housekeeping service, complaining about nobody showing up."

"Weird," I say. But I'm not sure what to make of it.

Autumn comes in, a copy of her first book – *Discordant Melody* – in her hand. "Hey, I got that autograph you wanted. And I have an awesome surprise." Her expression turns from happy to uncertain as she takes in me, Arlo, and Logan sitting glumly despite the sunlight streaming in through the window. "Who stole your puppies or whatever?"

Carmen is wiping down the counter in the coffee station. She says, "That's their *found another murder victim* faces."

From the doorway between the kitchen and the counter, Tracie calls for Carmen's help with something. Carmen goes into the kitchen to see how the pecan pie truffle masterclass is going.

I say miserably, "We found a pair of knitting needles sticking out of Mitch Eberhardt's chest."

Autumn's mouth falls open. After a moment, she composes herself and asks, "Mitch is dead?"

She sounds close to hysterical. Which feels like a bit of an overreaction, as she didn't even know who Mitch was before last night.

Arlo asks, "Autumn, were you friends with Mr. Eberhardt?"

"Goodness, no," Autumn says. "But last night, he offered to let me and Drake use the Wobble House ballroom for our reception. At no cost. It was going to save us so much money.

And I already told Drake's mama we could invite thirty extra people."

I say, "You were telling everyone Wobble House creeped you out. Why would you want your most memorable party there?"

Autumn says, "I never really looked at it before. Violet came and took your empty seat, and she explained some things about the architecture. And Mitch told us about some of the changes he had made to update the place behind the scenes. It's weird how once you get to know something, it becomes that much less scary, and can actually become cool."

"You must have had quite the conversation after I left the room," I say. Mitch had gone back out to his guests while I had still been speaking with Carmen and the others. But it had only been ten or fifteen minutes before I had rejoined the group.

Autumn says, "You missed quite a bit. You remember Pru?"

I nod. "She and Ben are frequent customers. You've probably seen them here."

"I have," Autumn says. "They have been here a couple of times when Drake and I stopped in for breakfast pastries and coffee before the library opens." Drake is an archival librarian at one of the local universities. "She called Mitch over when he came back into the room and introduced him to me, then suggested he open the ballroom for the reception. Then she introduced him to Sonya and suddenly he was interested in talking to her, after he blew her off when you tried to introduce her. I can't decide if Pru is Mitch's aunt from a whole other branch of the family, since they both have British accents – or if she's blackmailing him."

I protest, "Why didn't you tell me any of this when I got back to the table?"

Autumn shrugs. "The conversation had moved on. I was going to tell you about it this morning. As matron of honor, I assumed you'd be excited for me."

"I am," I stammer. "Or, rather, I would have been."

Because who knows what happens to Wobble House, now that the owner is dead.

"But this all brings me back to my surprise." Autumn's phone dings as she gets a text. She nods at her phone, then moves to the shop's front door. "I'm going to need you to add another bridesmaid to my roster."

She opens the door, and in bounds a familiar beagle wearing a familiar yellow vest.

"Satchmo!" I call, leaning over, and the dog rushes over to me and pushes his head against my outstretched hand. I'd gotten to spend time with Satchmo, a retired police dog in training to be a therapy dog, on board a cruise ship not terribly long ago. But he and his owner live in Baltimore, so I hadn't expected to see him again, after we had all disembarked from the cruise.

If Satchmo is here – then his owner Bea can't be far behind. Sure enough, she walks in the open door and says, "I see Satchmo hasn't forgotten his friends."

"And we haven't forgotten you." I give Bea a big hug, then ask her, "What brings you to Galveston?"

"I'm moving here, at least for a while" she says. Bea is in her mid-forties, and wears her brown hair cut into a bob. She has a wide smile on her heavily-freckled face. "I'm going to be working with the K-9 Unit here on training techniques. When I was offered the opportunity to spend some time at the beach – and to get some more of your delicious chocolate – I couldn't resist."

"That's awesome," I say. "You will finally get to meet Carmen in person." I gesture towards the kitchen. "She and my other employees are in the back, working on a giant order we took for truffles."

Bea waves in the general direction of the expansion. "What's going on over there?"

"We're going to have an open area for tours, where people can watch chocolate making in progress. It's going to be a draw for school groups from Houston and other surrounding areas, as well as women's groups, people who travel for foodie tours, and so much more."

Bea gives me the smile of a friend who wants to be supportive, but doesn't quite understand why something is making the person they're listening to so excited. "That's great," she says. "Sounds like a lot more work."

"But it's going to be worth it." I cut a glance at Logan. He's financing it, so I hope he still feels the same way, even if we don't wind up together after my moment of truth at Autumn's wedding.

Autumn says, "I've asked Bea to be one of my bridesmaids."

Bea says, "I hope it's not going to be too much trouble. I know the wedding is coming up fast, and you have a lot on your plate in addition to being maid of honor." She gestures towards the continuing construction sounds.

"It should be fine," I assure her. "Everybody's picking their own dress in Autumn's color scheme. I can take you shopping and show you the ones everyone else picked out, so you can match the feel. We're all ordering the same shoes, to tie everything together."

Bea looks uncertain. "Maybe you can pick something out for me. My taste in dress clothes tends to be a little offbeat."

Right now she's wearing jeans and a navy tee-shirt that says, *I'm owned by this spoiled rotten beagle*. Which isn't the height of fashion, but could hardly be called offbeat. I try to remember what she'd worn for formal occasions on board the cruise ship. I can't remember the specific clothes, just an impression of flowy floral fabrics and asymmetrical lines.

I tell her, "We're a fairly eclectic group. I'm sure you'll fit right in."

I mean, she hasn't seen Tiff's dress yet. My real-estate agent friend had chosen a green and teal peacock dress that Autumn had used as the basis for the whole color scheme.

Bea says, "I just don't want to be any trouble." She turns and puts a hand on Autumn's arm. "You're sure I'm not going to make your line uneven."

"It's not a problem," Autumn reassures her. She drops her voice to a whisper. "Drake wants to ask him himself, but he's going to ask Arlo to be a groomsman."

I glance over at Arlo, trying not to be obvious. I feel anxiety trying to settle into my chest. Now both of the guys I've been almost dating are going to be in Autumn's wedding. The very event by which I'd promised to make up my mind between them. Is Autumn trying to make my life more difficult on purpose?

Autumn takes in the stricken look on my face. She shrugs. "All is fair in love, right?"

"Sure," I say slowly. I'm not sure what she means. Did Arlo ask to be in the wedding? Or has Autumn maybe decided that I make a better fit with Arlo and wants to make sure he gets lots of time with me? After all, I had admitted to her that he's the one I keep kissing. But that's because Logan has backed off, and I'm not sure he'd even feel comfortable kissing me again.

## Chapter Six

Bea has a pending delivery at her new apartment, so she heads out. The guys start talking baseball while waiting for a call back from forensics, so Autumn and I wind up sitting at a table near the coffee station to finally talk about her book.

After pouring us each a cup of steaming java, Autumn sits back down and pulls her tote bag up onto her lap. She takes out a thick 3-ring binder and pushes it across the table towards me.

A sheet of paper has been slid inside the binder's plastic front pocket. It's a picture of me, but with red hair, obviously the result of one of those beauty apps that let you try out different looks. I'm holding up a whisk. I think I remember the shot. It was for an advertisement for a farmer's market in Houston, where we've sold Greetings and Felicitations chocolate a couple of times. And I remember, I'd just sneezed, so I wasn't smiling in one of the shots. What I don't remember is having a tattoo of a crow running across the back of my forearm, or the nose ring that has been carefully photoshopped into the image.

Autumn says, "This is my inspiration image for Fiona, a hot young chef with an attitude. She's been doing unlicensed pop-up dinners in abandoned subway stations under New York City. It's a ton of fun – until a mystery writer and a restaurant critic both wind up dead on the site where her last pop-up was held."

I blink at the picture, taking in the little details – like the black lace that has been added to my – Fiona's – blouse. Finally, I look up at Autumn and ask, "Did you combine me with Enrique to come up with this?"

Autumn nods, looking both proud and terrified that I'm not going to like it. "With just a hint of Violet, to keep things edgy."

I spend a few moments imagining how that might come together. Any way you look at it, you come out with a character with a good heart and a ton of self-confidence. Then I grin and say, "I have to read this book."

The title that's been added to the image is, "Ghost Kitchen," which is a clever pun – since a ghost kitchen is a space where caterers and virtual restaurants can operate in either a shared space, or by using a kitchen during the hours when the restaurant that owns it doesn't need it.

Autumn says, "I used the robots from the case you solved on the cruise ship. I think you'll appreciate what I did with them." She hesitates again, then takes a sip of her coffee before adding, "At least I hope you will."

"I'm sure it's spectacular," I say. "I've loved everything else you've ever written."

Autumn smiles, obviously pleased by the compliment. "I think we all need a couple of cheerleaders in our life. And for writers, it's great when those cheerleaders are also readers."

I sip my own coffee, thinking about why I like to read so much. I say, "I love being able to imagine I've become the protagonist of a book, seeing through different eyes, living a whole different life. Doing things I'd never dare in real life."

Autumn purses her lips. "But you've never gotten so attached to the characters in a book that you'd want to re-enact the plot, right?"

She's talking about Mitch's murder. I know that, but I say, "There's a couple of books I wouldn't mind starring in. Take Emma – you know how I feel about the relationship between her and Mr. Knightley."

I'd even named my pet bunny after the guy.

Autumn mimes fanning herself. "If we're talking Austen, I'm more for Darcy myself."

"Don't let Drake hear you talking that way," I tease. "He's too nice to be a Darcy-type."

She wrinkles her nose, playfully. "A Darcy would be too much maintenance in real life." Then her face goes somber. "But it's weird thinking about how this killer must be a reader. This is the opposite reaction that Doyle would have wanted for a fan of his Sherlock books."

It's something to seriously consider. Several people who were at the party yesterday are members of the book clubs that meet at the local book store. And that's just the people we know are connected to Mitch. Looking for people who love to read is not an easy way to narrow down suspects, though. We'd been discussing travel books at my table at the tea party. And even in the kitchen -- Yoli had asked for Autumn's autograph. And Enrique is at least a casual reader – what with the whole incident involving his copy of *The Invisible Man* in the course of a previous case.

"Hey, Felicity," Arlo calls from across the room.

I had been completely lost in thought. I jump a little, and Autumn giggles. She whispers, "It's almost like we're back in high school. Arlo always did make you a little nervous."

I had had the biggest crush on Arlo in high school, and Autumn had listened to me obsess about it, until Arlo had finally asked me out. Arlo and I had had a good thing back then – until I'd ruined it.

"Felicity?" Arlo says again. He sounds uncertain. He's probably just unsure whether I could hear him.

I move over to the table. "What is it?"

He shows me his phone. "Does this cat look familiar to you?"

The picture is clearly of Ruffles, Gently Drifting's emotional support cat. The big black and white feline is sitting on the table at a veterinarian's office, licking a back paw.

"Why are we looking at Ruffles? Is he okay?"

"He's fine," Arlo says. "But he was found in the pantry at Wobble House. It is unclear whether someone closed him in there, or if he went in on his own and the door closed behind him. I know Gently is your friend, but . . ."

Arlo gives me a significant look. Anxiety washes over me. I can't help but picture Gently's upset face last night, and those cat pawprints in the hallway leading away from the scene of Mitch's death.

If Gently has it in him to be a killer, then I have misjudged him greatly. And that means I failed him as a friend. I already feel responsible for not stopping Mitch's murder, after he asked me for help. But what could I have done? I'd asked Mitch to go to the police, or to talk to Logan, and he'd refused.

Thinking about what Logan had said about knowing Mitch, I reinterpret the look that had crossed Mitch's face when I'd given him Logan's card. If Logan knew Mitch – Mitch knew Logan. Which means – I'm not sure what. But maybe Mitch coming to Galveston hadn't been related to the art scene at all. Maybe he had wanted something from Logan but hadn't gotten around to asking for it.

But what could Gently have to do with anything between the two of them? Logan hadn't even known Gently until he had worked with us on the chocolate sculpture project, two months ago. But Gently is never far from his cat. So if Ruffles had been at the murder scene – Gently must have been there too.

Could something unexpected have happened? Something that had ended in murder? That certainly seems to be what Arlo is thinking.

The door to the shop opens and Violet, Carmen's roommate, comes in. She is also Gently's girlfriend, so it's not surprising when she stops in the doorway and gestures at someone still out on the sidewalk. After a moment, Gently appears behind her. He's holding a stack of paper.

They come into the shop. Gently spots Arlo and starts to back away, but Violet stops him. Gently's body language looks guilty. I have to give him the benefit of the doubt – after all, his anxiety disorder had made it difficult for him to talk to the police in the past.

Gently looks like he's forcing himself forward as he approaches us and hands me one of the papers – a lost cat flier. The picture of Ruffles is more flattering than the one Arlo showed me, clearly posed in the middle of the artist's workstation at the studio. Gently's hand shakes so hard that he almost drops the rest of the papers.

"Are you okay?" I ask.

Gently nods, though clearly he's upset. "Ruffles disappeared from my apartment last night. He was there when I went to take a shower, and gone when I got out. Somehow – I don't know – I never leave the back door open, but yesterday I must have because it was wide open, and there was no sign of the little guy. Violet and I have been looking for him since dawn. Ruffles has never been an outside cat. He must be so scared. He needs me – almost as much as I need him."

I get that. I have a lop-eared rabbit – the inspiration for the décor in my shop, which includes a neon sign of my bunny-shaped logo, an oversized chocolate sculpture featuring Knightley himself, and outlines of Knightley, which form the design on the wrappers of my chocolate bars. If he ever got outside – let's just say that domesticated bunnies aren't fit to survive on their own. And Knightley has gotten me through some of the roughest times in my life. I wouldn't stop searching for him, either.

Arlo says, "Gently, you can stop worrying. The police have Ruffles, and he is fine. I can take you to him. But first we need to talk."

"Why?" Gently looks terrified. "Are you sure nothing happened to Ruffles? You're not going to do the whole cat got on the roof thing, are you?"

Arlo appraises Gently before he answers. Finally, he says, "I have some questions about your whereabouts at the time of Mitch Eberhardt's death."

Gently gasps. "Mr. Eberhardt's dead? What does this have to do with Ruffles?"

He looks genuinely shocked.

Violet steps between Arlo and Gently. She says, “You can’t imagine that Gently killed someone.”

“I didn’t say that,” Arlo says. “Right now, there are just some things we need to clear up.”

“But you’re basically accusing him,” Violet says. “I’ve seen enough mystery shows to know that’s what you say when someone’s a suspect.”

Arlo leans back in his chair and crosses his arms over his chest, not denying it. It doesn’t sound like Gently has a verifiable alibi. If he’s been on the move all morning, nobody can account for a significant swathe of his time. Though if he could come up with enough different witnesses, it might give him the same effect as Eunice’s alibi, as there are still the issues of the amount of time needed to stage the crime.

“He didn’t say he’s the only suspect,” Logan points out. He means to be reassuring, but that’s not how Violet takes it.

Violet turns to me. “You have to fix this, Felicity. You’ve helped find the real killer when your other friends were accused. Please. I mean, look at him.” She gestures at Gently, and I notice a friendship bracelet on her wrist.

It’s made of green, scarlet and hot pink thread. I catch her wrist, to get a better look at the bracelet. This looks like the same type of thread as the scarlet one tied to the charm that Mitch had found in his pocket. I don’t know how common that is, but it seems like a big a coincidence. I ask violet, “Where did you get that bracelet.”

She blinks at me, obviously confused. “Gently made it for me, at some class he took at the yarn shop. Why?”

I look at Gently. He just plain looks guilty. I tell Violet, “I don’t think I’m going to be able to help on this one.”

Gently looks at me. He says, “It’s fine. I didn’t do it. I’ll just tell the truth. Maybe this time, someone will believe me.”

This time? I wonder what he means by that, but he doesn’t offer to explain. When he leaves with Arlo, Violet asks to go with them. At first it looks like Arlo is going to refuse, but he's always had a sympathetic streak – something I've always loved about him – so finally he says yes.

After the door closes behind them, there's a pause, as we all try to process what just happened, and find our way back to wedding talk and being happy about Bea's move. I start straightening things, checking over the bookcase to make sure nothing new has shown up. I haven't had any contact from the killer since the message I'd failed to pick up in time.

That could be because the killer had been Gently – who'd been out looking for his cat, that had wandered off after being kicked out of the murder room.

Or it could be because the killer was someone else entirely, and had decided I wasn't a worthy adversary. Which somehow makes me feel like I failed – though starting a timer like that based on a message you don't know if someone got doesn't seem like the smartest move. Or the most fair.

It almost feels like the killer had planned to kill Mitch anyway, while giving me the illusion I could have done something about it.

"Can we go to dinner later?" Logan asks, wandering over and handing me a couple of books that had been left on the sofa that is near the reading nook. "I'd like to talk."

I feel a different kind of anxiety. So much has been going on. What does he want to talk about? The business? Us? This murder?

"Sure," I say, trying to sound more confident than I feel.

## Chapter Seven

I can't remember the last time I had lunch out with both my parents. My mother, especially, prefers to cook and eat at home. I have dinner at their house about once a month, and it is always excellent. But Mom likes to take charge of the menu, as the kitchen is very much her domain in the house. Dad has his office – mom has the kitchen table by the window, where she writes articles for gardening and women's magazines, while drinking hot Earl Grey and simmering beef bourguignon. Her life is always organized and scheduled. Thinking about it, I probably come by some of my micromanaging issues honestly. Mom also volunteers at both the branch library near her house, and at a local animal shelter.

She's very particular about how food is prepared, and right now she's on a sugar cleanse. So the fact that both mom and dad wanted to do Mexican food at the restaurant I'm always telling them about is surprising. But I'd offered to treat for lunch, and for once none of us has a scheduling conflict. So, yay. Here we are.

Dad says, "I hear you got to see the changes inside Wobble House. Were they extensive?" He has salt and pepper hair, and a little goatee. He wears round glasses, and favors blazers, though today he's wearing a navy polo shirt with a conference logo, since it's a casual beach day. My parents will probably go walking along the seawall later.

I put down the tortilla chip I was about to pop into my mouth. Since my dad's an architect, it only makes sense that he loves old houses. I tell him, "It's been a while since I last visited the place." Like since I was in college. "So I don't remember for sure what was there. Mitch turned part of the first floor into a modern art gallery. But he kept enough of the traditional design elements and materials that it still felt as much a part of the house as any of the other changes over the years."

Dad says, "Nice. I'd love to see that."

"Maybe you can, once it's no longer a crime scene." I haven't asked him for my favor yet. Maybe I could take him on a tour and get talking about design elements, and then ask if he could design me something equally as cool. I lean forward. "I have an in with both the detective on the case, and the real estate agent who's likely to list the house if whoever inherits sells."

Dad says, "You really think so? I know a lot about the history of the place, so I could probably show you some things that weren't on the regular tours. The biggest renovation to Wobble House was in the 1920s. Some say it was to cover up a murder." Dad waggles his eyebrows at the preposterousness of this possibility. He, as far as I know, has never stumbled upon a dead body in his life. So it is easy to see why he'd take that info half-jokingly.

Mom rolls her eyes and takes a long sip of her margarita. She says, "Don't encourage her. Felicity gets into enough dangerous situations without you starting." Mom has long brown hair – dyed, of course to cover the grays, but it's dyed back to her natural shade, which is very similar to mine. She wears her hair parted in the middle, with waves that cascade down onto her shoulders in a calculatedly casual look. She's the only one in the family that has blue eyes, especially unusual since hers is the Cajun side of the family. Mom waves a hand and adds, "Besides, it was the 1920s, the height of prohibition, and of Galveston as a tourist destination, because this was one place that never took prohibition very seriously. Obviously, if a big empty-ish place got remodeled, it had to be to make it easier for rum running."

"Can't both be true?" Dad says, tapping her nose.

She bats his hand away. "Rob, that's embarrassing. Stop it." But she's on the verge of laughing.

My parents are a bit intense, but they are perfect for each other.

Dad says, "It's amazing that Wobble House is even still standing. Like a lot of historic structures, it went into decline, and with all the hodgepodged construction there were some issues with the foundation. If the Historical Society hadn't stepped in after old Doc Winters died, it probably would have been demolished in the late 1960s. It was the same with Ashton Villa in the 1970s, despite the effort it had taken to raise the mansion after the 1900 Hurricane. And with Moddy Mansion, after it was damaged by Hurricane Alicia in the 1980s."

He loves getting a chance to share things he's researched, and once he's on a roll, you're likely to get a lot more information than you bargained for.

Mom diffused his roll, saying, "You talk like you knew Doc Winters. You were just a little kid when he passed."

Dad says, "I did a paper on him, remember? It got abridged in that architectural magazine. He bought Wobble House from the family that built it for a song, after one of the family members was killed in the house and the grieving family wanted to move on. Learning about his fascination with optical illusion and the history of architecture, it was easy to feel like I'd gotten to know the good doctor."

Mom says, "Then he should have just been an architect instead of a doctor."

Dad says, "It's because he was a doctor that he could afford to do what he did with that house. It's like Felicity being a chocolate maker is what allows her to finance being an amateur detective."

My mom stops mid retort and silence falls over the table as she and I look at each other. I feel my face and neck going hot. Mom has never asked about anything to do with the cases I'd helped solve, as if she's in denial that it's even been happening.

She doesn't know about how much time I've been spending with Logan and Arlo while trying to unravel that crimson thread that keeps showing up in my skein of life, or the ultimatum I'd made with myself about my relationships with both of them. I doubt she's even met Logan.

Mainly, we've talked about the shop and how business is going, about the friends I've reconnected with since returning to the island. You know, about the whole normal side of my life. Even when I was young, I'd always looked up to my mom, wanted her to see the best parts of my life – while I just omitted to bring up the things that weren't going well. It was easier that way.

Mom looks at Dad and says, "Robert Antonio Marchetti. Our daughter is not an amateur detective. That's a fictional occupation."

"Um, she kind of is," Dad says. He turns to me, putting a hand on the table near my salsa dish. "I've been listening to that podcast your friend has been doing. I had no idea some of the things you'd been through. And he's only covered part of the first case."

"See?" Mom says. "It's worrying your father. You need to get your life back to normal."

"I'm not worried," Dad says. "I'm proud. Though I'd like to pay for you to take some self-defense classes. I have a client in Oslo where I designed a building where people can step back in time to the Victorian Era. It has a studio for Bartitsu, which I had never heard of. But apparently, it was practiced by Sherlock Holmes, and outside of fiction was a real defensive mixed martial art developed in England. So those sequences they show in the Holmes movies aren't that far-fetched, considering the source material."

"Stop," Mom says, putting a hand on Dad's arm as she interrupts him. She forces a smile. "Felicity, how are things going at Greetings and Felicitations? I understand your chocolate is up for several awards."

I force a smile, too. "That's right. They'll be announcing the "best of" winners soon. I'm a finalist for Best Dark Chocolate, and for Best Sea Salt Bar."

Mom relaxes visibly, as we head into this more comfortable conversation. She says, "I love that you are doing so well. And so many people compliment me, after visiting your shop. Let us know if there's anything we can do to help."

I know she means it. And I know she wants the best for me. After all, who wants their kid putting themselves in danger, no matter what the reason? And it can't be easy to rationalize why a previously normal daughter is suddenly stumbling over one dead body after another. I say, "There is something. I'm hoping you will come back with me to the shop after we eat. I want to show you the progress on the expansion."

Dad laughs. "It sounds like you're about to hit us up for an investment. Which we could do, no problem."

"No," I say, probably too quickly. I already have enough going on with Logan having a say in my business, without having to consult with my mom, too. "Nothing like that. Maybe just a little investment of time."

"As long as it's within the next three weeks," Dad says. "We can handle anything you want."

I pause with another chip midway to my mouth. "Why? What happens in three weeks?"

He sits up straighter and taps his chest. "I'm going to be leading a group of architecture students on a tour across Europe. It's a whole month of visiting ruins, and seeing museums, and taking gondola rides through crumbling neighborhoods."

"I'm going too," Mom says.

"Really?" I can't help but say. I explain, "I thought you hated hotels."

Mom shrugs. "I'll survive. I'm branching out into travel magazines. Speaking of which. I meant for this to be a surprise." She takes a glossy magazine out of her purse. It's the new edition of *Texas Go!* She flips it open, and there's an article about visiting Galveston – which features a stop at Greetings and Felicitations.

I'm truly touched by this. Obviously, this is her way of saying that she too is proud of me. But what I say is, "This is great! It's the kind of advertising you can't buy."

Mom beams at me. "I'm glad you like it." She licks at her lip, the way she does when *she's* nervous. "And I have a favor to ask you, too."

"What is it?" I ask as brightly as I can. Though Mom never asks for favors, and her expression has me bracing myself.

She says, "I'm in need of someone who can foster a dog. I have her at my house, but we already have Buster and Gizmo, and she just has too much energy for either of them. And the shelter won't take her back, because she bit one of the staff."

I say, "I can't take a dog. That wouldn't go over well with Knightley. Especially not one that bites."

Mom looks disappointed. "Maybe you can at least ask around? I need to find an arrangement before we leave. The kennel we use also won't take a dog with a history of biting. She's not mean, though. She just gets scared."

"I'll see if anybody is interested," I say. "Though I don't know anybody who's really looking for a dog."

Our food arrives, and we settle into more comfortable conversation, mainly about who all I've run into since I've returned to the island. A lot of people we all used to know still live here, so it's fun to reminisce and try to forget the horrible events of this morning, at least for a few minutes. Mom takes a packet out of her purse and pours special sugar-free dressing over her fajita salad.

Ash Diaz approaches our table and sits down at the empty chair on my side. He grabs a chip out of the basket and dips it into my salsa. I nudge the dish closer to him.

My mother looks startled, then frowns disapprovingly. "Felicity, is there something you brought us here to tell us? You know I don't like being blindsided."

Ash and I look at each other, surprised at my mom's assumption. We both burst out laughing.

I say, "Good God, no. Ash is engaged to somebody else."

And Ash says, "Felicity has enough love interests, without me."

Mom gives me a significant look. "Oh, really?"

I look down at the table. I'm not ready to discuss that topic with her. Definitely not in front of Ash, who might use the info for his podcast.

Dad says, "Wait. I recognize you. You're the guy with the *Crime, Island Style* podcast."

"Guilty," Ash says. "Always great to meet a fan."

"Ash," I say. "This couldn't wait until I got back to the shop?"

"I mean, I guess it could have," Ash says. "But I was hoping you could weigh in on a few things before I start writing the article on Mitch's murder."

My mom makes a small, upset noise. I haven't exactly told her that a killer challenged me. Or that I failed to rise to that challenge.

Ignoring Mom's distress, I turn towards Ash. "You can't mention me in your article. We're talking about a killer who thrives on recognition. Arlo thinks that if the media makes it look like this person won by killing Mitch, they might seek further attention by threatening somebody else."

Ash leans back in his chair, looking a bit deflated. "Oh."

"I do know something you can write about," I say. "My dad is well-versed in the history of Wobble House. And he's apparently a fan of yours, so I'm sure the two of you can figure out a way to capitalize on the new interest in the house as a crime scene."

My mother has gone pale, but my dad leans forward with interest. "What all do you want to know?"

I flag down a waitress to get Ash a menu, because obviously he's not going anywhere.

Ash and my dad talk about the house for a while, while I avoid Mom's questions about my love life, and manage to switch the subject to my parent's upcoming trip. Mom actually sounds excited. I guess I'm not the only one who's been focusing on personal growth lately. Good for her.

Dad gets my attention and asks, "Do you really think we could get inside the house? I want to show Ash the Art Deco bowling alley, assuming it's still there and not cemented over."

"Wait," I say. "I've toured Wobble House, and been to events there a couple of times. I would have remembered a bowling alley."

"It was never on the tour," Dad says. "The space was considered to need too much restoration. It was in a basement, which got heavily damaged during Hurricane Audrey in the late 1950s, and flooded again during Hurricane Alecia. But the Art Deco style inlay work surrounding the bowling lanes remained intact, and I was allowed in to photograph them for my research."

Mom says, "You'd have to wear a filter mask to go in there. There's bound to be a massive mold problem."

"And it's only two lanes," Dad points out.

"Still," Ash says. "My readers love things like that. If I could get photos, that could be its own story. *1920's Era Bowling Alley Hidden Under Local Historic Home*. That's a clickbait title if ever I've heard one." Ash elbows me. "Felicity, you have to get us in there."

"I'll see what I can do," I say. My phone – which I just charged before coming to the restaurant – is already down below 20% battery. I send a text to Arlo, asking when the house is going to be released from being a crime scene.

His return text says, *Why? Hoping to do a little breaking and investigating? If you are, you really shouldn't be telling me about it. I can empathize, but I'm still a cop.*

I tell Ash, "It doesn't sound like Arlo is going to give us a time frame."

So I try to finish my enchiladas, before they get completely cold.

But a couple of minutes later, Arlo texts, *Probably not until tomorrow, at the earliest. The place is huge. We released Gently, because there's nothing concrete connecting him to the crime scene, except the cat. It is his cat's pawprints, by the way. I just learned from the CSI guy that you can't identify an animal by pawprints – but noseprints are like human fingerprints, and Ruffles left his prints all over the hearth.* This is followed by a cat outline and several laughing face emojis.

And a minute after that, *I know you feel connected to this one, but it's a weird case. Hopefully, since you didn't rise to the bait, the killer will consider the challenge over. Try to relax.*

And then immediately after, *You haven't heard from them, have you?*

I reply to that one, *No, I haven't. But I'm very tempted to call back the number that left me the threatening message. Maybe I might learn something.*

The immediate response is, *Don't do that. DO NOT INITIATE CONTACT.* Followed by about nine frowny face emojis.

I text back, *Okay, I won't.*

But what am I supposed to do? I don't have any other leads, and I can't just let this one go. Silas had said that things happened at Wobble House at night, and I had passed that information on to Arlo, though it is likely that activity had stopped, with Mitch dead. Arlo promised to send somebody by just in case.

While it's possible the killer is Gently, it almost feels too obvious. Arlo had admitted he hadn't had enough to even arrest the guy.

It's creepy knowing someone with a fixation on me is out there. It feels unfinished. And I think I've hit the core of my unease.

I sigh, heavily.

"What?" Ash asks.

"You know a bit about Sherlock Holmes," I say. After all, Ash and his fiancé Imogen had organized a Holmes-themed live action role play – LARP – recently. They had to have done some research. "What do you think? Would someone obsessed with the Sherlock Holmes stories, and who basically imagines themselves as Moriarty, the craftiest villain Holmes faced, just walk away satisfied if they completed the crime without being stopped? Or would they call to gloat?"

Without hesitation, Ash says, "They'd gloat, definitely. Seriously, Felicity, how can you tell me that and then say I can't use it on the blog?"

"Because we're friends now. And you'll get the exclusive later and you know it."

"Fair," Ash says. But he still looks fit to pop.

But he agrees – Moriarty would gloat. So why haven't I gotten a call? I say, "There's something else coming. There has to be more to all of this."

Mom says, "Please stop talking like that."

I give her an apologetic look. But I can't keep my mind off this. I ask Ash, "In that situation, what would Holmes do?"

Ash says, "Holmes would review what happened, and then set a trap for the killer based on a minute clue."

"I don't think I can do that," I say. "My only experience is solving crimes after the fact."

My mom forces the conversation back to other topics, so by the time we leave the restaurant and head back to Greetings and Felicitations, I'm in a less morose mood. I'm excited to show my parents how much the shop has grown. And with Ash tagging along, I might get some non-murder related coverage on his blog.

When we walk through the shop's front door, the construction noises are still very much in progress, and Ash goes to check out what Logan and his crew are working on. Tracie is covering the counter. That seems a little odd, since she's the one who brought in the volunteer workers. Shouldn't she be supervising them?

Maybe things are going to well, that they are working on their own. Or maybe she swapped out with Carmen.

I get my parents each a cup of plain coffee – one thing they have in common, they take their coffee pitch black – and get them settled at a table, while I go to check on the progress. The volunteers seem to be ferrying full trays of truffles from the chocolate finishing room – which has a nice workspace for using the chocolate tempering machine. Each of the pecan pie truffles has to be dipped in dark chocolate and then have half of a pecan half pressed into the top. I had expected the volunteers to be rolling the truffles, and having staff dip them. But I guess it was easy to move the into the processing room, since there seems to be a meeting going on in the kitchen.

Carmen is standing with Enrique and Iris. She has her tablet computer open to some kind of spreadsheet. Iris likewise has a tablet, but she's using a stylus to sketch on hers.

I say, "I feel like I keep walking in on the middle of things."

Carmen says, "I tried to call. Your phone was off."

I groan. "I guess that means the battery died again. I have to find a minute today to go get that thing replaced."

Carmen says, "You really do." She shows me the spreadsheet, like the dates and numbers are supposed to mean something. "Enrique got a deal with a group who does event planning to do food sales for a series of summer concert nights. He wants to partner with us to do the desserts."

I say, "I thought you proved your brownie superiority and all that yesterday."

"But I made those brownies with your chocolate. Which is superb." Enrique plucks a truffle off a nearby tray. The chocolate hasn't completely set, so after he eats it, he moves over to the sink to wash chocolate residue off his fingers. "I think it could be great for both of us. I won't be able to bake on site, so hiring out to you guys saves me the cost of renting time in a ghost kitchen."

Iris holds up her tablet. "I've been helping Enrique out with graphic design. Check out the art concept I've been working on for the events." The sketched design is actually really cool, with smudges of orangey-red and dark blue representing the proposed color scheme, with Enrique's food being bright and hot, and my chocolate the deep dark of night. It's a bit of an obvious pun on dark chocolate, but I'm okay with it.

"I thought you were a cook," I say.

Iris points at herself with her stylus. "I dabble in a lot of different things. Anything to pay the bills when you freelance, am I right?"

"I guess so," I say. I remember Iris saying that she likes to travel a lot. Maybe she has trouble keeping a job. Or maybe she doesn't want to be tied down by having a regular job.

Enrique has brought back his oversized bag, with the cross-stitch design of himself on it. He takes out some pamphlets, from events the planning company has done in the past. He starts talking about how reputable the company is, and something about minimum guaranteed sales, but I'm not paying attention. I'm too busy thinking about that piece of cross-stitch – and the cross-stitched bookmark that came in the copy of *A Study in Scarlet*. They were both custom pieces – and given the uniform nature of cross-stitching, could well have been produced by the same hand. I know Enrique is a reader – though I don't know if he reads mysteries.

I'd been assuming that the killer had called me, and had arranged to send the book, before the murder had been committed. But what if that wasn't the case? What if the killer had committed the murder in the heat of anger – and then put the elaborate setup into place after, counting on the time of death being somewhat imprecise, since the body had been moved?

After all, Enrique was supposed to go by Wobble House this morning. And he hasn't said anything about it. Which is odd, given the murder. Most people want to talk about the slightest connection they have with a scandalous event. Maybe something hadn't gone as planned.

Carefully, I ask, "What happened when you brought Mitch the brownies this morning?"

Enrique snorts out a sort-of-laugh. "Nothing. I knocked on the door, and nobody answered. Presumably because he was already dead. I didn't know that at the time, so I just left. I didn't have an appointment with him or anything, so I figured he might have been the type to go for an early run on the beach, or maybe he was the type not to answer the door before noon."

Is he giving me too much detail? People sometimes do, when they're nervous. But this is Enrique we're talking about here. He tends to be detailed, in general.

I ask, "Did you notice anything unusual around the house?"

He pauses to think about the question. "That old guy who lives across the street was trying to peek into a window on the side of Wobble House. But he was being nosy yesterday too, so I don't know how unusual that is. He told me to have a good day, as I was leaving."

I'm going to have to make a point to talk to Silas about that. Maybe he can corroborate whether or not Enrique went into the house. Or maybe he saw whether anyone else did.

"Poor Mitch," Iris says. Then she asks me, "Having caught so many killers who have tripped up, what do you think would be the perfect murder? The one that would make the killer uncatchable?"

"I have no idea," I say. Does she think Enrique is guilty, too? If she does, being a true crime aficionado, she might try to find some evidence. So I warn her, "But killers are by definition dangerous, especially if they think you can expose them."

Iris starts to say something, but she is distracted by loud voices coming from the chocolate room. One of the volunteers storms into the kitchen and slams down a tray of truffles, causing them to roll around, smudging the pecan quarters with chocolate from other truffles.

The woman shouts towards the other room, “I never stole your boyfriend. Besides, we’re talking about high school.”

“No,” one of the other women insists, appearing in the doorway with her own tray of truffles. “We’re talking about my yogurt cup, at the office last week. I’m just saying you haven’t changed.”

Iris steps between the two women. “Why don’t we all just take a breath? I’ve listened to a lot of podcasts on therapy, and there’s this technique-”

Ignoring her, the first woman says, “You know what? One thing I’ve never been tempted to take is your clothes. You have horrible fashion sense.”

The second woman – whose jeans and black blouse look fine to me – lets out a growl. I can see her shift her weight to throwing stance before the worst even happens. She flips the tray sideways, catapulting the truffles towards the person who had just criticized her – only Iris is still in between them. Most of the truffles wind up splattering on her striped blue and white blouse, or sticking to her long blonde hair.

“Hey!” she shouts.

The woman who did the throwing bursts into tears and rushes out of the shop.

Her friend rushes after her, shouting, “I’m sorry. I was just mad. I didn’t mean that.”

Iris bends down and starts picking up the truffles, piling them back onto the tray. I help her, while Carmen and Enrique stand there and watch – possibly frozen with shock at the absurdity of what just happened. The chocolate is a mess, and I’m just grabbing it off the floor, which is the opposite of the way I usually work with chocolate, being careful to avoid smudging the pieces with my fingerprints.

And I have somehow streaked chocolate across the front of my pants.

My parents appear in the doorway.

Mom asks, “Is everything okay in here?” in a voice that clearly shows she knows it isn’t.

My cheeks flame with embarrassment. This was the one part of my life I told her I had under control. I step away from the shop during a big project or just a little while, and things start to spiral. I grab the tray off the floor and say, "Everything is fine," as I shove the tray onto the bottom shelf of a speed rack, so that it is out of sight and I can deal with the mess later.

I move to the sink and wash my hands. I rinse off my face, too, because I can't shake the feeling I have chocolate smeared somewhere on it. When I turn around, my dad is peering into one of the bowls of ganache ready for rolling, lined up on the counter.

He asks, "What's wrong with the texture of this chocolate?"

Panic jolts through me. Could they have been making truffles incorrectly all day? If even some of them are wrong, we'd have to start over, because there would be no way to tell which ones were correct. After all, you can't peek inside a chocolate coating without breaking it, and there's nowhere on a truffle where cracks wouldn't be obvious.

But when I look in the bowl, I am relieved. I say, "It's pecan pie ganache, Dad. You start with chocolate and cream, which would be smooth, but it has pecan gianduja to give it the pecan pie aspect."

"What's gianduja?" Dad asks.

I say, "It's a paste made by grinding together nuts and chocolate. Traditionally it would be hazelnuts, but I riffed on it with pecans and brown sugar. I wanted it to still have a bit of texture from the pecans, to make you think more of the pie, so it's not entirely smooth."

Carmen gives Dad a spoon with some of the pecan gianduja on it.

He tastes it and says, "This tastes like pecan pie filling all by itself."

I guess we're back on track, and he doesn't seem upset by the scene that just happened. So I say, "I want to show you the annex, and the space I want your help with. If you don't have the time to design it before your trip, it wouldn't be a problem to wait until you get back."

"Sounds good," Dad says. "If it's minor, I can probably get to it next week."

Mom says, "Felicity, have you been going into an indoor construction site?"

"Yes, Mom," I say, trying not to sound – or feel – like I'm a teenager again. "I told you, the asthma treatments worked, so I haven't had symptoms in months. And I have filter masks to wear when I go over there."

"You still have your rescue inhaler, though? Just in case?"

Enrique snickers. I give him a withering look – and my mom gives him a very similar look at the same time.

I move over to where I left my purse on the counter. I take out my inhaler and show it to my mom. I say, "Just in case."

Enrique says, "You seem busy. We can discuss the pop-ups when the shop is a little less crowded."

He and Iris leave – quickly. Cowards.

I take my parents over to the expansion. There's a couple of guys I don't know who are working with Logan as they all scrape up glue from the carpet they'd pulled out of the space.

There's an audiobook playing, loudly. I listen for a few seconds. It's a Dirk Pitt novel, in the middle of an improbable action sequence.

One of the guys asks, "Would that really work?"

Logan says, "Probably not. But it's still fun, you know?" He looks up and sees me and my parents standing there. His neck goes red as he moves over to his phone and switches the audiobook off.

That's what he's embarrassed about listening to? Adventure with inaccuracies? I have to choke back a laugh.

"Why stop the audio there?" Dad asks. "That's the kind of book I could get into."

Logan grins, a little sheepishly. "At least I'm not the only one." He holds out a hand to my dad, "I'm Logan Hanlon, Felicity's business partner."

"I'm Felicity's dad," Dad says. "And I have to say I like your handshake."

Awkward, Dad, awkward. But Logan plays it off like my dad is perfectly normal. He shows us around, explaining the work that's already been done.

"What's this?" my dad asks, pointing up towards the ceiling.

Logan says, "That is a light fixture installed by the tourist junk shop that used to have this space. It is a rusted bed frame bolted to the ceiling."

"I think it's a safety hazard," Dad says. "Those wires are just stuck up there."

"It's on my list to take care of, sir," Logan says. "I don't think I should pull it out myself, though, so I have a licensed electrician coming out."

Since when has Logan called anybody sir? Dad is nodding, though, looking approving. That look gives me a moment of déjà vu to when I'd brought Kevin over to meet them, when I'd been in college. And that parallel is not something I'm ready for at all.

I need to focus this meeting back onto the shop. I say, "Dad, let's go look at the space by the windows. I know you love cantilevered surfaces. Do you think we can make that work with chocolate?"

My mom appraises Logan and says, "I'm looking for someone to foster a dog, as a favor to Felicity. I'm having a hard time, since it has a history of biting, but you look like you could handle it."

A complicated look crosses Logan's face – and I remember his saying when we'd first met that he felt he had abandoned his childhood dog when he had to go to Europe, to keep himself safe. So maybe the idea of a temporary foster might be appealing – since he's not responsible for the dog forever – but might also feel like preparing in advance to abandon it. But what he says is, "I don't think it would work. Felicity has a bunny."

Mom looks surprised, then raises an eyebrow at me, and I look away. So now I'm not going to have a choice except to explain my complicated relationship with Logan to her later. But in front of him, she lets it go.

I notice Ash – who had been photographing pieces of the construction – looking at me curiously. He's just going to have to let it go, too.

Carmen comes into the expansion and says, "Kaylee couldn't get ahold of you, so she called me. She wants to make sure that you will still be there for the book club discussion of that book on the history of chocolate. She said don't forget the snacks."

My phone's dead, so I look at Carmen's to check the time. Somehow, lunch with my parents had taken an hour and a half longer than I'd estimated.

I say, "I've got to go."

Which means I'm leaving Logan alone with my mom's potential interrogations. He has experience with interrogation, from both sides of the table. So he can take care of himself here. Maybe.

But Logan and I will be at dinner in just a couple of hours. I hope she doesn't make it awkward.

## Chapter Eight

The rest of the day races past. I get back from the book club, minus the samples I had brought so people could, "taste the book" as Kaylee had called it. The volunteers are all back at work – how Carmen and Tracie had managed that, I'm not sure.

Logan has gone, and Miles wasn't able to stay all day. So I pitch in to get the last few truffles dipped, and then loaded into the catering van. Some of them haven't set. Carmen and I are carrying them very carefully, especially when we get to the venue and it comes time to unload. But the client seems happy enough, so I drop Carmen off and then rush to get my phone battery fixed, and get changed for dinner.

When I finally make it to the restaurant, Logan is already at the table. He's doing something on his phone. With his head tilted down at that angle, he's incredibly cute, in the way that makes me want to tousle his hair. He notices me and smiles, and I feel fizzy inside. I still don't know what Logan asked me here to talk about, but it feels like a date. Especially since we're at NaNa's, an upscale steakhouse not far from the yacht club. There's a small box on the table. Did Logan buy me jewelry?

Trying not to sound nervous, I sit down at the table and say, "Sorry I'm a little late. It took a while to get my phone battery changed out."

Logan nods, then asks, "So how did the book club go?"

I shrug. "There were two dozen people there. It's more proof that everybody reads, which makes everybody a suspect in a literary-inspired murder. Except for those who just pretend they've read the book, and get what they've skimmed out of context. And then sound foolish in front of the group. Kaylee doesn't let things like that slide, so I'm glad I actually read the text."

Logan says, "Remind me not to join book club. I've had enough being grilled for one day."

I wince.

"I'm sorry about my mom," I say. "She means well."

Logan says, "I'm sure she does. And that she wants to make sure you haven't gone into business with a crazy person. But let's just say I see where you get your deductive skills."

I laugh. I think that was supposed to be a compliment. Or at least that's how I'm taking it. It smells good in the restaurant, like seared meat and fresh-baked bread. Happy, I say, "I haven't been to this place in years. What made you think of it?"

Logan says, "I've seen you enjoy a steak or two while we've been places together. I stumbled across this spot a while back, when I was heading out on a fishing charter. It seemed like somewhere you would like."

I smile. "You're observant. I like that in a guy."

His green eyes crinkle at the edges when he smiles back. But then his eyes look sad. "I've been observing a lot of things, like between you and Arlo. It seems like you've been rekindling that old flame pretty effectively. Maybe I should have adopted that dog today, and be done with it."

Has he really been putting off getting a dog because he isn't sure if it would be a good fit with Knightley, if we did wind up together? And now he's changed his mind. I thought it felt like a date – but is he breaking up with me?

I feel my cheeks go hot. I hadn't expected Logan to be so blunt about it. Was this what he was already planning to say when he asked me to dinner? Or does this have something to do with whatever had happened with my parents after I left?

Logan had been the one who had told me I needed to make peace with my past, get closure over the disastrous breakup with Arlo, one way or the other. And to decide what I want my future with Logan to look like – even if that winds up with us just being friends. It takes me a minute to get my thoughts together enough to respond.

I say, "I told Arlo to give me until Autumn's wedding to make a choice. It's coming up quickly and-" I fall silent at his puzzled look. "What?"

He leans forward, studying my face. "Why do you still need time to make a decision? You're usually a very decisive woman. And not the kind who plays around with people's emotions. You love Arlo, just choose him."

"I can't," I say.

"Why?" he asks, genuinely puzzled.

How am I supposed to answer that? As honestly as I can. So I say, "You're the one who pulled me out of my depression about Kevin's death, and made me want to embrace life again. I fell in love with you, too, for your stubbornness and your brashness – and that sensitive side you try to hide. And I'm not sure I'm ready to lose that."

"Oh." He looks surprised. He leans back in his chair and crosses his arms over his chest. "So you're saying you love me."

"Don't be so shocked," I say. There's a vase of roses on the table. I pluck off one of the petals. "You've told me you love *me* before. Didn't you expect the feeling was mutual?"

"I've never been sure," Logan says. "I had hoped it was." His surprised expression is mellowing into something closer to bemusement. "Well, that complicates things."

"Exactly how?" I ask, looking at the dark spot on the petal, where I've crushed it between my fingers. I try to relax some of the tension out of my hand. But it doesn't work. I've been stalling so long about choosing a guy, what if I lose both of them?

Logan shrugs. "I had assumed that you were trying to find an easy way to break up with me. Not that we've been officially dating." He waves a flustered hand. "You know what I mean. But now – you can't say that you love me and expect me not to fight for you."

He's tinkering with the box on the table. I expect that he's about to give it to me. But he closes his hand around it and draws it back towards his edge of the table.

I gesture at the box. "Is that for me?"

"It was," he says. "I was going to give you the option to back out of our partnership, if me being there would make you uncomfortable. This is the key to the expansion, with the prepaid lease, and receipts for the improvements. I was just going to give it to you, no strings attached. But now . . . I think I should hold onto this." He taps it and gives me an ironic grin. "At least until Autumn's wedding."

I stare at the box. I say, "That's an expensive gift for someone you weren't sure even cared about you."

"Well, I know I love you. And that's enough for me to want to see you happy, no matter how you feel about me." He slips the box into his jacket pocket. Then He stands up, comes around to my side of the table, and pulls me to my feet. "There's been something I've been wanting to do for a long time."

I can tell from the way he is looking at my lips that he wants to kiss me. And I can't deny anticipation at the thought. I tell him, "We've done this once already."

"Barely," he says, even as he takes a step closer. "A mere brush of lips."

He's right – but it had been the perfect kiss for where I'd been emotionally at the time.

I look around, and yeah, people are looking at us. Including Ben and Pru, who are sitting at a table with another couple about their age. And Sonya, who is here with her twin sister Sandra. The sisters are sitting with two guys I've never met – but who also look a lot alike. Could the twins be dating twins? Surely Sonya would have shared news like that. But finding out the details about them can wait. Here I am, faced with Logan's expectant look, as he waits for permission to kiss me. I say, "So you're thinking right now, right here, in public."

"I don't mind, if you don't." He leans in, and I can't help but meet him. I've been wanting to know what a deeper kiss with him would be like, too.

The kiss is insistent and yet thoughtful and leaves me warm to my toes. And it's even worth the smattering of applause and the single wolf whistle we get when we break apart. The waiter approaches our table hesitantly, looking like he's not sure whether to take our order or tell us to knock it off. Logan moves back around to his seat and sits down like nothing has happened.

I stammer my way through ordering my steak, still feeling warm and off balance. Kissing Arlo yesterday had felt like going home. Kissing Logan now feels like leaping from a cliff into the ocean. Both of them feel right. But I have to make a choice. And soon.

I look down at my water glass, like there's some kind of answer there.

So it is only through the corner of my eye that I see someone in a white shirt and black pants place a tray on our table. The tray is covered with an assortment of fruit and small desserts. It's actually quite beautiful – if you ignore the fact that the word *Revenge* has been written in chocolate on the center of the tray. The letters are about three inches tall, written in the same calligraphic script as the writing on the wall in Mitch's study.

Logan and I look up at each other at the same time. I turn to try and spot the person who delivered the tray. But there's no one, except the other diners.

The wait staff are also wearing black and white, so in theory whoever had delivered the tray could be one of them. But I don't think the person I half-saw was as tall as our waiter. And he seems to be the only person handling our section.

"Don't touch that," Logan says.

"Like you have to tell me that," I say. As delightful as the lemon tarts and petit fours look, the person who assembled this tray is likely the same one who killed Mitch, so there's a chance the baked goods could be a temptation laced with poison. After all, poison was mentioned in the Holmes text. I add, “I knew this wasn’t over. I thought the killer might call and try to gloat. And when they didn’t – I’ve been on edge all day.”

“Stay here.” Logan gets up and moves quickly in the direction the person had gone. I see him reach into his jacket, reassuring himself that the gun he usually carries is there. And here I am, right back to having Logan as my bodyguard. Which is more or less how we met.

I stay where I am, but I’m scanning the room for any threat that might head my way, now that Logan is occupied. He’s right. It’s best to stay in the middle of this room full of potential witnesses. This killer doesn’t seem like the type to attack me in a way that would ensure they’d be caught.

Sandra and Sonya hurry over to me.

“What happened?” Sonya asks. “Are you okay?”

“I’m fine.” I gesture towards the table. “Did either of you happen to notice who dropped this off?”

“Sorry,” Sandra says. “We were too busy discussing the implications of that kiss you just shared with the entire restaurant. I didn’t realize how much chemistry you and Logan have. He always seems a bit stand-offish. I’ve been Team Arlo for you, myself. Now I’m confused.”

Sonya says, “I think whoever it was walked by from the direction of the pool room. I think someone might have gone in there earlier carrying a bakery box. But it was an impression. I have no idea who the person was.”

At least one of them had been paying attention.

Logan returns, not having found anything. The culprit either left the building or blended into the crowd. That’s the most unsettling thought. Could whoever had left this horrible tray be somewhere watching how I receive it? I try to be dispassionate and logical, like Holmes would be in this situation, but it is impossible to stop the goose pimples creeping up my arms.

NaNa’s has always had a room off to the side with ornate heavy wood pool tables, the pool room Sonya had referenced.

Sometimes people reserve the space for parties, since it is separate from the main restaurant.

I can easily imagine someone going in there carrying an innocuous bakery box and taking the tray out of it with no one watching. I tell Logan, "I'm going to check that out real quick."

He starts to protest, but I think he's decided that one of us needs to stay with the tray until the authorities can examine it and instead calls Arlo. So I go around the corner into the pool room, where there are around twenty people chatting and eating, and I see none other than Silas, the neighbor from across the street from Wobble House. Whatever party had been going on at his home earlier today seems to have moved here, en masse.

It is starting to feel weird that so many of the people who were at tea yesterday have shown up here today. Though of course, Silas wasn't actually at the tea. He was just in the vicinity.

Silas spots me peering into the pool room, and waves me inside. "Felicity, we just keep running into each other. Come in, join the party, and let me tell you my great news."

It turns out the news is he's about to become a grandfather – which isn't much of a surprise, given all those balloons back at his house.

I ask the room full of Silas's family in general, "Did anyone see someone come in here carrying a bakery box?"

"Yes," a young woman says. She's leaned over the pool table, about to take a shot at the two ball, over by the corner pocket. "I brought in a cake. There's still some left, if you want." She takes her shot, then gestures at a partially-demolished sheet cake over on one of the room's small tables. "And you can have next game, after I beat Silas Jr. here."

"Thanks, but I don't have time." Allowing a stranger to join in a family gathering is a kind gesture, but it is obviously not helpful in trying to figure out who left me a threat. If Silas's group brought the bakery box themselves, there goes the theory about the tray being hidden inside.

I want to ask Silas whether he saw Enrique at Wobble House this morning, but it feels like an awkward question to ask in front of all his family. Suddenly, it occurs to me that Silas could be the suspicious one – even without any evidence that he either reads or cross-stitches. Enrique had claimed to see Silas peering into a window. But Silas could have been securing that window, while making an escape. Given the timing, them bumping into each other had to have happened soon before I arrived. And neither one had been there by the time I reached Mitch's doorstep.

Tonight, Silas is wearing black slacks, but he has on a light blue dress shirt and a tie with tiny Tabasco Sauce bottles printed on it. I suppose I could have mistaken light blue for white with my focus still on other things. Maybe.

I ask Silas, "Can I have a word with you?"

He arches one bushy eyebrow. "What about?"

I gesture out of the room. "Perhaps in private?"

He says, "Whatever you want to ask me, you can ask it here."

I glance around at all these happy party guests. I hate to ruin the mood, but I say, "You were seen peering into one of the windows at Wobble House around the time Mitch was murdered. While you were there, did you observe anyone else enter or leave the house?"

Silas's eyes go wide. "He was murdered?" Silas says the word *murdered* as though it is in an alien language.

"Yeah, he was," I say. And the fact that Silas didn't know goes a long way in explaining why he could still be care-free at a party despite his neighbor's demise. "Why were you outside his house, around the same time? It was this morning, relatively early."

Silas says, "I wanted to see what all of the fuss was about, so I took a little peek inside. People came out of the tea party saying Eberhardt had made significant changes to the architecture. He might have ruined the building."

"So you went over there when you had a house full of family and friends?" I ask.

Silas looks confused. "What would that have to do with anything? I'm going to have family taking over my house all week."

"Fair enough," I say. "So you didn't see anything unusual?"

Silas says, "There was a cat, that came racing through the siting room. It seemed to be running away from something. But you know how cats do. Sometimes they spaz out over nothing at all." That much, at least, could match up with what I know already. Silas sighs. "And I heard a vacuum cleaner and shortly after that a repeated scraping noise, both coming from somewhere inside. The scraping noise had just started up when I left."

"Any idea what caused the noises?" I ask. After all, Mitch would have already been dead, and the hired help hadn't showed up. What would a killer need a vacuum cleaner for?

Silas looks at me like I'm a little slow. "Someone vacuuming and cleaning. I didn't stick around long to find out. My nephew came over and told me someone needed the pump for the air mattress, and I had to go find it. I didn't see anyone at the front of the house, but I wasn't looking." Silas gestures to a kid who's about fifteen. "Did you?"

"I saw some guy," the teen says, "But he was just standing on the porch. I didn't think it was important. We still had guests arriving, so I was more worried that somebody might hit my car." He looks nervous, like he thinks he might be in trouble

"Thank you for telling me," I say. "It could be important." Then I turn back to Silas and ask, "And tonight – you haven't left this room for the past ten minutes?"

Silas looks even more confused. "We've all been in here for at least an hour." He leans forward in his chair and asks, "What's with all the questions? Are you a detective or something?"

I shake my head, though that's getting harder to deny. "No. Just someone who needs to know the truth about what happened to Mitch." I don't say it, but I'm thinking, *Before the same thing happens to me*. Because I've just received the same kind of threat. I add, "I'm actually a craft chocolate maker."

Silas has a solid alibi, at least for the time when the threatening goodie tray had been delivered. He's likely not the killer. So I congratulate him on the newest addition to his family, and then I take my leave.

I return to the main room, where I take out my phone and photograph the tray. After all, this threat against me definitely relates to Arlo's ongoing investigation.

My phone's battery is already in the yellow zone again, even though it had shown as fully charged when I'd left the shop. The problem must be more than the battery, which is now brand new. There has to be something wrong with the phone itself. I wish I had just replaced the whole device while I was at the store.

Logan looks at me and says, "I don't like you being out in the open like this. Mitch's killer is obviously taunting you about having failed to stop them. This threat says you're next on their list."

I've already considered all that. I say, "Whoever it is will be a lot less likely to do anything with all these people around. Not to mention my former bodyguard." I gesture at the tray. "Besides, we need to make sure that no one is tempted to tamper with this evidence. Especially if it does turn out to be poisoned."

Our waiter comes hurrying over with a basket of cheese bread. He sees that we're both standing up again, but now we look agitated. He glances from me to Logan and back again. Then he asks, "Is everything okay over here?"

Logan gestures to the desserts and says, "We didn't order that."

The waiter studies the tray and asks, "Where did that come from?"

I verify, "So nothing like this could have been assembled from your kitchen."

"I wish," he says. "I'd certainly upsell a lot more desserts."

Logan tells the guy, "We'd like to leave as soon as the police get here to take this over."

"The police?" the waiter says. "Over a wrong dessert order?" He doesn't look like he believes Logan is serious.

I say, "The message written on this tray is the same as the one left for the man who was murdered this morning. This could be important to an ongoing investigation." I manage to keep my voice from quavering when I say that, but saying it out loud makes the threat feel so much more real. I can feel my anxiety throbbing in my teeth.

The waiter still doesn't look like he believes us – but his face betrays a hint of anxiety, wondering if we are telling the truth, and something has gone very wrong.

Logan says, "Can I go ahead and get our bill? Please." Never mind that we didn't actually receive anything to eat yet. He takes his wallet out of his pocket to get his credit card. Something falls out it, thudding heavily to the floor.

I bend down to pick it up whatever he dropped for him. Before I can touch it, I realize it's a charm, identical to the one that Mitch had found in his dressing gown pocket, of a silver heart with a knife through it, tied to a scarlet thread. I freeze, my hand close to the thread, not wanting to move this evidence.

Logan crouches down to get a closer look. "Now that's unsettling."

I glance around, more certain than ever that the killer is probably watching us. I whisper, "Logan, the killer was in your personal space, close enough to see the inside of your wallet. That's more than unsettling. It's downright creepy."

"I know," Logan whispers back. "Apparently that tray wasn't just a way of calling you out. The threat was meant for me." Logan takes my hand and helps me stand up. He says, "When we're done here, we need to find a shop that's still open and go get your phone replaced. We can't afford to have you missing any more messages."

My heart goes cold as I take in the implications. The guy I just kissed seems to be next on a killer's list.

A killer who has challenged me.

And it's a challenge I have no idea how to answer.

But if something happens to Logan because an unbalanced person is trying to get to me – that would break me. I've lost one person I care about due to an unfortunate accident. The meaninglessness of that had been hard enough to recover from. But to lose a second one to malice? It's unthinkable.

I try to stop my hands from trembling, as I stand up, but Logan sees, and I can't read the complicated look that washes over his face. Part of it is sympathy, which I don't want right now, since I feel like I'm the one who put him in danger.

Diners at other tables are still eating, though many are cutting glances over here to see what is going on – or outright staring. I'm not supposed to tell anybody that Mitch's killer called me out. When people inevitably ask, I suppose we can play this off as a threat because I'd been the one to discover the body.

Arlo walks in, looking very calm and at ease, an important skill for a cop wanting to reassure people, despite a crisis. I find myself blushing, like somehow he can tell I kissed Logan and came running. Though, of course, he's only here because Logan called him. Arlo looks so self-assured. Part of me wants to run into his arms, and look to him to fix this, like when we were teenagers and small things had gone wrong in my life. But I can't – because I'm still being indecisive, which makes me acting like a girlfriend when I'm not his girlfriend inappropriate. In this case, I probably couldn't hand over my problems, even if I wanted to. This killer seems interested in me personally. And now that this person has threatened Logan – I have even more impetus towards solving this case.

And Arlo couldn't help me with Logan, either. Logan is the kind of guy who is used to taking care of himself and protecting others. He's always pushing me to push myself, to be stronger and better, stepping in only when I'm in physical danger. He'd probably find it demeaning to have Arlo put a protection detail on him.

Arlo looks at me, obviously troubled. He pulls me off to the side and asks softly – so as not to alarm the people still half-heartedly trying to eat dinner – "Have you received any other communications from the killer?"

What he's really saying is, *You didn't call the killer, did you? After I told you not to?*

"No," I say. "This message was taunting me for not getting to the scene of the first murder in time to stop it. Not that we know where the real crime scene was. I'm guessing the killer just wants me to live with the implications of that for a while."

Arlo asks me to send him the pics I took of the tray. He zooms in on one of the desserts – a tiny heart-shaped cookie and asks, "Look familiar?"

It does, actually. Orejas are actually supposed to look like ears, as the dough gets folded in on itself. The cookies are also called palmiers in French, because they look a bit like palm leaves. But Carmen crimps hers on the bottom, to give them a point that makes the clearly look like hearts. And she studs the outsides with cacao nibs, which I've never seen anyone else do. This cookie is clearly her handiwork. And many of the other baked goods on the tray could easily be her style.

"Arlo," I protest. "There's no way that Carmen sent me that threat. Someone must have bought the palmiers from her because they thought it would be ironic."

Arlo looks at me sympathetically, yet he says, "She was there at the tea party, right?"

"Well, yeah," I admit. "But she was helping out in the kitchen the whole time. It's not like she had time to get into a fight with Mitch or anything."

"I'm still going to have to have a talk with her," Arlo says. "If nothing else, she may remember who bought the cookies."

I reluctantly nod. "It's better than arresting her."

Arlo had arrested Carmen once, for a murder she hadn't committed. The circumstantial evidence had been strong, but I hadn't felt right about it, so I'd kept digging and uncovered the real killer.

Arlo says, "You're never going to let that go, are you?"

"Probably not," I say.

Pru and Ben come over to us. Pru says, "I'm not sure what's going on, but is there any way we can help?"

Arlo asks, "Did you see who approached Felicity and Logan's table?"

"Unfortunately, no," Pru says. She moves a bit closer to me and adds, "Congratulations on that kiss, though. It looked fun."

Arlo raises an eyebrow and looks at me with curious brown eyes. I feel my cheeks flaming again. I can't meet his gaze, so I look down at the floor. I notice that there are paint drips on one of Pru's ballet-flat shoes. They must be doing some remodeling.

I ask Pru, "Are you sure you don't remember anything? It's important. It's possible that the same person who gave us the tray also murdered Mitch Eberhardt."

"Mitch is dead?" Pru asks, clearly alarmed.

Ben gasps and half-chokes, loudly coughing out whatever had gone down wrong. When he recovers, he says, "You have to be mistaken."

Arlo says, "It's no mistake. Mr. Eberhardt died today, in his home. I was wanting to speak with you anyway. I'm working my way down the guest list from yesterday's party, collecting statements."

"Now's not a good time," Ben says, putting a hand on Pru's shoulder and guiding her away from the conversation. ""We were about to leave. We need to run a few errands before the stores close."

"Maybe you can come by the station in the morning," Arlo suggests to the retreating couple.

"Yes, fine, of course," Pru says, while Ben just grunts in response.

Arlo leans in closer to me and says, "Anything about that strike you as odd?"

I try to ignore the heat from his body, with him right next to me. I clear my throat. "You mean the way that they looked scalded when you mentioned that Mitch is dead?"

"Pretty much," Arlo says.

I say, "At least that means that you can cross them off your list of suspects for having killed Mitch. It's hard to fake that level of shock."

"True," Arlo says. "But I still can't shake the feeling that they are guilty of something."

"Them?" I ask. "Ben and Pru are just a sweet old couple. They retired to the beach to get away from it all."

"Exactly," Arlo says. "Their story seems too perfect."

Since Fisk, the CSI guy that often works with Arlo, has commandeered the tray, Logan starts making his way over to us.

Arlo says softly, "Here comes the source of that kiss. And I'd say he looks pretty pleased with himself."

"Don't be ridiculous," I say. "Logan always looks like that."

"Exactly," Arlo says again, and this time I can tell he means it as a dig. Arlo had a wild streak when we were younger, but he's never been mean. But me kissing Logan has obviously hurt his feelings. I knew that it wasn't like he wasn't going to find out about it. Not as public as the display of affection had been. But I don't know how to deal with it. I've never been the type to have two guys trying to woo me at the same time, and I've always prized loyalty in relationships. I don't like the way all of this keeps making me feel like a bad person.

I try to focus on the less dangerous subject – the murderer. I ask around, but in a restaurant crowded for the dinner rush, nobody had noticed someone walking through with a tray. Nobody in the kitchen knows anything either. And the manager looks like he just wants us to leave. Arlo and Logan go to watch the footage from the cameras, but they report that there's only the one lady carrying a pastry box – which she opens to reveal a giant sheet cake -- and nobody else on camera who looks particularly suspicious.

After I get my phone changed out, I'm going to have to go and talk to the most suspicious person in this case – Gently Drifting. Only, none of the phone stores are still open, so we wind up going directly to Gently's small house.

## Chapter Nine

I've never been to Gently's home before. It's not what I expected. It's so . . . ordinary. All of the furnishings are mid-century, but surrounded by updated tech, like the giant flatscreen on the wall, and sound system speakers placed discreetly around the room. It all looks casual and worn – but some of the pieces are clearly reproductions. And gently looks perfectly at home sitting on the sofa with Ruffles in his lap, purring loudly.

"I like your place," I tell him. I've already apologized a dozen times for the fact that we'd shown up so late. He has assured us he's a night owl.

Gently says, "Thanks! A lot of the furniture belonged to my parents. I just had the sofa re-upholstered, but most of it is just well-maintained."

"Belonged?" Logan asks. Logan is sitting near me, and I'm sitting near the wall outlet, keeping my phone plugged in, so that in case I get another call from the killer. It would be bad if the device dies in the middle of the conversation. I think Logan feels like he's protecting me, but this time, I think I'm equally protecting him, because if he's with me, the killer can't strike without me witnessing it – which leaves me nothing to solve. Logan leans forward and asks, "As in they redecorated and gave you the old furniture? Or . . ."

"The second one," Gently says. "My parents disappeared when I was still a teenager. They are presumed dead, so I inherited the house. But I was a suspect in the disappearance. If there had been bodies, I'm sure I would be in prison right now. I had come home late from a party, and I saw a random stranger locking our front door, with a key on a fob I didn't recognize. I tried to talk to him, and he ran, so I chased him, and he kept shouting that he was unarmed and not responsible – like he thought I was trying to kill him or something."

Logan snorts a laugh, despite the seriousness of the situation. "You told the police the unarmed man had kidnapped your parents?"

"Something like that," Gently says miserably. "I'm sorry, but why is this funny?"

Logan says. "It's just – it's a sounds-a-like for that line from the Fugitive, where the guy claims the one-armed man killed his wife. It's no wonder the police didn't believe it."

This all sounds vaguely familiar, though it must have happened after I had moved to Seattle. Even there I had still gotten some news from home, and people had been theorizing. "You're talking about the Anders case. You're Perry Anders. That's why you changed your name."

Gently grimaces. "It seemed prudent, given the press and the way people were reacting. I felt lost, and couldn't find my footing anywhere in my life. The name basically suggested itself." Gently starts petting Ruffles rhythmically, probably trying to calm himself, and at first the cat is okay with it, but after a minute, Ruffles turns around and bites at Gently's hand. Gently moves his hand away. It doesn't look like the bite broke the skin. "I'm still convinced that guy with the key knows something. But the police never found him. I never got closure. Sometimes I still have these dreams that my family is still together. There's a recurring one where my mom just came home from the grocery store, and is calling me to come help bring in the bags."

"That has to be tough," I say sympathetically.

"Yeah," Logan says. "It's hard to not be able to escape into your dreams."

He sounds like he's speaking from experience.

Gently says, "I couldn't escape anywhere. At first, I stayed home all the time, just in case my mom or dad came back.

And then it got harder and harder to go out. And when I did – it felt like people were staring at me, or that the police were still watching, waiting for me to do something that would incriminate myself. For a while they were. I know they're not now – or maybe they are again, since Arlo seems convinced I know something about what happened to Mitch. So maybe that's a rumor going around now."

"If we thought that," Logan says, "We wouldn't have come here alone tonight."

Of course, that's not entirely true. I do still have some suspicions about Gently – possibly because he's the only solid suspect we've found. And Logan has expressed suspicions too. But neither of us are convinced Gently has it in him to plunge a weapon into someone's chest.

I feel empathy for Gently. It's hard enough to lose someone you love, under any circumstances. At least when my husband had died, there hadn't been suspicion of foul play. I can't imagine grieving while being considered a suspect. And the idea that no one believed his account of what had happened – it's no wonder he developed an anxiety issue. And now it must be opening the emotional wounds, knowing that he's being suspected and potentially not believed all over again.

Gently can't seem to stop petting the cat. Ruffles bites him again, this time more insistently, and jumps off of Gently's lap.

Logan says, "It must be a challenge to have an emotional support animal that walks off when you're in need."

"It's my fault for irritating him." Gently waves a dismissive hand. But then he grasps his hands against each other in his lap. "Ruffles never goes far. And I like that he's honest about his feelings. There's nothing ambiguous between us. And he always knows when I'm really upset. He'll come and sit on my chest and lick my chin. I'm not sure if he knows his weight helps calm my anxiety, but I like to think he does."

"Is that why you chose such a big cat?" I ask, half-joking.

Gently laughs. "I found Ruffles when he was just a kitten. He was lost and half-starved and so small he fit in the palm of my hand. It happened shortly after my parents disappeared, and the house was so empty – bringing him home added a little spark of life again. I may have saved him physically, but he kept me from drowning."

Ruffles comes back and plops down, stretching out across Gently's shoe.

"So what happened between you and Mitch yesterday?" I ask.

Gently scrunches up his nose. "He asked me to get involved with a little project he was working on. I told him absolutely not. Then he tried to bribe me to stay quiet about it."

I say, "Mitch tried to get me involved in one of his projects too. I told him I'd consider it."

Gently looks at me with shock and disdain. "Really?"

I hold out my hands, palms up. "It didn't seem like that big of a deal. I couldn't believe the profits he was talking about for just a couple of portraits. Despite the whole creepy side to it."

I mean, I would have thought Gently would think painting with chocolate on chocolate was cool. He had seemed to enjoy helping out with the project to build the giant chocolate sculpture.

Maybe Gently is turned off because of the true crime aficionado thing. I can see why Mitch would have wanted to include Gently in his portrait project, alongside me, knowing that Gently is really Perry Anders. I can also see why Gently would say no, because it might bring him more notoriety – but not why he would be that upset at me for saying yes.

Gently seems to be appraising me. "You're not an artist, but I can see why he would think you would be a good fit for some other tasks. After all, you travel internationally on a regular basis, and carry the kind of cargo that wouldn't get searched. Didn't you say you have an upcoming trip planned to Brazil? There's a whole segment of the population there who are very rich and a bit vain. I know because I've done some art for the cat magazines there. Cats are luxury pets in Brazil, and people with that kind of disposable income were right up Mitch's alley."

Alarm jolts through me. I don't like the way any of that sounds. "Now wait a minute," I protest. "Are you suggesting that Mitch would have asked me to do something illegal?"

"Didn't he?" Gently asks.

"No!" The word comes out more forcefully than I had meant it. "He wanted to do a portrait project, painting me using chocolate. Apparently, there's a market for that kind of art, and he thought I would be a draw as the whole chocolate maker – murder solver thing. Some of the example pieces he showed me on his phone were going for upwards of a thousand dollars."

"Really?" Gently says. "I wonder if there would be any interest in chocolate portraits of people's cats?"

I feel like we are getting off track, but I humor the guy with a, "Maybe?"

He says, "We could even do a class in your new space at your chocolate shop. People could have a go at painting their own cats. Or dogs. Or whatever pets."

"Like my bunny," I remind him, getting drawn into the idea, despite a few lingering doubts that he might still turn out to be the killer. "Since Knightley is the logo for the shop. We could even bring him into the studio so that he could model for the class."

Bunnies don't like to travel, but it would be for a good cause. And I could set something up where he could have space low to the ground, so he wouldn't feel too uncomfortable.

Gently says, "I could do a sample painting of you, to see how the techniques work. I can stop by the shop tomorrow afternoon if you have a few minutes to sit for an initial sketch."

"Are you sure?" I ask.

Gently still looks stressed. Haunted might not be too far a word. He nods, though, and says, "I need to force myself to leave the house tomorrow."

Logan says, "Hey, focus. Gently, what exactly did Mitch ask you to do?"

Gently says, "Mitch asked me to join his art forgery ring. I told him I wasn't interested, so he offered me a bribe to keep my mouth shut about his operation. And when I declined his money, he was none too happy. I told him not to worry, that I didn't plan to mention it to anybody anyway." He turns to me and adds, "See? I don't have a motive to hurt Mitch. It would make more sense if he had wanted to hurt me. You know, to make sure I didn't blab about his activities. But he didn't threaten me. He just asked me to come back for a chat, if I changed my mind."

Logan nods. "That sounds like the Mitch I remember. Violence was never his style. He was more about charm, and talking his way out of problems. Even when I led him into the trap that got him arrested, he didn't seem to hold a grudge."

I ask Gently, "Have you been home all evening?"

Gently says, "Yeah, Arlo dropped me off pretty early. I was supposed to go by the studio and then out with Violet, but I was too shaken by the whole police station experience to handle people today. So I just popped a frozen pizza into the oven and read a book."

Logan asks, "Violet didn't offer to come hang out with you instead, since you had a date planned?"

Gently says, "We were meeting some friends. I told her not to cancel."

Which is understandable. But also convenient, if he needed to be alone to say, deliver a threatening dessert tray to a restaurant at that time. Gently still doesn't have an alibi for any part of the crime.

But my instinct that he's innocent gives me yet another reason I have to solve this thing, because the easiest way to make sure Gently doesn't wind up in jail is to find the real killer. Preferably before Logan becomes the next victim.

My phone rings. I check and it's Arlo. He hasn't exactly told me to stay out of the case this time. Since the killer has communicated directly with me, it would be impractical for him to say that anyway. But I still don't want to advertise the fact that I'm at the house of one of his murder suspects.

I unplug my phone from the charger, and I tell Gently, "I'm going to step outside to take this."

I give Logan a significant look. He is, after all, being left alone with someone who, in theory, might be trying to kill him. Logan gives me a look back that means he is clearly aware of the situation and I should take my call before my phone stops ringing.

When I answer, Arlo asks, "Is Logan with you?"

Is that what he wants to talk about? Some form of jealousy? I'm honest. "We're not in the same room, but he's not far."

"Good," Arlo says. "You should try to get him to stay at the hotel."

I'm surprised at Arlo's response. Is he not jealous, after all?

"So you're okay with that," I say. "After what happened today?"

"I'm not happy about it," Arlo says. "But you know that. Still, it would be petty of me to do anything that could allow harm to come to someone just because it would smooth out my personal life. So I'm not going to ask you to leave Logan alone, not when both of you are safer together."

"I'm sorry I'm making everything so difficult," I say.

Arlo sighs into the phone. "Lis, Logan and I have become friends. Whatever happens between you and him, or you and me, I want all three of us to be happy in the long run. Happy and safe."

"Noble," I say. I explain my theory that the killer wants to leave me with mysteries to solve, then add, "I plan on keeping Logan in sight until we figure out who's trying to hurt him. It's funny. It feels like a reverse of the relationship I had with Logan when I first met him. He was protecting me, because I'd gotten in over my head. And now, I'm the only one in a position to protect him."

"Not the only one," Arlo says. "Just the only one he'll accept."

I try to bring the call to a close. "Okay. Now that we've gotten that all straightened out, the sooner you find the killer, the sooner I can stop shadowing Logan."

Arlo says, "Actually, Logan is not why I called. I wanted to talk to you about your friend Sonya."

He's the second person to phrase it that way. *Your friend Sonya.* Like Sonya isn't Arlo's friend too.

"Oh?" I say, like it never occurred to me that Sonya's initials were on the knitting needles used to stab Mitch.

Arlo says, "We ran the murder weapon for prints. Sonya's are all over those knitting needles – and no one else's."

"Somebody must have taken them from her shop," I say. Suddenly the night air feels damp and cold.

Arlo says, "That is a possibility. I'm about to head over to talk to her. Before I interview her, I wanted to ask you – do you think it's possible she did this?"

I say, "What possible motive could she have? She hardly knew Mitch. And she's not a violent person. Remember, someone else had to defend her when she had that date who got all pushy at Autumn's engagement party?"

"I heard about that," Arlo says. He pauses, obviously thinking, then asks, "How long have you known Sonya?"

"Just since after I moved back to the island. So about a year and a half. She used to have a corporate job, but it was too stressful, so she decided to move here with her sister and open the yarn shop. Art has always been her true passion, and working in fiber arts makes her happy."

Arlo asks, "Why did they move to Galveston, specifically?"

I have to think about that one. "I know Sandra got offered the job at the hospital. But as to why she applied to a hospital on a moderately sized island off the coast of Texas – I'm not sure I ever thought to ask that."

"I'll be sure to ask," Arlo says. He sighs. "Sonya was at both the tea yesterday, and at the restaurant where the threatening message was delivered tonight, right?"

I'm feeling a bit of déjà vu at that question. It's almost the same thing he just asked me a few hours ago about Carmen. Hesitantly, I say, "Yes, that's true. But there were other people who were also connected to Wobble House present at the restaurant. For instance, Silas, the neighbor who was none too happy about Mitch buying the place across the street. Though he seems to have an alibi."

"I'm going to need details on that," Arlo says, so I fill him in on the conversation I had with Silas yesterday, and what he'd told me about going over to Wobble House today. I also tell Arlo what Gently said about Mitch trying to get him involved in art forgery – only to find out Gently had already shared this information with Arlo himself. Reluctantly, I also tell Arlo what Logan had said about knowing Mitch, back in Paris. Arlo says, "Logan doesn't seem like the type who would fake a threatening message to himself. I don't think you have to worry about him becoming a suspect. But if you could get him to make a list of anyone he knows might have had a grudge against Mitch, I'd be much obliged."

"I'll do that," I say. There's one thing I've been thinking about, ever since Arlo mentioned Carmen, back at the restaurant. But I hardly know how to put it into words. I say, "Arlo?"

"Yeah?"

"Can I talk out a theory with you?"

"Of course," he says. "Lis, you know you can share anything with me, even if it is something I don't want to hear."

He's talking about a possible conversation where I might break up with him, even though we're not really dating. At least I think that's what he means.

I keep focused on the murder. I say, "Don't you think it is odd that my friends are all being implicated in the murder of someone they hardly know? Considering the phone message I got this morning, it feels like this might all be about making life difficult for anyone connected to me. Somebody stole Gently's cat out of his house, and Sonya's knitting needles out of her shop. And there's Carmen and the cookies. This person even put a trinket in Logan's wallet, which means they probably got past his paranoid security system into his apartment, too. So, shouldn't we be looking for someone who has a background as a thief?"

Arlo sighs heavily into the phone. "That's certainly one way to interpret the evidence. I hope that's not true, because it would mean that you are the one truly at risk here, because you would be at the center of the killer's obsession. It's enough to have Logan in danger, and not the woman I love."

Why are both of these guys determined to declare their love for me today? "Arlo," I start to say, but he's already started talking again.

He says, "But Lis, you can't consider that just because people are your friends, they are above suspicion. People have hidden pasts, and hidden motives. Even when you've known someone for a long time, that doesn't mean you know them well, and all of the people we're talking about are individuals you've only known since your return to the island."

I look down at Gently's sand-strewn driveway. I tell Arlo, "I've made so much progress since I came back, opening up to people, making real friends, repairing the relationships I'd damaged before I left – including the one with you. I don't think I could live by wandering around being suspicious of everyone. I've got to put faith in my friends, unless there's concrete evidence otherwise. Otherwise, I'll wind up withdrawing into myself again. Or I'll wind up like Gently – where it's a challenge just to leave the house and interact with people."

"I don't think anybody wants that for you, Lis," Arlo says. "Personally, I'm excited about all the progress you've made. I've changed a lot too, from the irresponsible kid I used to be when we were first together. I wouldn't want to take steps backwards in my emotional growth either. But you have to recognize that your friends may be your blind spot."

I say, “I’ll agree to keep that in mind – if you agree to look deeper for a suspect.”

He agrees. And I think he’s going to end the call. But then he says, “I have to ask. Who’s the better kisser? Me or him?”

“I don’t think there’s a safe way to answer that question,” I say.

## Chapter Ten

We're still in the driveway outside Gently's house when Logan's phone lights up.

Logan says, "Finally. Here's the phone information on the person that called you."

"Well?" I prompt. Logan may be a pilot now and part owner of a craft chocolate business, but he still has a lot of connections in law enforcement. So for him, finding out that kind of information is just a matter of calling in a favor.

"It's no help," Logan says. He looks disappointed. "It's a pre-paid burner phone, purchased a month ago with cash at a store in Amarillo. Someone drove out there to double-check for me, but they don't keep security recordings that far back. All it tells us is that this killer is a meticulous planner."

"Maybe," I say. "Except that they were counting on me getting a voicemail almost immediately. That seems sloppy."

Logan points out, "Maybe they just didn't care. They could well have sent the message after killing Mitch, just to muddy the time of death."

"That had occurred to me," I say. "I thought it might be Enrique, since he went over there this morning. But when we were chatting at the restaurant, Arlo admitted the police didn't find any gluten free brownies in Mitch's house, so maybe Enrique wasn't lying about not getting in. Besides, if the goal was just killing Mitch, then why threaten you?"

"I don't know," Logan says. "And I hate to think I might have given Enrique – or anyone – reason to dislike me that much.

But we're still at the beginning of this. You haven't received a call from the killer yet, not since the threat. So we don't know if there's a pattern for an intricate plan of multiple murders – or if the threat to me is simply a distraction to put you off balance. This case is so full of red herrings – I wouldn't believe that Mitch was really dead, if I hadn't verified it myself."

My phone rings. I look down, and the call ID says *Sherlock Killer*. Which is what I'd changed the burner phone number to, so I won't skip answering it. The timing doesn't feel coincidental, more like a response to Logan's complaint.

I answer the phone. It's that mechanical, altered voice again. The person says, "Of course there's a pattern. Of course I really want Logan dead. I expected you to have some concrete ideas by now. Instead of just mooning over your love life all day."

I put a hand over my phone – for whatever good that does – and whisper to Logan, "I think I may have figured out what's been draining my phone battery." Because, obviously, the killer has been listening and that's where the bug is. It sends a chill through me to realize the killer has been following along with me all day. And that we've finally goaded this person into responding. Uncovering the phone, I ask, "Who are you? Or at least, what should I call you?"

"If you need a name, Moriarty will do. Though, technically he doesn't appear until later in the series." The voice makes a huffing noise. "But the challenge aspect fits."

"Okay, Em," I say, shortening the name to something less threatening. "You have to give me a clue. Just one way into all of this. Please."

There's a long silence on the phone. Finally, there's a sigh. "The pattern is, I call the morning after I've left the charm on the scarlet thread. Maybe I've chosen the wrong adversary. If you can't figure that out, maybe I should just kill Hanlon today and get it over with."

I look over at Logan, alarm rising the hairs on the back of my neck. He's typing something into his phone – probably trying to get someone to trace the call to find the location of the burner phone. He gestures for me to keep talking.

I try to sound confident, though I'm terrified, when I say, "Look. So far, all you've given me are red herrings. You've been trying very hard to frame my friends – like, *all* of my friends – so I've been wasting my time following dead ends, to people I don't believe are guilty anyway. If you want to play a game, you need to play fair." I find myself gesturing with my free hand, though the murderer on the other end of the phone can't possibly know. "I get that the first message, with the scarlet thread, was supposed to point out how you were going to kill Mitch. But you haven't given me any hints about the threat to Logan. Or about your identity."

"We've met before," the voice says.

"And you feel I've wronged you somehow?" I guess. "So now you feel I need to pay?"

Laughter comes over the phone. "I like you, Felicity. Platonically." As though that might be something I'd be worried about. "I know you like to think of yourself as a kind, genuine, human being. Though sometimes you're kind of a snob. And sometimes you get really down about yourself. But I'm not challenging you to make you a better person. I'm challenging you because of your intellect. I need someone to play against at a high level, and it's too late to start over."

"I need more time," I say, not faking the pleading note that creeps into my voice. "I told you, I'm new at this."

The altered voice sighs in my ear. "Fine. I'll give you one extra day." The voice says louder, "You hear that, Logan? One extra day of breathing privileges. Maybe use it to put your affairs in order or something."

Anger courses through me. This whole thing is insane. I say, "So Logan's just a random choice? And he dies if I'm not good enough at a game I've told you I've never played before. That seems like high stakes, to be paid by a guy who has nothing to do with all of this."

The voice over the phone sounds bitter. "That's where you're already wrong. Your assumption is that all of this centers on you. But Hanlon isn't a random, innocent victim. He took a life that was important to me. The message of *Revenge* was genuinely meant for him. And one way or another, he is going to die. If I was cruel, I would have challenged Logan and threatened to kill you. And then made him watch me do it. Because it certainly would be closer to what he did to me."

I give Logan a questioning look. He shrugs. Obviously, this setup – him killing someone in order to hurt someone they care about – isn't ringing any bells. And that really doesn't sound like him. But Logan has been both a bodyguard and a cop – and who knows whatever he did in Europe. So he isn't able to say he never hurt anyone, either. The violence in his past is something that's always made me a little uncomfortable about my attraction to him. But I don't think he has ever been intentionally cruel.

I say, "Aren't you worried about perpetuating that cycle? You'd be taking someone I care about from me. It's one more wrong that doesn't add up to a right."

There's silence on the phone. I've hit a nerve. I have to get the killer talking again, because if they hang up, that's less chance of tracing their location.

I swallow, and realize my mouth has gone dry. I have to clear my throat, before I say, "You just said that one way or another, he dies. I thought you were giving me the chance to save him." I need to push the killer, even though it's dangerous. Maybe Em will slip and give me some information. "You're really not good at this, are you?"

There's a spluttering noise. Then the voice says, "Obviously, if you win, I don't get to kill Logan. I'll be either dead or in jail. But qualifying it like that doesn't make it sound like much of a threat, now, does it?"

"So what's my clue to get a real chance to save him? Instead of the hour lead nonsense where you don't give me anything concrete? You've been listening to the conversations

I've had with Logan all day. You know I love him. Wouldn't you have appreciated the same consideration?"

"Let me think," the killer says, then hums under their altered, electronic breath. "Okay, how about this? In *The Dying Detective*, Holmes says, 'I wonder how a battery feels when it pours electricity into a non-conductor?' Sorry I didn't have time to cross-stitch it onto a bookmark for you."

"Wait. What am I supposed to do with that?" I protest, in part to keep Em on the line, in case Logan is able to get a trace. Also, in part because I honestly have no clue what that clue means.

Em hangs up.

"Rude," I say to the bugged phone. "And I didn't even get a chance to ask about the vacuuming and the scraping noise."

It's hard to hide the quaver in my voice. After all, everything about this situation is pushing my psychological buttons, especially my need for a sense of control in my life. I don't like the idea of a killer pulling strings, and me just reacting, over and over. And – while I have learned to manage my grief over the loss of my husband – the potential loss of Logan, in just as sudden and meaningless manner, while I have no clear idea how to stop it, is hitting some of the same emotional notes, re-opening the same psychological wounds.

Logan takes the phone from me and puts it in his glovebox. He says softly, "Let's make a quick stop over at my place. We'll sweep everything for bugs ASAP – including our clothes, in case it isn't in the phone."

I whisper back, "I was going to ask if you wanted to stay at the hotel tonight. I still believe this killer is less likely to strike if I'm present."

Logan says, "I don't think either of us should stay there. I can get a friend to go by and check the hotel, but that's a lot of space for people to hide, and your aunt has minimal security. I'd suggest you tell Naomi to find somewhere else to stay until the killer is caught. You and your bunny can stay at my place, since it's obvious you're not going to let me stay alone tonight, no matter how much I protest."

I say, "I'd rather have Aunt Naomi come to your place with us. If someone is trying to get to me, she'd be an obvious person to try to hurt, if they can't get past your defenses."

Logan nods. "That's logical. The two of you can have my room. I have a reasonably comfortable couch."

Logan puts the car in gear, and we head towards his place, which is a luxury apartment on the Bay side of the island. It's actually not far from the hotel my aunt is refurbishing, so we can pick her up on the way.

Aunt Naomi has been putting work into restoring the crumbling hotel, with the intent to flip it when she's done. Since I've been living there during the remodel, I've come to think of it as home. And since a lot of my money is tied up in the project, I can't help but think of the hotel as partially mine. It's going to be so hard to see it go, when the project is complete.

Logan gets a text on his phone, and when we stop at a light, he glances at it then tells me, "They only got a partial trace. Just enough to guestimate that the phone is on this island. Which we already knew."

"That's disappointing," I say, hoping he doesn't think it is my fault that Em hung up.

We reach the hotel, and find Naomi still working on sanding a banister. I explain the situation to my aunt, who seems alarmed but not surprised on hearing I've been called out by a killer. She agrees that it's probably best for her not to stay by herself in the big building, and sends a message to Tiff, my friend who has been helping with the remodel project, not to come by the hotel for any reason.

Then I put clothes in my overnight suitcase, pack up Knightley's food, toys and treats and coax the bunny into his traveling carrier. Aunt Naomi brings his cage – which takes up most of the back seat of Logan's mustang – and off we go, her following us in her car.

I try not to think about the damage Knightley might do to the pristine baseboards of Logan's apartment. It will only be for a day, two at the most. I try to hide my shudder at the thought of that deadline, to force myself to believe that Logan is still going to be around after the deadline passes to worry about the looks of his apartment. A day or two. Surely I will be able to bunny-proof things tomorrow at least enough to minimize the damage Knightley can do in that amount of time.

When we get to Logan's place, he runs a sweep and finds a bug in the lamp in his living room. I see his jaw tighten, as he comes to terms with the fact that someone really did get past his security. He says, "Em must have gotten to my wallet when I was in the shower, when I got home from the gym. I used my card to buy a smoothie at the place next door after my workout, then I didn't open my wallet again until the restaurant."

He has to take my phone apart to get the bug out – clearly invalidating the warranty – but he doesn't find any other bugs or tracking devices on either me or my aunt. He goes down to check his car.

I tell Aunt Naomi about the line from the Sherlock Holmes story. Naomi pulls up a summary of *The Dying Detective* on her tablet and reads it. She says, "There's so many possible interpretations."

"I know," I tell her. "I've read the Sherlock Holmes novels, but I don't think I've gotten through all the short stories. I skimmed over *The Dying Detective* on the way over here, but I need to study it." The story is about Holmes pretending to be dying from some disease that would have been introduced by a gift – which he was smart enough not to touch. The line about the battery is just Holmes lamenting about being exhausted, from not eating for multiple days. I tell her, "Whoever killed Mitch took the name Moriarty – and is casting me as Sherlock. I used Em instead of Moriarty on the phone, and it stuck, in my brain at least."

Aunt Naomi takes this all in and then says, "With the reference to a battery, Em might be planning to electrocute

Logan. But there's also elements about unexpected packages, so there could be something to do with Logan's mail. Or directly copying the plot and somehow introducing a disease." She looks levelly at me. "Are you sure we shouldn't be putting some distance between ourselves and Logan, instead of staying with him? I hate to sound callous, but all of these methods of murder have a potential to hurt bystanders."

I sigh. Sensing my distress, Knightley looks up at me from the floor. He's nervous already about being in a new place, and I hate that I am making that worse. I tell Naomi, "The killer has made me a part of this, and I can't leave space for something to happen to Logan that Em could construe as a puzzle for me to solve."

Aunt Naomi points out, "And yet you let him go check out the car alone. And you left him alone in Gently's house."

I wince. "Logan wouldn't like it if I started acting like his bodyguard. He's always in control of the situations we've found ourselves in. He's more worried about you, honestly. Logan thinks that Em might make this even more personal if I don't figure out his or her identity by tomorrow. That if I don't save Logan, Em will turn towards someone like you as a new target to give me more incentive. If I leave, I can't protect you, and Gramma, and Mom – and who knows who else. This has to end with me solving Mitch's murder, while Logan is still breathing."

"Well, when you put it that way," Aunt Naomi says. She takes out her phone. "I need to call Greg and let him know what's going on."

Greg is my uncle, who is working offshore.

Logan, walking back in the door, says, "I'd prefer if you didn't do that. We've found one bugged phone already. Let's not advertise that you'll be staying here tomorrow. Just in case."

I ask, "Do you think Naomi needs to stay with us all day?"

Logan says, "Honestly, no. Em seems like a person who plays by the rules. I'm just trying to err on the side of caution, because first impressions aren't always accurate. If it was really Moriarty we're dealing with, it would be different. After all, Moriarty cheats."

"Wait a minute," I say, "When did you read Sherlock Holmes?"

"I read one or two of the short stories," Logan says. "I wanted to see how close the TV shows were to the source, especially the big deal everybody made about Reichenbach Falls. I blame your influence for that."

It's weird that night, leaving Logan on the couch so that Aunt Naomi and I can have his room. His bed frame is modern, the sheet threadcount high. There's the smell of lavender-scented laundry detergent. It's hard not to wonder which side he sleeps on.

Aunt Naomi says, "This room reminds me of a hotel I stayed at once in Sweden, with your mom."

By the time it registers to ask when this trip might have happened – since I certainly don't remember it – Naomi is already asleep. I guess she believed Logan when he said we weren't in any danger tonight.

I, on the other hand, have a hard time drifting off. There's so much to process about everything that happened today – and Logan's room certainly doesn't feel like a comfortable place to do that. So I try to just blank everything out. When I finally do fall asleep, it's fitful.

I wake to a noise in the other room, and I hear Logan cry out. The noise isn't repeated, so I'm not sure what happened, but I'm groggy and on edge at the same time. Naomi is still asleep. I don't wake her. Fearing an intruder, I grab the can of hairspray that Aunt Naomi left on the edge of the dresser and ease open the door. It's not the mace Logan gave me, which I never remember to carry, but it will have to do.

I tiptoe into the living room, scanning for danger.

Relief floods through me as I realize that Logan is simply waking from a nightmare.

I put the hairspray down and close the door to Logan's room. He's sitting up, so I go and sit next to him on the couch. "Everything okay?"

He runs both hands through his hair, looking both frightened and embarrassed. "Yeah. I haven't had a nightmare that vivid in a long time."

"Do you have nightmares a lot?" I ask, trying to be sympathetic. It's hard to see Logan looking this vulnerable, fear from his dream still evident in his eyes. He always seems to be put together and in control.

"Frequently, yes." He sighs. "When I was a kid, I used to sleep like a rock, through anything, even the worst of storms. But it's hard to sleep at all when you've had to be alert for danger for long amounts of time – especially when I worked protecting people."

I look at Logan, seeing his features differently as I realize how hard it is for him to feel completely safe.

"Is that what the nightmares are about?" I ask, putting a hand on his to try and steady him. "That woman you weren't able to save?"

The one that he had been in love with, but never found the words to tell her.

"No," Logan says, gently pulling his hand away from mine. "They're about things I've had to do, to keep others safe. You know I don't like to talk about it – I don't even like to think about the violence in my past. Even if it was justified, and exonerated, there are faces I will never forget – faces that pop back up in nightmare form. It used to happen all the time – but I've had some healing, and some distance. But what Em said today has made me have to think about each of them – and the people who cared about them. It's complicated. There's nothing noble in the fact that if you live by the gun, you accept dying by the gun. It just gives you a sense of dread. Which I've been pretty good at leaving behind – until today."

It hurts me, seeing Logan in so much pain. He's the one who pulled me out of depression, when I'd moved back here still lost in the grief after Kevin's death. I wonder if now I will need to return the favor.

I say, "Dwelling on the past can destroy your future. You're the one who taught me that."

Logan picks up the stabbed-heart charm – which I would have thought would have been taken for evidence, but he has it sitting on the coffee table near him. He says, "But ignoring that anything bad ever happened is just as much of a problem."

I put my hand on the sofa, close to him, but not reaching out for his hand again. I say, "Surely there are good things to remember, too. With me and Kevin, we had so many good memories. They're bitter-sweet now, but I wouldn't have wanted to have miss out on them."

Logan says, "Know where my favorite place in the whole world was, when I was growing up?"

I shake my head, indicating that no, he has never told me that.

He says, "Duluth. Actually, the whole North Shore of Lake Superior. My Dad used to take my family out there. We'd go agate hunting, and watch the bridge rise. It's where I learned to scuba dive, and how to handle a sailboat."

"I assumed you learned to dive later," I say. "Since Minnesota isn't near the ocean. You always talk about the ocean like it represents second chances. I didn't even realize you could dive in a lake."

Logan chuckles, softly, obviously not wanting to wake Aunt Naomi. He says, "Not only can you dive – you can wreck dive. Superior is big enough – with storms nasty enough – to break ships in half. Some of those wrecks – well, you're not supposed to dive them, because they're considered graves. Some of those are where sailors completely disappeared. After everything that happened, when I had to leave the country, I went out to the lake by myself, before my flight. Watching the perfect, glittering water that day, all I could think about were the graves."

"Oh, Logan," I say. I need to comfort him. I scoot closer to him, leaning against him. I take the charm out of his hand. "You don't deserve to die. You know that, right?"

He leans his head against my shoulder and says, "I wish I could just fall asleep like this. I've never been able to just fall asleep against another person. It feels like too much of a risk."

Logan needs someone he can trust and really relax around. I can't be that for him, not entirely, until I make my decision between him and Arlo. But I can still sit with him, offering as much comfort as I know how.

# Chapter Eleven
## *Monday*

Logan wants to see the sunrise. He barely slept last night, but it is important to him. I get it. He wanted to go down to the beach, by himself, but that would defeat the purpose of us sticking close to him so far. So he's out on the balcony, which overlooks the bay, doing breathing exercises or something. I can see him moving, through the partially open blinds, and I keep checking he's okay, lest he disappear.

Aunt Naomi and I are bleary-eyed, sitting on the sofa in Logan's living room, trying to cope with such an early start after such a stressful day. We've let Knightley out of his cage. The poor lop had to spend the whole night in there, since we hadn't had time to bunnyproof Logan's place. I realize that we haven't brought any supplies to do so.

Aunt Naomi leans her head against mine and says, "It seems like your life keeps getting more complicated at every turn. I miss the days when the biggest thing I was worried about was getting you a date."

I get up and go into Logan's kitchen. It's spotless, if a bit spartan – except where the coffee corner is concerned. He has one of those coffee makers that takes the plastic pods, but beside it there's a high-end home espresso maker. I don't quite dare to go rummaging in his cabinets for the espresso, but I feel comfortable enough to stick a pod in the other machine and grab one of the mugs from the hooks on the wall to make Naomi a cup of coffee.

I tell her, "I know things have gotten complicated – especially with Logan – but honestly, I don't miss those days. I just felt stuck."

Aunt Naomi arches an eyebrow. "Really? Tell me what's going on with Logan. I thought you were all Team Arlo lately. Didn't you make his mother an apple pie?"

Heat blazes into my cheeks. I say, "I told you. Arlo and I aren't dating. I'm still-" I think how to say it. "Weighing my options."

When Logan comes back in a few minutes later, Aunt Naomi gives him a long, appreciative look, and I can see her weighing the scales in his favor. She's wanted to see me together with Logan practically since we met.

Logan catches her looking and says, "What?"

Naomi starts to say something, but before she can, I say, "We really need to get going."

Naomi gestures with her coffee cup. "Don't worry about me. I just downloaded a copy of the Sherlock Holmes collected short stories. I want to get up to speed on the detective, and see if I can actually help out. That means I have a book to read and a bunny to keep an eye on until you two get back."

"Why?" Logan asks, giving Knightley a skeptical look. "Is he likely to go on the rug?"

"No," I say, taking a moment to lean down and pet one of Knightley's soft ears. The bunny rubs his face against my hand and licks my palm. Logan loves animals – especially my lop. But I guess when it's an animal invading his space, it's enough to give him pause. Logan had talked yesterday about getting a dog, but maybe there's more to his reluctance than just the possibility of having to integrate pets if he does get together with me.

Maybe it's because he's gotten used to the quiet of living on his own. He's so self-sufficient – it's easy to wonder how adaptable he'd actually be in relationship. Or what he really needs from one.

Aunt Naomi says, “If Knightley has an accident outside his cage, it’s usually just a few pellets, which are easy to clean up. What you have to watch out for is your baseboards. Rabbits tend to chew, so at home, we spray all the wood we want him to leave alone with a bitter apple spray, and we use PVC cord protectors to make sure there’s nothing tempting for him to chew on except his toys.”

Logan nods, looking much more comfortable. “Obviously, you have to keep the little guy safe.” He leans down and holds out a hand, and Knightley hops over to him.

I say, “The spray doesn’t work for all rabbits. Some of them even seem to like the taste – like some people like really astringent coffee. But Knightley tends to stay away from it.”

“Got it,” Logan says, as he types something into his phone.

“What are you doing?” I ask.

Logan says, “Ordering bitter apple spray for pickup at the pet store.”

And that’s Logan for you. Ready to solve the problem and move on.

We head for Felicitations, hoping to talk to Carmen before we open, so that we don’t have to deal with the distraction of customers.

It’s a gorgeous day. There’s still that early-morning new freshness to the air, and the tang of salt that always comes from ocean breezes. Still, Logan exudes an air of melancholy, like he believes tomorrow really might be his last day on Earth, and he has to soak up everything this day offers. I’ve never seen him be negative like that. But then again – I’ve never seen him have a threat on his life.

He’s a little jumpy, too, as we walk down that alley behind the row of shops. He’s always felt the space was too unprotected and out in the open. But it seems perfectly innocent today. It rained heavily overnight, so there are puddles in the gravel.

I unlock the back door – Carmen keeps it locked when she's there alone. The lights are on, and there are trays in the oven and dough on the counter, but no Carmen. I try not to panic at the unusual nature of this. She could just be in the bathroom.

I hear soft voices in conversation from the front of the shop. If someone's in here, Carmen had to let them in. She's careful – so theoretically, this situation should be fine. But I have to force tension out of my shoulders. I realize I'm on edge too.

Logan and I go through into the front of the shop, and at the table closest to the coffee station, Carmen is sitting opposite Arlo. They each have a cup in front of them. Arlo also has a chocolate muffin, which he hasn't touched.

Arlo makes eye contact. Obviously, he's there on official business. He'd told us yesterday that he intended to question Carmen. But the empathy I see in his expression tells me he's not going to send us away.

I make my way over to the station and pour myself a cup of coffee. I say, "Ironic that we both had the idea to talk to Carmen, before the shop opens."

Without asking, Logan takes a seat at the table with them.

Carmen says, "Felicity, you know I didn't do this. You have to convince him."

I look at Arlo, who is trying to keep a blank face and hide what he's thinking, but I know him too well. "I don't think that is going to take much convincing. There's only the most circumstantial evidence connecting you to Mitch, and no motive for you threatening Logan. You two work so well together – if you had a grudge against Logan over getting you arrested that one time, or your roomate winding up in jail because of evidence he gave, we'd all know about it. You've never been the type to hold that kind of thing in."

Arlo sighs. "You know I have to keep looking for connections. After all, Carmen's fingerprints are on the book. And on the dessert tray."

"And Sonya's are on the knitting needles," Logan points out. "Obviously, that doesn't mean anything clear in this case."

Carmen says, "I handed Felicity the book, after I found it on the floor. Plus, that tray should have been at my house. I use it for parties. It's no surprise my prints were on it."

"What about the palmiers?" I ask. "Did you sell any recently here in the shop? Having a description of anyone who bought them, especially if they also had a connection to Mitch, could really help."

Arlo's lips are all scrunched up. He says, "I already asked her that."

Carmen ignores him and says, "Like I told Arlo, the ones I baked were for Paul. Half of them disappeared from my kitchen at home. I though Paul got into them before I'd actually given them to him. You can ask Violet, I was complaining about it yesterday."

So there's no money to trace, and no description. Just some thief slipping into Carmen's house.

There's a loud knock on the window. I look over and see Ash on the other side of the glass, holding up his phone and gesturing to be let in. I get up and go to the door.

Immediately, he says, "I think the killer left a comment on my podcast."

"What?" I take the phone from him, looking at the screen. The comment is from CumberbatchJunkie3. It says, *Felicity just got lucky with her first case. I have reason now to know that her deductions aren't as brilliant as you make them out to seem. V disappointed. Pick a better subject for your next podcast, please. I could just drown in your voice, so I'd hate to stop listening.*

"Oh, yeah, that could be Mitch's killer, all right." I bring the phone over to Arlo. I feel a sense of déjà vu as I remember Enrique telling his cooks that I had just gotten lucky, solving the cases I had dealt with.

Arlo says, "Ash, if you're right, that means Mitch's killer is a fan of your podcast. I need you to turn over the identity of CumberbatchJunkie3."

"Can't," Ash says, plucking the phone out of Arlo's hand. "I don't get that information, even for accounts that have subscribed to my podcast. And Cumberbatch Nuthatch hasn't. Which isn't unusual – a lot of people who listen to podcasts never subscribe."

I look over at Logan, but he gives a little head shake and says, "It would take too much time."

I guess there are limits to the information he can procure.

I gesture at the phone. "Ash, it's fair to say that whoever it is has a little crush on you."

The lemon-pucker look on Ash's face is priceless. I guess he didn't factor in the unpredictability of fans when he'd decided to start a podcast.

Arlo says, "The only solid suspects we have are Gently, Carmen and Sonya. And that message doesn't sound like it came from any of them."

I want to tell him that's because he's looking for suspects in all the wrong places. But he already knows I feel a little nonplussed that he's looking into all of my friends.

Logan says, "I don't see how any of those three could have a grudge against me. Especially not one worth killing over."

Carmen asks Logan, "Aren't you from Minnesota?"

"Yeah," Logan says, looking puzzled at the question.

Carmen says, "I was hanging out with Gently and Violet a while back. Gently had a few wine spritzers – usually, he never drinks – and he started telling us about this private detective he'd hired after his parents disappeared. The detective had come up with some whacked out theory that Gently's parents had been trafficked across the border, into Canada, aboard a boat. The only place that makes sense for that to have happened is at one of the Great Lakes."

"Unless the boat was in the open ocean," Logan points out.

Carmen says, "It didn't sound like that kind of boat. What if Gently thinks there's some kind of connection between you and what happened?"

"There isn't," Logan says without hesitation. "For one thing, I never worked that kind of case. For another, I have never heard of anyone being trafficked into Canada. It's not that kind of place."

"I told you it was a weird theory," Carmen says.

"But what about Mitch?" Logan asks. "He couldn't have had anything to do with the Anders disappearance. I'm pretty sure he's never been to Minnesota."

I think about it for a minute. "Technically, Em never said that Mitch was responsible for the death of the person that Em cared about. Just that Logan was. Logan wasn't a random choice – but Mitch might have been. Just someone to get me drawn into the case. So, theoretically, it could still be Gently." Even as I'm saying it, though, I'm not feeling it. It seems like such a stretch – especially since Logan doesn't seem to have any actual connection to the abduction. I wave away the thought. "Okay. I realize how ridiculous that sounds. But there's no motive for anyone else who was at the party to want Logan dead. At least that we know of."

"Including me," Carmen reminds us.

"Including you," I say.

"The threat said that you caused the death of someone?" Ash asks.

Logan says, "That's right. But if you can't be more specific?" He shrugs and makes a hopeless gesture with his hands.

I say, "So far, there's been evidence leaning towards Sonya, Silas, Carmen, Gently and Enrique. All very circumstantial."

Ash says, "Enrique had a sister who died in a car accident in Florida, about six years ago."

Logan looks thoughtful, and a little guilty. "I was on a protection detail in Florida around that time. We were involved in a car chase which resulted in a pile-up wreck that involved fatalities. The car I was driving wasn't in the accident. But the guy chasing my client was."

"It would be easy enough to check if that accident involved Enrique's sister," Arlo says. He takes out his phone and starts texting, presumably a request for information.

I feel farther away from a solution to all of this than ever. All of the suspects either cross-stitch, or are close to someone who does. And all of them could have found access to Carmen's cookies – if they were good enough thieves to break into her house undetected, which they aren't, unless one of them has been hiding a secret past. Which means they have exactly half the skills to pull off what has happened so far.

I ask Arlo, "Did Pru and Ben show up at the station to give their statement?"

Though it is early in the morning, and they might not have had time.

Arlo hesitates. He's a cop, and he tries his best not to give out information about his cases. But this case has extenuating circumstances. Finally, he says, "They're each other's alibi for the murder. They say they don't know anything about Mitch, but I tell you, they're lying about something."

"Maybe they've never been questioned by the police before," Logan says. "People tend to freeze up during unexpected interrogations."

"Maybe," Arlo says. "But I don't ignore it when I get a vibe. I'm going to be checking into them some more."

"We'll be trying to follow up some other leads," I say.

"Right after we stop by the pet store," Logan says. He tells Arlo, "We still need to Knightley-proof the baseboards at my apartment, before that bunny has time to get bored. Otherwise, what's the point?"

Arlo gives Logan a skeptical look. "Knightley is at your place?"

"We should go," I say, before this gets awkward. "I still want to go see Sonya. You said you were going to question her yesterday." I hesitate until Arlo gives me a slight nod. He doesn't seem inclined to elaborate. I add, "She must be shaken up."

"What should I do?" Ash asks. "I mean, should I reply to the comment, try to get more information?"

"Never reply to the comments," Carmen says, and I have to stifle a laugh.

Arlo says, "You do nothing. Enough of you are already involved in this case, I don't need anybody else volunteering to be the next victim." He turns back to me and Logan. "I wish you two could-" He shakes his head, then looks directly at me. "Just be careful."

"I will," I say. "I promise."

So we get ready to head out, just as Carmen flips over the open sign, and the first few customers start moving into the shop. Tracie's at her other job. Miles said he would come in for a little while, before going to class, to help us get caught up after the truffle project, but he isn't here yet. I hope Carmen will be okay on her own until he gets here, because obviously the word is out that Mitch's murder is somehow connected to me, and hence to the shop, so there's going to be a line. The police have been keeping the specifics quiet – so no one is supposed to know the killer challenged me – but the news did report last night and this morning that I was the one who found the body.

A group of the customers head over to me, two guys and three girls. One of the guys is wearing a shirt with Edgar Allen Poe silkscreened on it, and one of the girls is holding a copy of *Murder on the Orient Express*, and a Sharpie. She wants me to sign it, probably with something about solving the cruise ship murder. It freaks me out that someone similar to these people, a fan who sees my shop almost as an entertainment venue, could well be the killer. It isn't one of these specific people though, as I've never seen them before in my life. I've got to take Em's word when this killer said we've already met.

"Felicity!" the fan says, holding out her book. "You're actually here! So cool to meet you in person. I've been listening to the podcast."

"I'm heading out, actually," I say, side-stepping my way towards where Ash is standing. "But the voice of the podcast is right here. Ash is always excited to meet his fans."

Let Ash get a taste of what I've been dealing with, since he's put me into the spotlight. Ash is smiling when he gestures her over. Let's see how long that lasts.

Logan and I make our escape out the back.

When we stop at the pet store, Logan says he's just going to run in. He's in there for a while, though, and then comes out with a bag that is bigger than just a bottle of spray. As he closes the car door, he says, "Have you ever heard of a foraging box?"

I say, "I know bunnies like to forage. Knightley really gets a kick out of nibbling on live plants."

Logan nods. "Right. Like the lavender plants you have him eating in the chocolate sculpture in the shop."

I smile, thinking about how determined Knightley can be, if there's a plant he wants to eat. "He loves herbs and flowers."

"Perfect," Logan says as he reaches into the back seat and pulls a cardboard box out of the bag. He hands it to me, and I open it. It's filled with dried hibiscus flowers, rose petals, chamomile flowers, lemon balm and strawberry leaves.

I say, "Well, I can't say you never gave me flowers."

Logan looks at me, and there's a sense of vulnerability in his expression. "Maybe I should have done that sooner."

I put a hand on his sleeve. "I was kidding. Knightley is going to love this."

"Good," Logan says, as he puts the car in reverse, and pulls out of the parking lot. "At least something is going right today."

He's quiet, all the way back to his place. At the door of his apartment, I can hear a hacksaw cutting through plastic. Logan knocks loudly – he told Aunt Naomi to set the deadbolt and not open it for anybody except us.

The noise stops, and Miles opens the door, holding a mug. Logan looks past him, to where Aunt Naomi is busy making cord protectors. Logan doesn't look happy. He's probably not used to people just making themselves at home in his apartment.

Miles says, "I wasn't staying. I just dropped off the tools and supplies, and Mrs. Thibodeau made me coffee and eggs for my trouble. I can still make it by the shop before class."

"Don't worry about that," Logan says. He walks over to Naomi. "What part of don't call anyone wasn't clear? Mitch is already dead. We're trying to keep everyone else from being next. This is a serious threat."

"I know that." Naomi points with the hacksaw in the general down direction, presumably several floors past the wood floorboards of Logan's apartment. "That's why I went downstairs and made my call from the phone in the lobby. I saw Knightley sniffing a lamp cord, and I already feel useless enough. I had to do something to help."

"I get it," Logan says, looking at the new cord protector. "I really do."

## Chapter Twelve

We still need to find out what Sonya knows about those knitting needles, so we leave Miles and my aunt to finish bunny-proofing the apartment and head for the yarn shop.

At A Knit in Time, there's a class in full swing, but Sonya isn't teaching it. Instead, it's a petite Latina girl I've never met who looks about sixteen years old. So, where's Sonya? Is it possible she's been arrested? If that was the case, surely the class would have been cancelled. And Arlo would have said something when we left him all of an hour ago, at my shop – instead of just being vague about what had happened.

It's difficult to tell for sure, but I think the students are knitting oversized baskets. Which I would have thought would be too floppy to be functional, but apparently, I was wrong. I also assumed knitting had to involve needles, but I soon learn that if you're dealing with chunky enough yarn, you can "arm knit," which involves wrapping yarn around your wrists and using your arms to form the shapes you would have used needles to create.

Bea is here taking the class, with Satchmo sitting at her feet. The beagle wags an enthusiastic tail when he sees me walk in. He doesn't move from the spot where he's been told to sit, though. He looks up at Bea, but she's too focused on her project to notice.

For a second, I can't help but wonder. Bea moved to Galveston so suddenly. And I know she loves solving puzzles – we'd even been on the same team on a Sherlock Holmes themed LARP. Could us meeting, and her coming here have been something other than coincidence? Something far more sinister? I try to shake away the thought. Bea hadn't known Logan before the cruise we'd all gone on. And she had seemed to get along with him well enough. It's hard to imagine she's that good of an actress, and that she would have gone through so many convoluted steps to set up a murder. It's highly unlikely that she's the one who killed Mitch and threatened Logan. Right?

I turn towards Logan to get his reassurance that that theory is impossible, but he's started walking towards something at the other side of the shop. He's checking out red threads, presumably to find a match to the one that is in his pocket.

I stay near the class, trying to get a feel for Bea's state of mind.

Iris is here, too. I recognize her, but it takes me a minute to remember her name, or why I know her. She'd been the cook at the tea party who had been interested in the cases I'd helped solve. She's nosy, so maybe she'd be the one to ask about Sonya's whereabouts. She's also the only one who seems to be at a stopping point in the knitting project, as she prepares to join a new skein of yarn to the one she's been working with.

I walk over to her and gesture towards the basket-in-progress. "I like the color you're working with."

It's a pale pink with teal specks in it. Of all the yarn people are using for their projects, it is the one I would have chosen for myself, if I ever decided to dabble in the fiber arts.

Iris looks startled. "Oh, Felicity." She gives me a forced smile. I think she's going to say something else, but she doesn't. She seems to be waiting for me to say something, and she looks both frustrated and excited.

I ask her, "Have you seen Sonya?"

The excitement seems to fade. She purses her lips and points a lilac-manicured finger towards the back of the shop, where there's a restroom and an office. Iris says, "She's been in there crying for at least an hour. Somebody leaked a photo of her leaving the police station to the AP wire, and now the fact that

that the yarn shop owner's prints were on weaponized knitting needles has made national news."

I'm not sure if she means the office or the bathroom. I guess it doesn't matter. At least Sonya's not still at the police station.

"Are you here to talk to her about the case?" Iris asks.

I glance over at Logan, who seems captivated by the embroidery floss. I say absently, "Something like that. I know she didn't kill Mitch, or threaten Logan. I just have to figure out how to prove it."

"Oh?" Iris asks. That glint of excitement is back in her eyes. "How do you plan to do that?"

I stifle a grumble. I get so frustrated with these true crime nuts, who want to glorify murder. Iris is talking about this as a case, but doesn't she realize that Mitch was alive yesterday, and now he's gone? Everything that he was snuffed out and all his dreams and plans brought dramatically to a close. She must never have lost anyone close to her.

"I'm still working on a plan," I say. I take a step away from her. "Excuse me. I need to go comfort my friend."

"Wait," Iris says. When I turn back to her, she says, "Aren't you going to ask me if I know anything? If Enrique or Carmen or Yoli might have forgotten to return a key to Wobble House?"

"Did they?" I ask, carefully. Arlo already half-suspects Carmen is wrapped up in all of this, so I hope there's not going to be any more circumstantial evidence pointing to her.

Iris shrugs. "Maybe? Enrique sent me a text message this morning asking if I had seen a key to the back door, leading into the kitchen. But who knows? Maybe he found it."

I already believe Enrique is a possible suspect – though it still seems shaky why he would swear revenge on Logan. I'm sure Carmen is innocent. But I don't know much about Yoli. Or about Iris herself for that matter. I ask, "How long have you and Yoli been working with Enrique?"

Iris looks down at her yarn, rubbing the two ends between her fingers to join them into one seamless piece with easy dexterity, the precision that comes from working as a cook. Iris says, "I've only been in town a couple of months. I followed a guy." She scrunches up her nose. "It didn't work out."

"Where were you before that?" I ask.

She flutters a hand, "Oh, here and there. New York, mainly." Iris wraps the yarn around her wrist, ready to start knitting again. "I get bored staying in one place too long. Not enough challenge, you know?"

"So how did you meet Enrique?" I ask.

"I went to one of his pop-ups," she says. "I was impressed with his cooking, so I asked for a job. He put me on a list of people to call when he needs extra help."

"And he just happened to get the job with Mitch because the other caterer became sick," I say slowly.

Iris nods. "At least he says that's all there is to it." She gasps. "You don't think he's the one who killed Mr. Eberhardt? Why? What's his motive?"

"I didn't say that," I say quickly. In fact, part of me still doubts Enrique is capable of killing anyone, especially not so directly as stabbing them through the heart. But the timing of the job with Mitch – it does make him suspicious. Especially if he really did wind up with a key to Mitch's house. Enrique could have stood on the porch until he made sure someone noticed him and then gone inside the house through the back door – done whatever caused the vacuuming and scraping noises – and then disappeared. Just – why? The odds of Logan's traffic accident being the same one that had involved Enrique's sister are so small.

"I can see your mind working," Iris says. "You're so close to figuring it out. I want to be able to tell my friends I was there, when Felicity Koerber solved the case."

Iris is creeping me out – like I haven't had enough of that at the shop this morning, with the other murder book fans.

I take a step away. "Look, I need to go to talk to Sonya. Unless there's anything else you want to tell me?"

"No," Iris says. "I hope the case works out."

"Thank you," I say, even though it is hard to feel sincere. I go to the back of the store. Sonya's office door is open, and Logan is already in there, sitting across the desk from my friend. As I approach, I watch him lean forward and hand Sonya a tissue from a pack in his jacket pocket. Logan keeps a go bag in his car, so it's not surprising any time he's prepared for an unexpected need.

I move into the room and sit in the green bean-bag chair in the corner, as the only two real chairs in the space are occupied.

Sonya says, between sniffles, "I'm so glad you're here!"

I manage to extract myself from the chair to get up and go give her a hug from behind. She grasps the arm I've wrapped around her, holding on like I'm a life preserver. I tell her, "It's going to be okay. We're going to figure this out."

She nods, and I feel her hair tickle my cheek. Sonya says, "Logan just told me he's been threatened. You know it wasn't me. I would never – how could anyone think I hurt Mitch? I've been getting calls all morning, asking for interviews, hating on me for ridding the art world of such an enigmatic icon – even a few threats. If Arlo hadn't made me go to the police station, none of this would be happening."

I let her go and move back to the beanbag chair. "Arlo admitted the evidence against you is circumstantial. But he wouldn't be doing his job if he didn't follow up. I'm sure he didn't mean for this to happen."

Logan says, "We're probably going to ask you a lot of the same questions the police did. I'm sorry if that's upsetting."

Sonya blows her nose into the tissue. "I don't have a lot to tell you. I didn't even realize my knitting needles were missing until Arlo showed me that picture of them. I keep my knitting bag here in the shop, back behind the crafts counter. That's where Zoe should be standing to teach today's class. But that counter is not locked up. Anyone could have gotten to it, when I was helping a customer, or organizing things on the other side of the store. You would not believe how many people pick up yarn in one spot and stick it back somewhere else."

"Okay," Logan says. "But was there anyone in the shop acting suspiciously over the last couple of days? Especially anyone who might have been at the tea party?"

Sonya bites at her lip, obviously trying to think. Finally, she says, "Gently was at the party, and he came in a couple of days ago, for a class we did on knotting friendship bracelets. But he didn't seem particularly suspicious. He was on edge – but he always seems on edge." She pauses, then leans forward. "You know what? Pru came in here on Monday. She bought pearl cotton thread for a cross-stitch project she was working on. Some kind of heart-shaped pillow."

I shudder, remembering the caller on the phone saying, *I don't have time to cross-stitch that onto a bookmark for you.* I ask, "What color thread?"

Sonya says, "Red, I think. And gray. There was one other color. Maybe lavender?"

A scarlet thread of murder, running through ordinary life. Just like the quote said.

Arlo had his hunch that Ben and Pru are hiding something, and they have such a flimsy alibi. Still. I hope Pru's not the murderer. She seems so sweet, coming in together for dates with the guy she's been married to for thirty-two years. She doesn't seem the type to stab someone. But then again, neither do the others who seem to have a connection to Mitch.

I ask Logan, "Have you ever seen Pru before she and Ben started coming into the shop?"

Without hesitation, Logan says, "No. But she seems harmless. And she's retired. It makes sense that she's the type to actually do cross-stitch."

"That's my point," I say. "Remember the bookmark that showed up with that copy of *A Study in Scarlet*? Mitch's killer does cross-stitch."

He says, "I realize that. But come on – it's Pru. She's been really kind to me. I can't see her wanting me dead."

I wonder why Logan has a blind spot when it comes to Pru, when he's able to stay so logical about everyone else. I ask him, "Do you think she might have recognized you, the first time you saw her?"

Logan leans back and crosses his arms over his chest. "I thought about that. Not Pru specifically. Just the fact that because Em knows me, that doesn't necessarily mean I know him or her. I wasn't there at the trial of every bad guy I arrested as a cop. And in my other lines of work – you don't exactly follow up with the families of people you have to stop from hurting your clients." He sighs. "That wouldn't be good for anyone's mental health."

"I know," I say gently. "But we need to figure out who might be obsessing about you. So? Was there anything odd about meeting Pru?"

Logan says, "I remember thinking that her accent sounded a bit London, when she said they'd retired to Galveston from California, due to the cost of living. But lots of people take jobs in different cities than where they grew up. Pru and Ben were personable and talkative, from the first time we met. Pru always gives me one of those puffy peppermints when she comes in. She tells me to save it for my next long flight. And Ben always asks about flight conditions and airplane facts. Pru reminds me of my grandmother, honestly."

Suddenly I get why he's got a block on this one. It's hard to imagine being killed by your Gramma. And Logan is so far from his family, he needs the connections he can make. I say, "You can't underestimate anyone here."

Logan says, "True." From the expression on his face, he's thoughtful, but I can't tell what he's thinking so deeply about.

Sonya asks, "Did you recognize anyone in the class today? A lot of the same students were at the friendship bracelet class earlier in the week. They would have all taken home skeins of floss. I don't know how many of them would have been red.

And the piece of thread you showed me could have come from any craft shop – or even a Wal-Mart."

Logan says, "I saw Bea, but I didn't recognize anybody else. Not that I was looking all that close." He brings a hand up to his temple, as though rubbing away a headache. "I'm having a hard time wrapping my brain around the type of person we're looking for. I always thought that if my life ended by violence, it would be protecting somebody else. Probably looking down the barrel of a gun. It's hard to imagine dying as a pawn in a twisted game designed by a bookworm who does needlecraft. There's something just undignified about that. I can't accept it."

I take Logan's hand in mine. "You don't have to. We know there's going to be a threat to you. That means we can figure out how to protect against it."

Logan closes his eyes and brings his hand to his temple again. When he opens his eyes, they look sad. "Fee, it's hard enough to protect someone when you know when and where the threat is coming from. This is so vague. And the story reference to *The Dying Detective* was about a threat that came in the mail. Whatever method of attack, it is going to be executed from a distance. You can't stop something you don't see coming. I should know. I've lost clients before." His gaze hardens and he reaches out to take my hand. "None of this is your fault. And you aren't trained in tactics. If something does happen to me, promise me you won't blame yourself."

My mouth opens to reply that of course I won't, but just a weak noise comes out.

Sonya says, "Why don't you both just leave town? Logan, you own several airplanes. Just go see your family in Minnesota."

Logan sits back up straight. "That's the last thing I'd want to do. There's no guarantee the killer wouldn't follow me, and then more people I care about would be in danger. And if Em stayed here, this killer might choose another target Felicity cares about. Or Felicity herself. And I won't risk that."

That sudden intensity, the willingness to risk anything to protect others – that's the attraction. Logan's big heart is the part of him I fell in love with. Despite the darkness in his past.

And that's the part of him that I find myself in the singular position to protect. I've solved mysteries before. I've found myself in danger before, even saved the lives of several of my friends while stopping killers. But I've never felt this kind of urgency to solve a puzzle.

I say, "I feel like we're missing something obvious. Em claims to be someone I've met." I hesitate. I just said that no one was above suspicion, but I also told Arlo that I have faith in my friends. Still, I have to ask it. "What about Bea? What was her initial reaction when you two met on board that cruise ship?"

Logan studies me for a long time before he answers. "Bea knew who I was. She had met my father at a training session, where she was lecturing about how to more effectively use K-9 units. So she knew about me leaving the force."

Logan has told me before that his father is a police chief, and his sister is also a cop. They've never visited him in Texas, so I've never met them.

I ask, "What was Bea's reaction to meeting you?"

Logan says, "She seemed sympathetic. She said she understood how easily an operation could fall apart. I admitted it was my fault, and she said that in a team, nothing is ever a hundred percent one person's fault."

Sonya asks, "What operation?"

I wave away her question. The specifics of what happened aren't important, and I don't want Logan to have to relive one of the most painful experiences of his life. I ask, "Do you think Bea could have sought your father out on purpose? That she might have had a connection to one of the officers who got killed that day?"

There's pain in Logan's intense green eyes. "You don't really think she would have gone through all the trouble to make friends with us, and then wait months to follow up? There would have been plenty of opportunities to take her revenge on board the ship."

"Except Mitch wasn't there," I point out. "And he's obviously part of this somehow."

"That doesn't make sense," Logan says. "Mitch didn't have anything to do with the operation I botched here in the States. I met him in Paris. I got him arrested in Paris. The first I saw of him on the island was his dead body, yesterday."

"So why did he move to Galveston if he has no connection here?" Sonya asks.

Logan says, "He may well have been following me. I did some research last night, called in a few favors this morning to get more information. Mitch Fontaine only got out of prison six months ago. His alter ego – Mitch Eberhardt – is known in the art world for going through reclusive phases. Apparently, Mitch was able to use electronic communication inside a French prison to keep his businesses going, and to keep making philanthropic donations, so that he appeared active, even if he wasn't appearing publicly. The rumors were that he had been ill and didn't want to be photographed in that state. If he hadn't been killed, and I hadn't happened to be able to connect the two names, he probably could have continued his work as an above-board art collector without there being a whiff of scandal."

I say, "Bea wasn't invited to Mitch's tea party. It's possible she had no connection to him, which would mean that I'm being incredibly unfair thinking such a delightful person might be a killer." I look in the direction of the class, thinking about how good Bea is with Satchmo, how kind and gentle she seems with both animals and people. "Or it's possible there was some reason Mitch didn't want her there."

Logan stands up and moves to open the office door.

"Where are you going?" Sonya asks.

Logan says, "If we want to know what Bea was doing yesterday, the easiest thing to do is just to ask her."

I follow Logan as he strides purposefully towards the class space. Unfortunately, the class has ended, and many of the students are gone. I spot Bea though, looking at project kits. We make our way over to her and find she's looking at a boxed kit for cross-stitching a sea turtle. Well, that answers that question. Bea's a cross-stitcher. A chill runs down my spine at this not-so-innocuous piece of information.

Bea smiles at us and shows us the kit. "What do you think?" she asks. "It's not one of the local sea turtles, but it still looks like fun, right?"

"I guess," Logan says. "I've never tried cross stitch myself."

"You should." Bea picks up an identical kit. "I'll get you this one, so you can try it. We all know how much you like sea turtles. Right, Satchmo?"

Satchmo looks up at his name, and his tail starts wagging, but he stays put beside Bea.

Logan smiles and straightens his jacket. "I did name my business Ridley Puddle Jumpers after all."

I have a hard time making myself ask, "Where were you two days ago around two o'clock?"

Bea's eyes widen, then she looks skeptically at Logan. Then she looks back at me and says, "I was at the police station, introducing myself and talking up the therapy dog initiative I'm helping to launch at the hospital. Satchmo was a big hit."

I ask, "So you weren't invited to Mitch Eberhardt's tea party?"

Bea looks confused. "Who's Mitch Eberhardt?"

I don't even bother asking her where she was yesterday morning. Every one of the threads we've followed – every one of the suspects – seems to be leading to a beige dead end.

## Chapter Thirteen

As we're leaving the yarn shop, we get a call from Arlo, saying that he'd like us to come to discuss the case. But he wants us to come to his house, instead of the police station. Which I find a little odd, especially considering we just talked.

Logan tells Arlo that he needs to go by his hanger at the little airport first, to grab information on a client whose upcoming flight he needs to cancel. Driving all the way to the hanger feels like a waste of time – considering the less than twenty-four hours we have left on the time limit the killer gave us. But the fact that Logan is showing interest in his business is actually a good sign. He's not completely convinced he's going to die after all.

So I slide into the passenger seat of the Mustang, and try to quiet my anxiety about time ticking away.

Logan says, "You know what I like about flying? The sense of control, paired with the absolute freedom. There's no feeling like it."

I smile. "I think you've said that before."

"Probably," Logan says. "But when I get anxious, I think about what it feels like to fly. My heart rate goes down, and there's a sense of peace, no matter what else is going on."

"Even now?" I ask.

"Even now," Logan says. "What I'm trying to say is, you need to find that feeling somewhere in life. So on days like today, you have a place to go in your mind, just for a few minutes. If you think it would help, I could take you flying."

"I don't think we have time for that, Logan," I say.

He says, "There's always time for the important moments. Especially if there might be no time left later."

Those words squeeze at my heart. I tell him, "I already have a happy place. It's always been the ocean. That got clouded after Kevin died. And you were one of the people who gave the peace of the ocean back to me."

It's a complicated journey, and has taken a long time, but the feeling of being on a boat, looking out at the crystalline specks of sunlight dancing on the waves, while all the cares of life remain back on shore – yeah, Logan's right, just thinking about it helps my anxiety fade to a manageable level. We start talking about Mitch, and what Logan knows about Mitch's past.

Logan says, "I don't know of anybody who would have hated Mitch enough to kill him. Mitch was a gifted painter who found out there was a lot more money in copying old paintings than in trying to sell new ones. Although his original works are some of my favorite paintings. He had a way of capturing modern Paris that just felt timeless. But joyous and playful, too."

"Mitch was your favorite painter?" I ask.

Logan thinks about it for a second. "Yeah, you could say that. I doubt he knew."

I say, "Mitch asked me who my favorite painter is. I told him I don't know. He seemed very disappointed. I hate that me disappointing him is one of his last memories."

"That's not your fault. Just because this killer is trying to make this personal for you doesn't mean that it is."

"We still haven't figured out who it might be personal to," I point out. "Think. Who had even the slightest disagreement with Mitch?"

Logan says, "Under his guise as an art dealer, Mitch sold forgeries mainly to people who wanted paintings for private collections. As the real paintings were all ones that had been stolen – or were rumored to have been stolen and quietly replaced with replicas – the collectors would be hesitant to have them authenticated, and even more reluctant to show them publicly, or even to friends. I suppose someone could have found out they'd been sold a fake and been angry enough to hold a grudge. Mitch liked to live dangerously, so he actually exhibited several of his fakes. I'm guessing that all the paintings in that gallery he showed you are his work, forged or original. When he asked for your favorite, he was probably hoping you'd choose one of his."

By the time we get out to the small airport where Logan's private hanger is located, Logan has come up with four names of individuals who might have held grudges over Mitch's actions: Luis Oakenthorne, the collector who had tipped Logan off to Mitch's operation; Maggie Gold, a painter who had been working with Mitch and had also gotten arrested; Rupert Hertz, the courier who had been sent to fetch the painting, who had never gotten paid; and Cassidy Blanc, the girlfriend Mitch had dumped shortly before his arrest, for reasons entirely unconnected.

Logan says, "I haven't seen any of those people in Galveston. And I have no idea who was in Mitch's life when he was in prison, or since. I don't know how much that helps."

I get out of the car, and as we enter the hanger, I say, "Maybe we can figure out what these four folks are up to now. I can do basic searches and check their social media."

Logan says, "These aren't the kind of people who have social media."

I say, "Well, then maybe you'll have to call in a few more favors and see if any of them have a rap sheet for being a thief. But the killer said on the phone that I'm supposed to have more ideas by now. Which means Em is expecting me to be finding some kind of clues, somewhere."

"I doubt it's going to be that easy," Logan says as he goes over to the workbench where he stores his maintenance tools. There's a sticky note stuck to the side of a multi-tiered tool chest. Logan plucks up the sticky note, types a number into his phone and texts the cancellation.

I say, "We came all this way just for that?"

Logan gives me a lop-sided smile. "I usually put bookings into my phone right after I take them, but I was busy, and then I forgot."

"You don't use a computer to take them?" I ask. "You know there's software you can use that lets people make their own appointments."

"I prefer talking to potential clients first," Logan says. "I don't like surprises."

"I get that," I say.

Logan moves over to the first aid box on the wall and opens it. He takes something out of it that I can't see. When he closes the box, he's holding surgical gloves and a filter mask.

"What's that for?" I ask.

Logan says, "Checking the mail. Considering what happened in that Sherlock Holmes story, I'm not taking any chances."

I nod, though I wonder if even that is enough preparation. I ask, "Where's the mailbox?"

Logan says, "In a post office box, at a shipping store down the street."

I ride with Logan to the shop, but he asks me to stay in the car – just in case. I get that he's worried about dust or fumes on suspicious mail, and that one person potentially exposed is better than two. But I don't know what the point of being with him is, if he's going to sideline me when things get dangerous.

While I wait, I start searching for Mitch's associates, using the scant information on them that Logan has given me to work with. I've drawn complete blanks on Luis Oakenthorne – assuming he's not a thirtieth level bard in QuestMuch, an online role-playing game that seems geared towards fourteen-year-olds. And while there are a number of Maggie Golds on the Internet, none of them seem remotely like the person Logan had described.

Before I can get to the other two names, Logan gets back into the car. He's no longer carrying the mask and gloves. He is, however, holding an envelope. I can only describe the look on his face as bemused.

"What's that?" I ask, trying to match his tone and expression.

He pulls a piece of paper out of the envelope and hands it to me. "It's from Mitch. I think it was meant to be a threat. He challenged me to figure out the secret of Wobble House, since I was the only one ever smart enough to catch him. It's postmarked before his murder."

I unfold the letter and skim it. Mitch's writing was neat, and practical, not at all like the calligraphic style of the person who had written the threats on the wall and on the dessert tray. The letter is long and rambling. When I finish reading, I say, "This clears up a few things. Mitch got interested in this island because of you, but he found out about Wobble House because of an open house right after he arrived on the island. He decided he had to have it, because he fell in love with it. He says it spoke to his soul."

Logan says, "I'm choosing to interpret that as, I'm the one who introduced him to the place where he could finally be happy."

Which explains Logan's bemusement, despite the anger expressed in other parts of the letter. I get it. We can't change the fact of Mitch's death. But we can re-interpret the context of his life.

Once we're headed toward Arlo's place, which is actually on the way back to town just past the State Park, I can't get a specific line from Mitch's letter out of my head. He said there's no right or wrong about art, and no such thing as best – it's just what you like.

I pull up a list of famous painters and famous paintings, and start trying to evaluate each one, to find a piece or an artist that speaks to me. I hadn't felt a lack in my life when it came to art or artists – not until Mitch had pointed it out. There are plenty of paintings I find interesting, plenty that are attractive enough that I would hang on my walls. And some are obvious nos. I just don't get Cubism or melting clocks. You can keep your soup cans and kitschy modern art. There's nothing wrong with them, as expressions of that artist's heart and vision – but if I'm looking for a favorite, I need to narrow it down to favorite types of art first.

I am drawn to the portraits, of people with searching eyes and depth to their rendering and their worlds. Paintings of groups like the *Luncheon of the Boating Party*, and Mary Cassatt's tea party scenes seem to tell a story that make me want to know more – especially once I read a bit and realize that that luncheon party was made up of the artist's friends, many famous in their own right.

And I like the landscapes. From Monet's muted watercolors, to Van Gogh's haystacks. They all transport me somewhere, through space and time.

But to call one of them my favorite? In a way, to claim one of them as my inspiration, to make it part of me? None of the images speak to me that way.

When we get to Arlo's place, Arlo is sliding sandwiches onto plates. They're traditional Cuban sandwiches, thick with mustard and Swiss Cheese and multiple variations on pork. The smell of them sets my mouth salivating.

Arlo says, "Now that's timing."

We all sit at his neat dining table. He says, "I know, with Bea in town, that it's going to be tempting to get her to help you on the case. But she's part of the police, so try not to make her have a conflict of interest."

"Is that what you brought us here to say?" Logan asks. "You could have just said that over the phone. We're not entirely sure Bea's not a suspect, so we probably weren't going to reach out to her anyway."

Arlo's eyebrows rise with skepticism. "Bea?"

Logan shrugs. "It's just a theory."

Arlo says, "Then hope it's not her. I've asked her to bring one of the police dogs to attempt to do some scent tracing off that skein of yarn, starting in Mitch's study at Wobble House."

"What good will that do?" I ask. "The killer is bound to be long gone."

"I'm trying to do something you taught me," Arlo says. "When you run out of leads, think outside the box."

I can't help but smile at that, and Arlo smiles back at me. There's warmth in his brown eyes that makes me warm inside, too. I say, "I guess, what's the worst that can happen?"

"Why are you telling us this?" Logan asks.

"If you happened to want to meet us at the house, first thing in the morning, Bea is going to need someone to watch Satchmo, maybe even take him for the whole day. And if you happen to observe the scent tracking while you're there, or explore parts of the house since it has been released as a crime scene, who am I to complain?"

Arlo is usually such a stickler for following the rules. I don't think he's breaking any here, but he's bending them enough that he wanted to talk about it in person, away from the station. It's kind of him to let us have this information, giving Logan the best chance to survive – though it is going to be a last-minute tactic, as tomorrow is when Em is slated to strike.

Logan says, "Usually you're reminding me that I've officially quit the police force."

Arlo replies, "And you're usually reminding me that you're still quasi-connected to the force. You could make a call, and I'd have the governor telling me to let you observe."

"That's fair," Logan says.

"Besides," Arlo says, "If anything happened to you, I'd miss our little chats."

Logan says, "What about the leads we were talking about earlier?"

Arlo says, "Nothing has really panned out. Enrique's sister's accident wasn't a multi-car pileup. So we're back to him not having a motive."

Logan's jaw relaxes in a way that looks relieved.

We get Arlo caught up with the little that we've discovered so far about the case, and we give him Mitch's letter – which I have already photographed.

Logan says, "I've checked the rap sheets, and none of the suspects we've come up with so far have ever been arrested for theft."

"You checked up on Pru?" I ask, surprised.

Logan says, "You told me not to underestimate anyone. So I checked out Pru, Bea, Gently, Sonya and Enrique. Except for Enrique's issues with the illegal pop-ups, they're all model citizens. Although, Pru did get arrested about twenty years ago for streaking."

"Really?" I study Logan, trying to tell if he's serious. I think he is. "Kinda makes it hard to picture her as your grandmother now, doesn't it?"

Logan laughs. "You've never met my grandmother."

We all dig into our sandwiches. A really well-made Cuban sandwich is a work of art – and it's surprisingly easy to encounter bad ones, even on restaurant menus. Arlo's are some of the best. Authentic Cuban bread with the richness of lard, from a bakery in Houston, and just the right amounts of high-quality ham and roasted pork.

I savor this unexpected treat. He has an extra sandwich, over on the counter. Maybe I can talk him into letting me take it to go. After all, it has been a long day, and I still need to get back to Greetings and Felicitations.

Arlo says, "I've checked with the housekeeper at Wobble House, and Mitch's personal assistant about why they were no-shows. They both received e-mails from Mitch's account unceremoniously firing them, with time stamps during the tea. We believe that someone snuck into Mitch's study and sent those emails, then wiped all the prints off the computer and the desk. That's why Mitch was alone this morning."

"Such a considerate killer," Logan says. Then his face goes serious. "It means we're dealing with someone who doesn't want to hurt any more people than they have to."

"It also makes it that more obvious that the knitting needles with Sonya's prints had to have been planted," I point out.

"Yes, we get that too." Arlo wipes his hands on a napkin. "She's dropped down to the bottom of the suspect list. The personal assistant has made her way up to the top. She was really angry when we contacted her, and had no alibi for the time when Mitch was shot. She claims to have stayed home all morning, writing angry fan fiction and baking comfort cookies."

"Fan fiction of what?" I ask. It couldn't be so simple as for him to say Sherlock Holmes.

Instead, Arlo says, "Dr. Who. She let me read it. And let's just say, the Daleks are not very kind to a character who looks and acts very much like Mitch." He shudders.

I haven't seen a lot of Dr. Who, but my nephew is a fan, so I have a passing acquaintance with the worldbuilding. "Sounds – graphic."

Arlo nods. "Very."

I say, "That doesn't mean the writer's a killer. Besides, how would she have the motive to write the email firing herself if her motive for wanting Mitch dead was having been fired? And what about the call to me and the threat to Logan?"

Arlo taps a finger to his own nose. "And that's exactly why I didn't arrest her. It only makes sense if there was another motive. And so far, I haven't been able to connect her to you or Logan."

Well, I'll leave that wild-goose-chase to Arlo. I really want to find a suspect that isn't Pru or Bea or Enrique– but I don't have time to try and connect in things that are that much of a stretch. I say, "If you find someone who writes Sherlock Holmes fan fiction, let me know. Because that's the killer's real obsession."

That gives me an idea, and I do a quick search to see how many people are writing such fan fic – and the hits are immediately overwhelming. Entire archives of stories loosely based on the original characters, serious Sherlock Holmes research societies, traditionally published retellings, discussions of the films with Robert Downey Junior and Basil Rathbone, comparisons of Benedict Cumberbatch and Johnny Lee Miller's modern takes on the detective and the liberties taken in the course of their series. Comic spoofs. Articles that pick apart the references in Star Trek – complete with gifs of Data as Holmes – and images as obscure as stills of the collection of Holmes memorabilia from the opening credits of Diagnosis Murder.

Even if I sat here at Arlo's table, with him feeding me Cuban sandwiches all day and into tomorrow morning, until the time limit for Logan runs out, there would be no way I could even scratch the surface of the people involved in creating all that content.

There's a knock at the kitchen door, and I jump, realizing I'd gotten caught up in the content I'd been looking at. I've lost track of the conversation between Arlo and Logan.

Arlo gets up from the table, "That will be Drake. He wanted to talk to me today. I didn't realize it was going to take you two so long to get here, so I told him to come after I thought we'd be done."

Well, now I know who the extra sandwich is for.

Drake comes in, still dressed for his job at the library in a long-sleeved plum shirt and black tie. He doesn't look surprised to see me and Logan sitting there, and doesn't look nervous, even though he's obviously come here to ask Arlo to be in the wedding – in front of Logan. Maybe Autumn didn't tell him about the potential conflicts, which have been brewing since I'd asked Logan to be my plus one at the wedding, before Logan had even been added to the list of groomsmen.

Arlo hands Drake the sandwich, and gestures to the fourth chair at the table.

Drake gives the sandwich an appreciative look and takes a seat. He tells Arlo, "I know this is late notice, with the wedding just a month away, but Autumn is letting me add a groomsman to my side of the wedding party. The first person I thought of is you."

"I'm always up for a party," Arlo says. "And that day is bound to be more meaningful to me than you could ever imagine." He gives me a significant look.

I feel my face go hot with embarrassment. Drake doesn't seem to notice, as he takes a first bite of his sandwich.

Logan says, "You may not have to wait that long, if we don't solve this case."

Now Arlo's looks embarrassed. The implications of what Logan just said are pretty dark: if Mitch's killer removes Logan from the picture, then Arlo has no rival for my affections. And Arlo doesn't seem to know what to say to that.

Drake doesn't seem to know the subtext of what's going on. He just looks confused as the awkward silence falls. After about a minute, he says, "It's been a crazy week at the library. You know we had a break in?"

"Oh?" Arlo leans forward, looking relieved to be back on ground he knows how to navigate. "Did you report it?"

"Of course," Drake says. "But the books disappeared from my department, so my boss keeps asking me in different ways if I might have left the door unlocked."

"Which books did the thieves take?" Logan asks.

"They didn't take everything on my processing shelf, but everything they took was valuable. There were a few volumes of psychology texts that I'd just finished repairing, and a donation of rare books we'd just taken in – including early editions of Robison Crusoe and all four of the original Sherlock Holmes novels. It's a shame. The books were all in easily repairable condition. Mostly it would have been a matter of removing a bit of grime from the covers."

I say, "I have a feeling I know where one of those books wound up."

I explain about how the copy of *A Study in Scarlet* had shown up on my shop's bookshelf, and about the threat.

Arlo tells Drake, "I'd like to take a look at your office, to see if there's any forensic evidence left behind after the theft. You may change your mind about wanting me as a groomsman, after you're dealing with fingerprint powder on your desk."

## Chapter Fourteen

I pick up a book off Drake's desk. It's an anatomy book I'd used back when I was in college.

"Careful," Drake says. "I had to re-do the binding, so the glue hasn't had time to cure yet."

Logan says, "And you're getting prints on it. Arlo is going to need to take yours now for exclusion."

I say, "He already has them on file."

Arlo comes back into the oversized office. "Didn't I say not to touch anything?"

"Sorry." I put the book down. We only have a short time before the CSI guy gets here.

I step to the middle of the room. I'm not sure what we're going to gain from checking out the scene of a theft that happened days ago, but Logan and Arlo both wanted to see it. So I study it too. Drake has a bookcase against one wall, and it's stacked with books – some obviously in need of repair. One shelf is for decorative items – where he's lined up frames with photos of his mom, him and Autumn, and him on skis with a mountain in the background.

I'm seeing art everywhere now that I've started looking. Drake has an oversized print on the wall behind his desk. It's of a painting in riotous red and gold and black, of two musicians, one with a violin, the other a guitar, both wearing old-fashioned hats and suits. It makes sense – Drake and Autumn share a love for jazz and blues music. Autumn had been the one to turn me onto jazz, too. So maybe finding a favorite artist has to come from the other things you love. Or the things that you just feel.

Drake also has an expensive looking globe over in the corner, next to a brown leather club chair with short legs. There's something shiny under the chair, by one of the front legs.

"Hey, what's that?" I bend down, resisting the impulse to pick up the object.

Arlo grabs a tissue from the box on Drake's desk and uses it to edge the shiny object out from under the chair.

It's a key on a flat keychain. The keychain is engraved with WH – in the same font as the sign for Wobble House.

Drake says, "I've never seen that before."

I say, "One of the cooks working with Enrique told me there was a key to Wobble House that went missing after the tea party. Whoever broke in here must have dropped it."

"That seems careless," Logan says.

"Or maybe we were supposed to find it?" I say.

"Probably just another red herring," Arlo says.

I say, "Iris – the cook I was talking about – thinks Enrique took the key himself, that maybe he killed Mitch. But if the key is here, that falls apart because the theft happened before the tea party."

Arlo says, "Not necessarily. He could have made a copy of the key. Or he could have figured out another way in."

Logan says, "How would Enrique even have known that specific book was in this office?"

Drake says, "Books go into the catalog, no matter where they are in the library. That's how we can find them, even if they've gone in for repair or are in a special collection. It would have been searchable by anyone visiting the library – or even from home, through our remote catalog, or through WorldCat, which indexes which libraries have what book."

"That doesn't narrow down anything," Logan says.

Drake taps a finger to his chin, thinking. "I did mention the book to that couple that Autumn and I sometimes have breakfast with when we're all at Greetings and Felicitations."

"Are you talking about Ben and Pru?" I ask.

Drake nods. "They are such a cute couple. So literate. They love talking books with us, and they've read everything Autumn has ever published. Ben was so excited about her new project. Especially after he got to read the first couple of chapters."

"I haven't even had time to read those," I protest. Though, really, I have no claim on the book, even though Autumn asked for my input.

Arlo says, "Mysteries. As in Sherlock Holmes."

Drake says, "I was the one who brought up Sherlock Holmes. Both Ben and Pru had read some of it. But I wouldn't say either one of them was obsessed with the detective."

Arlo gives me a significant look. He still thinks the elderly couple had something to do with Mitch's death. And I have to admit, this does make them look more suspicious, knowing they've read Holmes. But that's hardly unique to them.

I ask, "Were there other people in the shop at the time?"

Drake says, "A lot of the tables were full. But I don't think anybody else was listening to our conversation. Not that I was really paying attention to anybody else." Drake fiddles with the end of his tie. "Felicity, this was days ago. I'm sorry, but it didn't seem important at the time."

Arlo says, "That's normal. Most witnesses don't remember details, even immediately after the fact."

I say, "Say Ben and Pru are secretly master thieves, and they took the book. That still doesn't explain how Ben and Pru would have wound up with the missing key."

Arlo says, "Were they still at the party when you left?"

"Yes," I admit. "I guess they could have somehow wound up going into the kitchen."

Logan says, "We really should make sure that's the same key."

I take out my phone. The battery seems to be working fine, now. I call Enrique and ask him, "Did you ever find the key that went missing after the tea party?"

He asks, "How do you know about that?" Then before I can answer, he says, "Oh, wait, Carmen, right?"

I tell him, "Actually, Iris mentioned it."

"Really?" Enrique sounds surprised. "I didn't realize you two were friends."

"We're not, really. I just happened to run into her."

Enrique says, "I never found the key. The caretakers are charging me for replacing the lock on the back door. Which stinks, because they're going with the most high-end expensive lock they can find."

I ask, "Did you keep the key on you? Or could your employees – or even one of the guests – have borrowed it?"

Enrique says, "I'm sure it was in the pocket of my jacket, when I hung it up to change into my chef's whites. Once we had everything cleaned up and our equipment carted out, I put my jacket back on, and there was no key."

I start to tell him that we just found the key, but I don't know for a fact that it is the same one. And even if it is, and he returns it after the police are done with it, there's no guarantee that nobody made a copy of it while it was missing, so these caretakers will likely go ahead with replacing the lock.

I ask, "What do you know about Yoli and Iris?"

Enrique says, "Just their qualifications, mainly. I work with a dozen different cooks when I do events, and as long as they do good work and show up on time, I don't ask a lot of questions. Yoli graduated from El Centro, in Dallas, a couple of years ago. And Iris did some coursework at the CIA before becoming a personal chef. She handed me a list of references from hoity-toity families when she asked for work, but I never got around to checking them."

CIA in this case stands for Culinary Institute of America. It's a prestigious school. Less prestigious if Iris didn't graduate, but it matches her model of getting bored with things and then moving onto the next task. I ask, "Do you think you could take a picture of that list and text it to me?"

"Sure," Enrique says. "I'm going to need a minute to find the file folder."

Before he can hang up, I ask, "How do you decide which cooks to work with for each catering job? Especially the tea party."

Enrique says, "I usually plan out who I think would be a good fit for the menu and the venue. But this one was last minute, so I just started calling. Apparently, this flu bug is going around the culinary community, because some of the first cooks I called were also too sick to work. Yoli and Iris were the first two healthy bodies I contacted. Probably because neither of them seems to have much of a social life."

That sounds weird and a bit of a coincidence, especially if someone specifically wanted access to a key to Wobble House, or to case out the place to get the layout for staging the murder.

"One more question. Where were you the night of the tea party, between 10 p.m. and midnight?" That's the rough time Drake gave us for the theft of the book.

Enrique says, "I was at a concert, in Houston, with some friends. Why?"

I tell him, "That gives you a pretty good alibi."

He asks, "For what?" but I'm not sure how much Arlo wants me to tell him. And Arlo is looking this way, probably already frustrated that I'm taking it upon myself to question his suspects. So I cut my conversation with Enrique short.

After I hang up, I tell Logan and Arlo, "Enrique has an alibi for the theft of the book, and the motive we thought he might have against Logan doesn't hold up. I don't think he did this."

My phone dings with a text from Enrique with a picture of Iris's resume, and her references page. It looks legit. I call the first number on the list, and the woman who answers gives a glowing review of Iris's services. Just because she's a true crime fan, and happened to get asked to work the tea party, doesn't mean she's connected to any of this. We're getting nowhere hopping down all these rabbit holes.

My phone rings and I assume it is Enrique calling back, but when I look at the caller ID it says Sherlock Killer. I answer it, saying, "Hi, Em," loudly enough to alert everyone in the room that now would be an excellent opportunity to trace the call.

The same altered mechanical voice says, "Made your way to the library, I see. Finally tracing where I got the book."

Chills creep over my skin. This killer is following us. I guess that makes sense – giving Logan an extra day must have left Em with time to kill. Stalking us is at least better than throwing us an extra victim. And without a bug to listen in, Em must be bored and frustrated about being left out of the investigation.

"Yeah," I say as casually as possible. My voice still squeaks a little. "We also found your key. I'm guessing that would be another red herring?"

The electronic voice laughs in my ear. "Actually, no. I was wondering where that got to. It would have been so much easier to slip in quietly to Mitch's place if I had held onto that key. There was so much to be done, and I'd only been able to bring in part of my supplies the night before."

So Em had been at the party, or had snuck into the house while the party was going on. We hadn't found anything in the way of supplies – unless the killer means the knitting needles and yarn. So presumably they took whatever else they'd brought away with them. Unless that explains whatever got burned in the fireplace.

"How did you even know that the book you needed would be in a nearby library? You could have had to drive for hours to find a copy. Committing the theft the night before the murder was cutting it close, don't you think?"

There's a tutting sound – I think – the mechanical altering makes it weird. "It wasn't until Mitch showed he had no remorse when I confronted him that I was sure I had to kill him. Books have always been my solace. And the fact that I'd overheard someone talking about the very book that had resonated with me, just days before I could strike, when I was finalizing my plan for revenge – it seemed absolutely serendipitous. How could something so right fail?"

I feel chills on top of chills. This murderer had been in my shop, days before the crime, probably trying to catch a glimpse of my face, to decide if I was truly worthy to challenge. Unfortunately, I wasn't there that day. I'd had a dentist appointment Monday morning. Not that I would necessarily have spotted the killer in my group of customers, even if I had been there, or that I would remember the details. If the killer is someone I would know on sight, Em could have come in disguise. Or if Em is someone I have only met in passing – they could have just been in the shop, another customer that no one really noticed.

I ask, "What about the vacuuming and the scraping sounds that were heard at the house? Care to share what that's all about?"

"Not really," the altered voice says. "Some things you have to figure out for yourself."

I sigh, loudly, into my phone. "But why? Why go through all of this? Why even challenge someone to a battle of wits? Why not just kill Mitch and Logan if all you want is revenge?"

Logan's eyebrows go up at this suggestion, but he doesn't try to stop me asking the question.

The mechanical voice says, "I need for this to mean something. I need there to be justice, even when there's no recourse through the courts. And I need it to be remembered. The news and the crime podcasts don't cover boring cases."

So whoever Em is, this killer wants the story told. Potentially, this person feels underappreciated, or is crying out for attention as much as justice. I'm not sure which of the suspects might feel that way. Potentially, all of them, from what little I know about their lives.

I say, "You know that none of this will bring back whoever you lost. Or stop the pain."

The altered voice says, “That’s one reason that I picked you. You’ve lost someone, but through accident. It helps complete the mirror between us.” There is a mechanical laugh. “And also, Ash said some things on his podcast about you and Logan working together. After that, it had to be you. There was no choice. So you need to start living up to the hype.”

I say, “I’m trying my best. None of this is about the fact that Logan is from Minnesota, is it?”

“What? That’s random.” Em sounds mechanically offended.

“It was just part of a theory,” I say. I’m more reassured that Em is not Gently.

“Stop wasting time,” Em snaps. And then hangs up.

Again, the call is too short to get a trace.

What am I missing? Logan had said Mitch’s associates are not the type to even have social media, so it’s not likely that any of them are attention seekers.

“Maybe this is all Ash’s doing,” Logan quips. “All of it just to boost his ratings.”

I give him a pointed look, since he’s joking when I just got off the phone with a killer. Maybe that’s why Logan is joking, though. To get us back to a better mood.

“I need a minute to think,” I say. “But I don’t want to go outside. Em is probably still somewhere outside, waiting for us to leave.”

I take a seat at one of the work carrels near Drake’s office and try to wrap my brain around what I know. The CSI guy shows up and goes into the office. I feel like I need to find a different way to analyze things.

I realize I never got back to searching for information on the other two names Logan gave me as Mitch’s associates. I search the ex-girlfriend, Cassidy Blanc. If it’s the same person, she’s a model now, and her Instagram features blooper photos of herself from a shoot in Milan – six hours ago. There’s no way she could be on Galveston Island.

That just leaves Rupert Hertz, the courier, who turns out to be a thin white guy in his thirties. He has a Facebook account with a ton of photos, though he hasn't posted anything in years. Near the top of the list, there's pictures of him with a girl, though she's hiding her face from the camera – even in pics where she's showing off her ring. I wonder what happened for him to stop posting. Maybe the girl broke off the engagement.

Rupert also has a business Facebook account for his legitimate business as a travel agent. The last post to that was years ago. It's a picture of Rupert, smiling, wearing a blue suit. The caption starts, *The Hertz Family regrets to inform everyone of Rupert's untimely passing.*

That explains why he stopped posting. He had died, somewhere near the time that Mitch had gotten arrested. That can't be a coincidence.

I have to find Logan.

He's not far – just leaning against a pillar, staring off into space, probably upset that we're wasting time here when we could be trying to follow some other lead.

I blurt, "Did you know that Rupert Hertz is dead?"

"Why would he be dead?" Logan asks, looking alarmed. "He's just a courier. Is Em after everyone Mitch knew?"

"It wasn't recent." I show him my phone, with the message Rupert's family had posted still visible.

Logan takes the phone, staring at the picture, scrolling through the entire caption. Eventually, he says, "I had no idea." There's pain in his piercing green eyes. "This could be my fault. After Mitch was arrested – they just let Rupert go. There wasn't enough connecting him to the case to make it worth prosecuting him. I didn't think anything of it. But he was a courier, who didn't show up with what he was meant to deliver, and the guy he was supposed to pick it up from had wound up in jail. There are several ways that could have gone badly."

I show Logan the Facebook page, with the engagement photos, and ask, "Did you ever see Rupert with a girl? Can you recognize who this is?"

Logan shakes his head. "I never really took an interest in his life. I'm beginning to regret that now. I should have at least sent flowers."

A voice from behind us says, "Regret what?" It's Autumn.

I turn. She's carrying a picnic basket and a binder full of fabric swatches. I say, "You're here to see Drake."

"It's a surprise," Autumn says, opening one flap of the picnic basket. "Want a Jamaican meat pie? I took a shot at Drake's mama's recipe, and I made way too much getting the shapes right."

We just ate at Arlo's place, but who can resist the delicious smell wafting out of the basket? I look over at Logan. "Want to split one?"

"Sure," he says.

I reach into the basket and draw out one of the rectangular hand pies. The crust is flaky, and yellow from the turmeric. When I break it, the layers reveal the spicy meat mixture inside. The key to this kind of meat pies is enough habanero peppers to clear the sinuses, but not so much as to make the experience unpleasant. I take a bite, and Autumn has nailed it, perfectly.

"Look at you, learning to cook," I say.

Autumn looks both pleased and embarrassed. She says, "Girl, you know I am highly skilled at dialing a phone for any cuisine of takeout you want. But Drake likes to spend time in the kitchen. I thought I'd try to see what you all get out of cooking. I'm still not sure I get it. These were seriously a lot of work."

"But they're divine," Logan says. "Forget the over fancy wedding food, and just put these on the table."

"I might have to. I am still looking for a caterer," Autumn says. "The one we booked says they can't accommodate the additional guests."

I say, "We already know a good caterer – who could probably get tiny versions of these on the menu. I might be working with him next summer – assuming he didn't murder Mitch."

"You're talking about Enrique, aren't you?" Autumn says. "At this point, accused of murder isn't a dealbreaker."

Logan says, "He's got a pretty decent alibi."

"Even better," Autumn says. "I don't know why I didn't think of calling him earlier. Those little salmon puffs he did for the tea party were absolute perfection."

"Man, I missed those!" I guess there had been another course of food at the party that I'd entirely missed by wandering off to chat with Mitch. "I guess you found a venue that can fit the extra guests?"

Autumn says, "I'm still working on getting Wobble House. It's being overseen by caretakers assigned by the Historical Society, while Mitch's will is still in probate. But I'm going to approach them with the idea that Mitch gave me a verbal contract – in the hearing of the person set to inherit the house, once the legal stuff gets sorted."

"Who exactly is supposed to inherit?" Logan asks.

"Ben Burton." Autumn flips the picnic basket closed. "As in Ben and Pru, who I have breakfast with at least every other week at your shop. There's no way they'll say no to me and Drake using the ballroom."

Autumn seems excited. She's supposed to be a mystery writer, and has always been savvy about picking up clues in the past, but she's so blinded by wedding plans that she doesn't seem to realize that that gives Ben and Pru a mighty powerful motive for murder.

## Chapter Fifteen

"I still don't think Pru killed Mitch," Logan says. We're heading back to the shop to regroup, but we're taking the long way around, as Logan is determined to lose any possible tail. The way Logan's driving, I bet Em's day just got a lot less boring.

I say, "Maybe Ben is the one who actually killed him. They're the only ones who fit all the clues, have no alibi – and now they're inheriting Mitch's estate. Think hard. Is there any reason they might want you dead?"

Logan looks sullen, but he thinks about it. "I never met them before coming to Galveston, and Em said this didn't have anything to do with Minnesota. If the two of them are Em – and I'm not saying I think they are – then maybe I'm another red herring. It would be easy to use my past to make this look like it's about revenge, when it's really a grab for money or control."

"I don't know," I say. "Em sounded sincere about the need for justice. If this killer picked you as a second target, I doubt it's random. Possibly misguided, of course."

"There's no way I can have wronged that sweet old couple," Logan insists.

The car in front of us is still going about five miles an hour, and the road is too narrow, with too much oncoming traffic for us to easily go around. I watch our surroundings as Logan tries to find a gap in the traffic. As we come to an intersection there's a carriage waiting to make the turn. The horse tosses its head, and I recognize the gray and black marking running down the side of its face. It's the horse that was out in front of Mitch's house the morning he was killed. I didn't think much of it at the time, but surely, the carriage driver had to have seen something.

Given the plot of *A Study in Scarlet* – where a major plot point involves a disguised person leaving Sherlock Holmes's home in a cab -- it's possible that Mitch's killer would have gotten a literary thrill out of driving away in a carriage. Could it be possible that the carriage had left carrying the very person that we're looking for? That Mitch's killer had walked across the street behind us, while we'd been flustered by the gong at the door?

"Stop," I tell Logan. "Stop the car."

I have my seatbelt off, and I'm out of the car moments after the tires stop rolling.

I rush over to the carriage, forcing myself to slow down as I get closer, lest I spook the horse. The horse still lets out a nervous snort.

"Don't worry about Asta," the carriage driver says. She's wearing a white dress shirt adorned with lace and a calf-length black skirt, which look rather old-fashioned – likely a part of the carriage ride experience. The driver adds, "She's usually quite curious. Want me to come down so you can pet her?"

"Sure!" I say. There's no better way to get someone talking than to ask about their pet – and this woman sounds genuinely affectionate about the 1,500-pound animal. I also find people like to talk when they're hoping for referrals for their business. "I'm Felicity Koerber, of Greetings and Felicitations." I point in the general direction of my shop. "My friend is planning a wedding."

Logan has parked the car and is catching up to me.

The woman gives him an appraising look. Logan gets that a lot, since he is quite handsome. She asks, "This your friend?"

"No," I say. "I mean, yes, Logan is my friend – but he's not the one getting married next month."

Logan doesn't comment on this, just says, "Nice to meet you."

"I'm Fran." Fran comes around to the horse's head and holds the bridle while I come up and pet Asta. Asta's cheek feels velvety, though she has a distinctly horsey smell. She pushes her head against me, nibbling at my sweater. Startled, I take a step back.

"Asta!" Fran says, pulling on the bridle to dissuade the horse's attention. "I'm sorry about that. She usually only goes for tote bags."

I had left my purse in Logan's car. "It's okay," I say, despite the fact that there is a small hole in my sweater where Asta chewed through a few of the threads. "But can I ask you something?"

Before she can respond, Logan says, "This has to be the same horse we saw out in front of Wobble House yesterday morning. Do you remember seeing us going up to the steps?"

Fran rubs the horse's forehead, calming the mare, who is starting to look like she might want seconds of my sweater. "I remember somebody being there. I was more concerned with my fare. She was crying and trying to shove a wad of cash at me."

"Please," I say. "Can you tell us who she was? It's important."

Fran's thin face takes on a wary expression. "I don't know if that's a good idea. Privacy and all."

Logan says, "A man was murdered in Wobble House that morning. We're investigating the case, on behalf of the bereaved. If you can just tell us what she looked like, it would be a great help."

Fran hesitates, for a moment seems to be looking to the horse for guidance. Then she looks at Logan and says, "Her hair was all wrapped in a silk scarf – like the ones you'd expect a 1940's film actress to wear. She was older, so that made sense. She was black, and everything was well-put together about her clothes, except her shoes, which had a couple of paint splotches."

The carriage driver is describing Pru. I take out my phone and pull up Autumn's Instagram feed, and find the set of photos she posted the day of the tea party. I find one with Pru in it and show it to Fran. "Is this the lady you're describing?"

Fran squints at the image. "Maybe? I more vividly remember the clothes, but it could be her. Though people look a lot different when they're laughing than when they're crying."

I give Logan a significant look, saying, *She was there. It has to be her.*

Logan shakes his head, not convinced.

Fran says, "You know the odd thing? She walked over from the group of cars at the party next door. Who hires a carriage ride if they've already got a car? And who leaves a party in the middle to go to an art gallery?"

"Is that where you dropped her off?" I ask.

Fran says, "Right in the middle of the arts area, between two galleries. But you never know why passengers do the things they do. It's not the oddest thing I've seen, by far."

Before she can launch into a story, Logan asks, "Did she leave anything in the carriage? Even something small?"

"Not in the carriage, no. But I told you Asta has a bad habit of grabbing things out of people's tote bags. The lady had a white, lace-edged piece of cloth sticking up out of hers, and Asta grabbed it. After the horse had chomped on it, she didn't want it back. I can't say that I blamed her. There was a bit of slobber."

"You don't still happen to have it, do you?" Logan asks. "We have access to a scent dog, and it might help eliminate a suspect."

"I stuck it under the seat. It might still be there." Fran turns back to the carriage and rummages around. "Yes. Here we are."

Fran holds out the cloth with two fingers, obviously due to dried horse slobber. Logan takes it just as carefully, trying to preserve the scent.

I take down Fran's phone number, in case we have other questions – and obviously to forward to Arlo. I'm not about to try to impede his investigation. Then we return to the car, where Logan goes to the trunk and takes a gallon-sized zipper topped bag out of his go-bag, which he seems to always have with him. He places the handkerchief inside and puts it in the trunk, then he pulls out a container of hand sanitizer. He offers me some, too, and I take it gratefully, since my hands do now smell of horse.

Back inside the car I say, "You still think that it wasn't Pru, leaving the house at the same time as Mitch's murder?"

Logan shrugs, both hands on the wheel. "Call it a vibe. The same as Arlo has – I follow mine too. Maybe she was there. Maybe she *is* hiding something. But I still don't think Pru is a murderer."

"Okay," I say gently. "There's not enough solid evidence yet to accuse her of anything."

Though the circumstantial evidence is growing to be the size of a large carriage horse. I'm pretty sure that Logan's vibe is wrong. I just need to figure out how to prove it, in a way that Logan won't be able to question. I need to figure out what wrong Ben and Pru hold against Logan, what connection we have yet to see.

Logan says, "What we need to figure out is, why does Ben inherit the estate? Is it possible that he's Mitch's grandfather or something?"

That would make it extra cold if he actually had a hand in orchestrating the murder. "I hope not."

Logan gives me a sharp look. He can pretty much tell what I'm thinking.

I say, "We need to talk to Silas again. Maybe he or somebody at his party saw something and didn't realize the significance of it."

This feels like grasping at straws, but seems to make Logan happy. Logan says, "Ask him to come by the shop. We're already supposed to meet Gently there, and it's cutting the time pretty close."

Autumn is the one who took Silas's card, so I text her to get the information. She sends me the number almost immediately. Then I call Silas, telling him we have a gift for him, to celebrate him becoming a grandfather. This isn't entirely a lie – I have a gift basket in stock that will be perfect for the occasion. He seems pleased, and agrees to meet us. I hang up with him and text Autumn a thank-you.

My phone rings in my hands, but it's not Em wanting to gloat about incorporating the horse. Maybe Logan's efforts to lose any possible tail had worked, and Em doesn't even know we've discovered this new evidence.

Instead, it is Enrique calling back. When I answer, he says, "You're not going to believe this. I called all of Iris's references, and there's no way she is who she says she is. So I checked her out with the CIA, and they've never heard of her."

Logan asks, "What did he say?"

I explain, then put Enrique on speaker phone, so I won't have to double the conversation. Logan looks super intrigued at the thought of another suspect that isn't Pru.

Enrique says, "That makes her suspicious, right? Since she showed up here so suddenly?"

"It does," I say. "Though we just found some evidence that suggests she probably isn't responsible for Mitch's death."

"We don't really know that," Logan says. "I wish I had a fingerprint for comparison."

Enrique says, "You could swing by the ghost kitchen. I'm there now. They clean the equipment frequently, and we're expected to clean up after ourselves too, but there must be a fingerprint of Iris's on something somewhere."

I say, "It would be easier to look at the messy truffles back at Greetings and Felicitations. Since Miles didn't make it in this morning to tidy everything up, and Carmen looked like she was going to be slammed, there's probably still a whole tray of chocolate with mine and Iris's fingerprints on them."

"You're right," Logan says. "That will be easier."

After I manage to get Enrique off the phone – he's convinced that he's hired a murderer and is now freaked out about it – I check my text messages.

Autumn has sent me several. She says, *Having lunch with Bea. Did you know she knew who Logan was before we got on the cruise ship?*

I did know that.

But Autumn has also texted, *I think you need to hear this. You were still planning to take Bea dress shopping, right? Can you meet us there in an hour?*

And after that, *Seriously. Bea knew one of the guys who died in the failed operation Logan was a part of in Minnesota. I am freaking out right now. What if she's planning to kill Logan? I can't have that bad of taste in bridesmaids, can I?*

And then, *I need to wait she's coming back from the bathroom have to go now.*

That's the last text. What if I am wrong about Pru? Pru still has to have been at the house – but what if she wasn't the only one?

What if Bea and Pru were working together? One of them with a grudge against Mitch – and the other against Logan. It would make sense of some of the things Em had said, and also cover any gaps in the alibis. It seems elaborate, and I can't prove a connection between the two of them. And I really hate the idea of Bea as a bad guy. But why is she just now revealing this connection to Logan's past – unless she is one half of Em, taunting me for not figuring all of this out?

I call Autumn, who, thank goodness, answers. From the discombobulated wording of that last text, I was worried that she had been in the middle of being abducted.

She says that they are at the dog park, with Satchmo, and I get her to convince Bea to bring the dog by the shop, before we go dress shopping. That way, I can see if Silas recognizes her, and Logan can ask about borrowing Satchmo for a scent test.

I need to tell him my theory, and he's not going to like it. Bea and Pru are two of his favorite people. The idea of those two plotting against him has to be a serious blow to his self-esteem.

## Chapter Sixteen

Gently is waiting for us by the time we get back to Greetings and Felicitations. So is Silas. Neither of them seem to see me peeking through the doorway from the kitchen.

Tracie has showed up for her shift, so I tell her to help Gently get set up for the sketches.

Tracie says, “I’m still jazzed to have a job with this much flexibility. Who knows what I’ll get to do here tomorrow.”

I say, “Probably it will be your turn to mop and sanitize everything in the back.”

“I’m okay with that,” Tracie says.

“But not today,” Logan says quickly. He still wants to get a fingerprint off those ruined truffles. I follow him into the kitchen, to make sure they’re still there. Sure enough, the mess is still there, on the bottom shelf. Logan bends down to it and takes out his phone. He uses an app that allows him to scan the visible print directly into the phone. The first print that comes up is mine.

Logan gives me an apologetic look and tries again.

Carmen walks up behind me and asks, “What’s going on?”

I ask, “What’s going on with the line out front?”

We’re still pretty slammed. Carmen says, “We’re out of conchas out there, so I’m grabbing some to restock. I could use some help on the coffee station.”

“I can’t.” I gesture towards the front. “In fact, it would be great if you could help me out for a minute.”

Carmen gives me a look that clearly says, *you have got to be kidding me.*

"I'm sorry," I say. "See the old guy looking lost, over by the book nook? I need to get a gift basket for him without him noticing that we just grabbed it off the shelf. And I need a card."

Carmen half-laughs. "I'll go get it for you, in the name of good customer relations. But then somebody has got to help me out front."

"I will," Logan says.

I start to say absolutely not. If Logan is supposed to be staying away from potential attackers, then customer service is the last thing he should be doing. But one look at his face tells me he's not going to back down here.

He picks up a tray of chocolate conchas and marches through the doorway to restock the case.

Meanwhile, Carmen grabs me the gift basket, and I quickly fill out the card.

Carmen says, "Don't worry. I'll put Logan as barista, so he won't be touching any money or anything directly."

A chill goes through me at the thought of Logan suffering from a contact poison – like the disease in the short story.

"Thanks," I say weakly.

Carmen goes out to work on whittling down the line.

I force a smile and go to talk to Silas. Gesturing him to sit at one of the tables, I say, "I'm glad you had time to come in today."

Silas snorts out a laugh. "My house is overrun with family. I love them, but at some point, any excuse to get a few minutes of alone time in the car is a precious relief. Plus, you offered chocolate."

I hold out the gift basket. "Congratulations, Grandpa."

Silas grins, which completely transforms his face. "You have no idea how excited we all are." He looks down at the shrink-wrapped basket. "Do you care if I open this here? Whatever I take home, I have to share."

"Sure." I make a sweeping *go ahead* gesture with my hand.

Silas pops the shrink wrap. He gives me a conspiratorial look. "What's the best thing in here?"

I say, "My favorite in this collection is the Madagascar bar. Cacao beans from that area are known for fruity notes, so this bar tastes like there's cherries in it – even though it's nothing but cacao and sugar."

"Really?" Silas opens the bar and breaks off a piece. He pops it into his mouth. "I taste cherries, like you're talking about it. And also walnuts, and orange. Maybe something woody, too."

"That's all what I taste, too." I give him a genuine smile. "I didn't realize you were a craft chocolate connoisseur."

Silas breaks another piece off of the bar. "I'm a wine guy. I've never had chocolate like this before. I always though dark chocolate was bitter and bland."

"I'm glad you were willing to try something new. Craft chocolate is a lot like wine. You're going to taste the differences in the soil, and the growing conditions, and the variety of the beans." I take a deep breath, getting ready to switch from one of my favorite topics to a most uncomfortable one. "Look, the basket isn't the only reason I asked you to come in."

"Yeah, I got that. You know you aren't very subtle." He taps his hand on the table. "Come on, out with it."

I ask, "Did anyone unexpected showed up at your party? I talked to a carriage driver who said someone came from your driveway and hired a carriage ride."

Silas says, "That's weird." He pops the square of chocolate into his mouth, which gives him time to think. "I don't know about the number of people actually invited to the party, and I didn't know half of the people who showed up personally. Some were family friends, some are people my wife invited, some my daughter and her husband invited."

"Basically, you're saying that nobody in your house knew everybody who showed up." I sigh heavily. "I guess that would be too easy."

"One thing, though." Silas breaks off another piece of chocolate and points with it. "Chelsea didn't open her gifts during the party. She didn't want to make it feel like a competition. So we had the family party at the restaurant, and she opened gifts with us after. And there was a gift with no card, that no one has been willing to admit to, even though we've asked around. It had to be a gag gift. Because no one would show up at a baby shower with an expensive reproduction of Munch's *The Scream*. Can you think of a better way to emotionally scar a baby?"

I can't help but picture that creepy image hanging over a crib and feel creepy-empathy for the hypothetical child having to deal with that. I ask, "Are your daughter or son-in-law fans of Munch? Maybe it was meant for them."

"Doubtful," Silas says. "Any other questions?"

I ask almost playfully, "I don't guess you're into fiber arts?"

Silas says, "Do I look like the kind of guy who does macrame?"

The very fact that he specifically said macrame instead of knitting or crochet makes me think that he actually might be. Of course, I'd never get him to admit to that.

I say, "Why don't I get you a latte, and you can relax for a few minutes before heading home into the fray?"

"I'd be much obliged," he says.

I go around the counter and join Logan at the coffee bar. It's a tight squeeze – and I'm very aware of how close to him I am – but I manage to pull a shot of espresso while Logan finishes a couple of hot drinks with swirls of whipped cream.

Logan tells me, "I got a hit on the fingerprints off the truffles that aren't yours. I think you'll find it interesting who Iris really is."

"Let me get Silas his coffee." I steam milk and pour it into the drink, finishing the top with a simple flower in latte art. I take the coffee over to Silas, then rejoin Logan, who shows me his phone.

It's an image of a somewhat younger Iris, wearing a leotard and holding her hands over her head, showing off a gold medal on her chest. Logan says, "Meet Lisa Banks, a diplomat's daughter, who was raised in Austria, and educated via an American homeschooling service. Articles paint a picture of a shy girl, who spent a lot of time lost in books, who learned to cook from a series of servants and refused to become the public figure her father wanted her to be. She was a gifted gymnast – who wasn't shy about competing. She could have gone to the Olympics, except she broke her toe a few days before the qualifiers. There's not much about her after her father retired."

"So then there's no obvious connections to Mitch."

"Absolutely none," Logan says. He sounds disappointed. "She doesn't sound like an attention seeker, does she?"

"Not really," I admit. "But I didn't really think she was Em anyway."

"Why do you think she lied about her identity?" Logan asks, as he starts prepping the next espresso order.

I think about this shy girl, who didn't seem to fit in her life – but has a nosy need to know what is going on in the lives of others. "Maybe it's like Gently. Maybe she wanted to distance herself from being the girl who almost made it to the Olympics, and who disappointed her father. Maybe she really did take that last gig as a personal chef, and follow some guy to Galveston."

Logan says, "I used to think I was the only one who felt alone like that. I never had an urge to change my name, or hide my past – except when I had to, since I had bad guys looking for me."

I say, "We haven't even considered that. None of those guys are suspects here?"

"Uh, no. They weren't exactly the literary type. More the shoot now, bury you later, never ask questions type." His expression says he finds this amusing.

I don't. I shudder. "Don't talk like that."

"Don't worry. They're in jail now."

Somehow, that's not exactly comforting.

Logan says, "I also checked. Ben and Mitch aren't related, and they aren't business partners. There's no obvious reason why Ben would inherit anything."

Tracie comes back and says, "Gently says everything is set up. I can do coffee if y'all are ready to pose?"

I ask Logan, "Are you sure we have time for this?"

Logan says, "I think I'd like to talk to Gently again."

I tell Tracie, "Let us know if Bea shows up."

Tracie says, "I have no ideas who that is."

I say, "She should be coming in with Autumn. And with a beagle."

"Oh-kay," Tracie says. "That shouldn't be hard to spot."

We go into the annex. I have to put on my filter mask – which I don't think anybody really thought about when we set up for me to pose in a construction site. The dust has settled, though, and Gently has blocked off the space near the windows with tarps.

Gently is standing in the middle of the annex space, peering up at the odd rusty-mattress-springs light fixture. He says, "You really need to do something about this. All the exposed wiring in here is garbage. All you'd have to do is plug a microwave and a coffee pot into the same outlet, and you're bound to blow the whole circuit."

Logan says, "These quote-unquote improvements are the main reason the previous tenant got kicked out of this space. I had to sign that it would all be removed or upgraded before we can open to the public."

"You didn't tell me that," I say. There are a number of homemade fixtures in the space. Some of that work is bound to be expensive.

Logan shrugs. He doesn't offer an explanation.

Gently has left a bunch of chocolate-finishing supplies on the table near the doorway, and there's some chocolate shavings on the table's surface, which must be left over from leveling the chocolate slab Traci had given him to work with. He completely ignores the mess. "Come on through into the studio. I've had an air filter going in here, to keep dust off the chocolate. No guarantees, but you can probably take off the filter mask."

Even Gently knows about my former troubles with asthma. I say, "In theory, the experimental treatments have completely cured my symptoms. I'm actually able to exercise like an almost normal person."

Still, it's hard to trust my cured state as I make myself take off my mask and sit in the chair that Gently has set up in the window. It's flattering light, but I can't help thinking about being watched from outside. We may have lost Em, when that person had been tailing us earlier. But it wouldn't be exactly hard to figure out that we would eventually come back here.

Ruffles is sitting on the table where Gently has set up the slab of chocolate, plus several shades of milk and white chocolate to sketch with.

"Careful," I tell Gently. "Cats can't eat chocolate."

"I'll make sure he leaves it alone," Gently says. "But I need him there. Unless you want to hold him?"

"Sure," I say, holding my arms out for the cat. Gently brings Ruffles over to me, and the big tuxedo cat settles in my lap. But after a few minutes, Ruffles changes his mind and jumps to the floor. He at least seems content to sit by the chair, grooming himself with one back leg in the air. That doesn't make me feel particularly elegant, especially considering the horse-nibbled sweater. But Gently said I didn't need to be wearing the final outfit that would be detailed in the painting. And I'm sure the details of my expression will come later, too.

How must all the people who had sat for the famous portraits I had so admired felt about someone studying them enough to paint them? I try to think serene thoughts about the ocean as Gently stares at me for a very long time, then dips his brush in the chocolate.

He's using one of my silicone molds as a paint tray. The cups are shaped like cats, so it's not a surprise why he chose that one. Silicone molds are cheaper, and for a lot of uses they're harder to work with. Polycarbonate molds are stable, so you can just flip the whole thing over hard on the counter to crack the chocolates out all at once. But silicone molds are great for making delicate pieces, like isomalt lace for decorating chocolate cakes and sculptures, or thin, filled chocolate cats.

This whole serene-model mode becomes immensely more difficult when Logan asks Gently, "Do you have any problem with me? If you have any reason to want to see me dead, I'd like to hear it now."

Gently makes a splatter across the chocolate's surface with his brush. "Logan, what are you talking about?"

Logan says, "I heard a rumor that you might think I had something to do with your parent's case, in Minnesota or in Canada. I don't like dealing in rumors."

"Neither do I," Gently says. He takes a paper towel and wipes the stray chocolate off the slab. I guess that's one advantage over working with paint. "Look, I've made my peace with the past as best I can. I don't have a grudge against anybody. And I'd never threaten anybody." Gently points with the paper towel. "And I don't believe my parents wound up kidnapped into Canada."

Logan says, "Good enough." He claps Gently on the shoulder. "You should go deep sea fishing some time with me and Arlo. Get a little sun on your face."

I think Logan is trying to make a connection, with someone who's been just as lost as he has been. He seems really awkward about it, but there's something vulnerable there.

Gently picks up his brush again, looking a little intimidated. He says, "Ruffles isn't really a boat kind of cat."

I say, "Gently, you know the local art scene. An artist's work usually goes up in value after his death, right? Is it possible someone was collecting Mitch's paintings, and then killed him to cash in?"

Gently considers this. "I don't know of anybody local. But people collect art from around the world these days."

I ask, "Do you remember Pru Burton? She was at my table at the tea party. She was dropped off at a local gallery yesterday, and since she was at a party for a famous art collector, I thought you might have some insight."

"Are you saying you think Pru might have killed Mitch, and then headed to one of the local galleries to buy up his work before the news of his death hit?" Gently reaches out towards Ruffles, who accepts Gently's hand across his shoulders. "I seriously doubt it. I love Ben and Pru. They've been at a lot of gala openings since moving to Galveston, and they're good at approaching people and getting them to talk. They're always more interested in the people they're with than in their own opinions. Which is sweet, since they know a ton about art. Pru once told me she majored in art history, at the Sorbonne in Paris."

Pru and Ben are certainly adaptable, and well-rounded. I had assumed Pru was being greedy or cheap when she'd asked for the banana bread that Mitch had turned down. I hadn't minded – who can fault a retired couple on a budget? But I realize now that it was her way of showing enthusiasm for me and what I do.

They've been trying so hard to carve out a space for themselves in the community. It's incredibly sweet.

Or – maybe incredibly fake. If they came here to take advantage of Mitch – somehow talk him into handing over his estate to Ben – they could be master manipulators, manipulating the rest of us almost out of habit.

## Chapter Seventeen

Once Gently has finished his sketches, we head back into the shop.

Gently nods over to the line trailing towards the front door and says, "Look. Ben and Pru are here."

Of course they are. I'd forgotten that I'd promised them truffles today.

The line of customers is finally starting to dwindle, and they're at the very back of it, so likely they haven't been here long.

I catch a weird glance between Pru and Silas, of all people. They both look a little flustered. Silas's ears go crimson, and he fumbles his coffee cup. What's up with that? It isn't a romantic look, and Pru hasn't let go of Ben's hand. So no worries there. It's the look of two people who wish they didn't know each other. Then they break eye contact and each pretend that they don't know each other.

I have no idea what to do with this information. I doubt either one is going to want to explain it.

Pru lets go of Ben's hand and moves out of the line of customers to come over to us. She reaches into her purse and offers Logan a puffy peppermint.

Logan takes it, saying, "Thanks," calmly, like he doesn't suspect she might have designs on killing him. Maybe he still doesn't suspect her, and the confidence isn't an act.

She says, "Now, promise me you'll save that for your next flight."

"Of course I will, Ms. Pru," Logan says. "I'll be out to help with the community garden next week, like I promised." This is a somewhat different side of him than I've seen.

The peppermint is wrapped, but I still can't help but suspect it might be tampered with. Logan had a flight scheduled for tomorrow – when the deadline Em had given him is up. He's canceled that flight, but if Pru really is secretly a master thief, she might have waltzed into the airplane hangar and only seen the sticky note – and not realize he's grounded himself.

I take the peppermint and tell Logan, "I'll hold that for you."

No way am I taking a chance that he might naively eat it, when it could well be poisoned. I mean, I don't *think* he would take that kind of chance – but just in case.

"Oh, dear," Pru says. "You can have one too. I never thought someone who makes candy would want something you can buy at the corner shops."

She reaches into her purse again and produces another puffy peppermint.

I take it from her and put both of them in my pocket, telling her, "Actually, I love these. They remind me of being at my grandmother's house, before she moved into the assisted living condos. She always had them in a covered candy dish on the table. I have no idea what happened to that dish when she moved. I think I owe you something in return." I go into the chocolate finishing room and get the box of tea-infused truffles out of the cabinet, where I had tucked it so it wouldn't accidentally get sold.

When she sees the box, Pru claps her hands with delight. She says, "I have learned so much about chocolate since we've been coming here. If you had asked me before if white chocolate could be made into something special, I would have said no. But I've seen you work miracles."

I can't help but smile at the flattery – even while I'm questioning whether or not it is sincere. I ask, "Would you like a cup of coffee while you're here?"

"Ordinarily I'd love one. But we just popped in for a minute, since you promised us truffles. Ben has a doctor's appointment, and I'm off to do some shopping."

I convince them each to take a complementary cup of plain coffee to go. I watch through the window as the couple step outside and embrace, before each walking different directions.

Pru really is our most viable suspect, and I still know nothing substantial about her. Impulsively, I tell Gently and Logan, "I'm going to follow her."

Tracie overhears this and says, "But what about Bea?"

I say, "Stall." I turn to Gently and say, "Offer to paint Satchmo, or whatever, but don't let her leave."

I grab my purse from the back and sling it over my shoulder. Logan starts to follow me out the front door, but I shake my head. "I should be relatively safe, but you are staying put. Em needs me alive to solve the mystery, remember?"

"Fee," he says, "I really don't think this is a good idea."

"I know." I kiss him on the cheek, then while he is standing there startled, I slip out the door and onto the street. Pru is already a good way down the Strand, turning the corner onto one of the less busy streets. I follow, having to move quickly to keep up as she goes a couple of blocks, then turns again, then goes into a building. It's an entryway between two shops, leading to loft apartments on the second floor.

I just wait for her to go up the stairs and turn at the landing, then I follow. I plan to peek and figure out what door is hers, then take a look inside when she leaves again. I'm not sure what I'm going to do if she just goes into her apartment and waits.

I tiptoe up the stairs, and my plan actually works – the apartment is three doors down on the right. I return downstairs, and move to a shielded spot around a corner, congratulating myself for how much better I've gotten at following people. I never intended to become a detective, and the time I had followed Enrique had ended in disaster. This had felt like a triumph. Then it occurs to me that I shouldn't be happy about that – not if I'm still hoping my life is going to go back to normal as soon as I figure out who killed Mitch. Surveillance isn't a skill any chocolate maker should actually need.

Pru comes back down the stairs, without the chocolates, but carrying several reusable canvas grocery bags. I guess she wasn't kidding about going shopping.

I wait for her to turn a corner, then I head upstairs to check out her apartment. If need be, I can catch up with her at the grocery store. I move over to Pru's door and look down at the knob. I've never done this without Logan before. He's the one who can open locks like they were made of cream cheese. He actually carries lockpicks.

But everything feels flipped this time around. I'm going to have to try and make do with a credit card from my purse and what I've seen on TV. Thank goodness I'd taken the time to grab said purse. I take out the store card I almost never use – just in case I damage it, I don't want to risk my debit card. I shift the knob, trying to gauge how the lock works – only, the knob turns easily under my hand, and the door opens.

I can't believe it. No one leaves their door unlocked anymore. But that sense of disbelief is overshadowed by the shock that comes once I actually look inside the apartment. The walls of the living room are studded with paintings, in various sizes. More paintings are stacked against the walls. There's a sofa on one side of the room, which has several cross-stitched pillows on it, but on the side nearer the windows, there are two easels, set back-to-back, and each have a half-finished canvas on them. The canvases are dry – probably haven't been touched today. But I am pretty sure that one canvas is in the process of being turned into a reproduction of Vermeer's *The Girl with the Pearl Earring.*

I'm having a hard time processing this. But the fact eventually penetrates my brain. Ben and Pru are part of Mitch's ring of art forgers. Or were – presumably they stopped painting after Mitch was dead. Maybe out of respect. Or maybe because they murdered him and are now free. It's hard to tell.

There are footsteps outside in the hallway, that stop right outside the room I'm in.

I can hear Pru talking to herself as she comes in the door. "Forgot to lock the door, forgot my shopping list, I'll forget my head next."

There's no place to hide, so I try to take positive ground. I say loudly, "Just what has you so distracted today?"

But the way she's dabbing at her eyes tells me why she's distracted – raw grief, in an unguarded moment when she'd assumed she was alone.

She freezes, a tattered Kleenex up against one cheek. Slowly, she drops her arm to her side, then raises her hands in surrender. She says, "Oh, love, I never thought it was you."

I tilt my head, trying to get a better angle on what she's saying. But it doesn't become any clearer. "Thought it was me what?"

Now she looks confused. "Aren't you here to kill me? First Mitch, then dismantling the rest of his operation."

"What?" I make a sound that is close to a hysterical laugh. "I though you killed Mitch. I came here looking for proof."

Pru slowly lowers her hands. She sees me glancing back at the canvas with the almost Vermeer. She says, "You know I could never sell that one, with or without Mitch's connections. The original is too well known. But sometimes the paintings call out to be remade. For me to understand each brushstroke, each angle of light. I had to paint her, for me."

I say, "Mitch asked me if I had a favorite painter. Since his death, I've been trying to figure it out, but I have no idea how to choose."

Pru says, "You have to wait until you find a painting that fills you with a sense of longing, or a sense of joy. I've had a number of favorites over the years. Right now, I'm in love with Vermeer. I think it is because I've gotten old, and he captured youth so well. Look at the clothes she has on. You can tell from the way she stands that they're not what she's used to wearing. So maybe she's traveled, for the first time. I can remember being this girl's age, thinking that life would be a beautiful adventure, just as she does here. And it has been, in a way. The painting is a tronie, not a portrait, which means it was painted from the artist's imagination. So she can have whatever adventures I can imagine."

"I've never felt anything like that deep of a connection to a painting," I say. "I guess I've always been too busy trying to think what paintings match the room where they will hang to pay that kind of attention."

"I find that hard to believe," Pru says. "If you weren't paying attention, you wouldn't have wound up here."

"But I misread the situation," I point out. "I took your reactions for suspicious behavior – not as they were, a mix of fear and grief." Because if Pru had had anything to do with Mitch's death, she wouldn't have been so genuinely terrified to see me. "You really miss Mitch, don't you?"

Pru brings the tissue back to her eye, dabbing away a stray tear. "He was very dear to both me and Ben. We were probably closer to him than to either of our own sons."

I ask, "Is that why Ben inherits Mitch's estate?"

Pru bows her head. "We didn't know that was Mitch's plan. Not until after he was gone, and a lawyer called. Mitch didn't have family. He grew up learning to be charming in order to survive. Ben and I saw beneath that veneer, took the time to make a connection with him."

"That's how you wound up working with him?" I ask. "He talked you into turning into forgers?"

"Oh, goodness no. We were the ones who helped him get his start. Though he far outpaced us both in both scope and ability." Pru gestures around at the paintings stacked against the walls. "We were the main reason Mitch was able to continue his philanthropic activities from behind bars. Now, we're semi-retired."

I try to take that in. It flips everything I had thought about what might have happened to Mitch. "But you were there," I insist. “I talked to the carriage driver who was outside Wobble House when we discovered Mitch’s body. She described you, said she saw you coming away from the cars near Silas’s party.”

Pru nods miserably. She goes and sits on the sofa, gesturing for me to take a seat on the other side. She suddenly looks likely to collapse. She makes several noises, like she’s trying to speak, but the emotion is too thick in her throat. When she finally can, she says, “I came by the house early that morning, through a hidden side door. I had two very small paintings to deliver, which I had in a big tote bag. Right away, I could tell the house felt too quiet. Then I found Mitch’s body, in the study. I was so discombobulated, I broke a vase, and wound up Hoovering up the bits.”

That tracks with what Silas had said he had heard.

I ask, “What about the scraping sound? Silas was snooping around outside, and he said he heard a scraping sound.”

“Of course he was,” Pru says. “I caught him snooping around inside the house once, though who knows what he was looking for. No one is supposed to know I’m connected to this place, so I couldn’t exactly report him for trespassing. And he wasn’t supposed to be here, so he couldn’t say anything about me. But I doubt he’s the one after Mitch’s organization.”

I shake my head. “It’s not about that. The police are keeping the details quiet but-” I think how I can say this without giving details away to someone who is still Arlo’s favorite suspect. “There is evidence of a different motive.”

“Oh,” Pru says softly. Then as the implications hit home, she manages a wan smile and adds, “That’s a relief.”

But if Silas had been snooping in the house – maybe I should re-evaluate his alibi, and seriously check if he might have a grudge against Logan.

But first I need to understand Pru’s version of what happened. “So, the scraping noise?”

Pru says, “I heard it too. I have no idea what it was, but it startled me into hiding, in case the murderer was still in the house.

But when that gong sounded at the front door, I knew I had to get out, before anyone else discovered Mitch's body, leaving me trapped inside for the authorities to find and get the wrong impression, so I made a break for it through a side entrance. I was so upset, and a bit of a mess, and when I got to my car, it was completely blocked in. I panicked. I was spotted by a woman taking a gift out of the back of a car – obviously headed towards Silas's party. She saw me crying into my sleeve and handed me a handkerchief. It was embroidered with flowers and edged all in white lace. I'd never seen anything so elaborate. I told her, 'That's so lovely.' But by then I'd gotten snot on it, so she said, 'You know what? Keep it.' So I put it in my tote bag. But then it got eaten by a horse, and I completely fell apart."

I put this together with what Silas said about having a painting unexpectedly show up as a baby shower gift. It could have seemed like the killer was headed to Silas's party, especially if she was carrying a wrapped item. And to complete the illusion, she might have gone into the house and joined the party, letting Pru live rather than eliminating a potential witness.

I ask, "Can you describe what that woman looked like?"

Pru says miserably, "I never actually looked at her. I was crying so hard, and trying to make sure she didn't get a good look at my face. I think her hair was brown."

Which describes both Bea and Iris. "Try to remember anything."

The penny drops and Pru realizes I think she had crossed paths with the killer without realizing it. Her mouth widens into a surprised o. She says, "I'm lucky to be alive, aren't I?"

I say, "Only because this killer is big on not having collateral damage."

Which, unfortunately, sounds like something Bea would do. And Autumn is still with Bea.

Maybe coming here was a mistake, because it means I left Logan alone, and increased the time for Bea – if she is Em – to uncover that Autumn has started to suspect her. I begin second-guessing every decision I've made since that phone message from

Em. So much of this is out of my control. I want to figure out a way to be with everyone at once, though that's impossible.

Would the killer who spared Pru also spare Autumn? Especially if they happen to be friends? Even if it means her identity has been compromised? I hope I don't have to find out.

"I have to go," I say, racing for the door, taking the stairs down two at a time. I feel a little tickle in my lungs as I power-walk back to the shop. I refuse to have an asthma attack right here in the streets, after so long feeling cured.

## Chapter Eighteen

When I get back to the shop, everything seems fine. Logan is still pulling lattes, and Bea and Autumn are playing Scrabble, from the pile of board games we keep in the cubbies near the coffee station.

True to my instructions, Gently is in the expansion, painting Satchmo on another chocolate canvas.

I ask Logan to come with me to check on the progress. I put on my filter mask to go back into the space, but I still feel that tickle in my lungs, not a real attack yet, just a little warning. And after a bit, it goes away.

Satchmo and Gently both look up as we come into the tarped-off space. Ruffles is draped around Gently's shoulders, asleep, his leash trailing down Gently's chest. He doesn't even bother waking up.

As we've eliminated Gently as a suspect, I decide to tell Logan what had happened at Pru's place in front of him. It's the most privacy we're likely to have without leaving the shop and arousing suspicion.

Logan says, "We should visit the galleries Pru went to. Try to figure out of someone there knows if she bought any of Mitch's original art. Or if there's anyone else who has a large collection. We're running out of suspects. Maybe we're missing someone."

I say, "I already promised Bea I'd take her dress shopping. And I really need to try and find out what *she* knows." I show Logan Autumn's texts.

He winces. "I wonder what she means by 'knew one of the cops.' If Bea was in love with one of the people I got killed because of my mistake – I deserve for her to hate me." He brings both hands to his temples. "Murdering me is a bit extreme, though."

Gently says, "Then you and Autumn should do the dress thing. Ruffles and I can go with Logan to the art galleries. I know people who will likely talk to me."

"No," I say. "We are not splitting up."

"Then what do you suggest?" Logan says.

"We are all five going both places, together. That way I can keep an eye on everyone, which is safer anyway." I point at Gently and Logan. "You two will wait patiently inside the dress shop, then we can go to the galleries."

Logan lets out a loud laugh.

"What?" I ask.

He says, "Now you know how hard it is, trying to keep assets safe. You have to second-guess every decision, and then deal with the fact that people have free will, and are going to want to do things that jeopardize their safety at every turn. And that it is impossible to be with everyone, all at the same time. With more than one asset, it's like herding cats." He nods at Ruffles. "No offense."

"None taken," Gently says.

Autumn is obviously on board with the idea of taking the guys with us. She's been freaking out about being alone with Bea, who she doesn't know whether to treat like a friend or a potential killer.

Bea seems to like the idea too.

Logan goes up to her and looks her in the eye and asks, "Are you sure? You don't mind spending time with me?"

"Why should I?" Bea says. But she looks a little nervous. Of course, that could be the fact that Logan, who is physically imposing, is staring at her.

We all pile into Bea's van – the only vehicle with enough seating to accommodate the five of us, plus Satchmo and Ruffles. I wind up in the mid-row seat, between Autumn and Logan, two of the people I am usually the most comfortable around. Nobody talks. It gets awkward.

We all practically jump out of the van as soon as Bea parks. The dress shop owner arches her eyebrows as we make our way inside, with a leashed Ruffles in Gently's arms and Satchmo trotting happily beside me, his vest showing his status as a therapy dog. I guess we're not the most unusual group ever to visit her shop, because she recovers quickly. Logan asks if there is a bench for waiting.

She says, "Unfortunately, no."

So he and Gently stand against one wall while I show Bea pics of the dresses the others have picked out, and show her how the brightest dress has all the colors in Autumn's wedding color pallet.

Bea grabs a couple of possible dresses and ducks into one of the changing cubicles. Autumn and I gather up some other options in Bea's size.

As I am handing the dresses over the cubicle door, Bea asks, "Do you mind telling me what Logan's problem is today?"

What should I tell her? Logan isn't being exactly subtle that something's wrong. But – assuming she's not the killer – she has no way of knowing that Logan was the one who was threatened at the restaurant, rather than me.

I admit, "Autumn and I told him you had a relationship with one of the cops who died on the botched mission. He assumes you hate him."

"What?" Bea bursts out of the cubicle wearing a dramatically tiered teal dress that looks designed for a Flamenco dancer. She marches out of the changing rooms and over to Logan. "You assume that I secretly hate you over something that happened in the line of duty, a lot of years ago? After I have been nothing but kind to you. Actually moved here because you were one of the friends I was looking forward to seeing again." She steps close into his personal space, looking up at him. "Well?"

Okay. So I guess Bea is just as blunt as Logan is. Maybe it's good that they're getting this out in the open. Though it is seeming a lot less likely that Bea is Em.

Logan says, "I lost somebody I cared about, too. And I hated the guy who took her life for a long time. I wouldn't blame you-"

Bea interrupts him, saying, "There's a big difference between taking a life and making a mistake. Yes, I went on a couple of dates with a guy who died on an operation you survived. Yes, it was an unmitigated disaster. But you know what? I broke it off with Christoph because he was stubborn and impulsive. And your dad read the reports afterwards – before it was all sealed. He believes that Christoph's actions may have been a contributing factor to the failure that day. And honestly, that sounds like him. No one person on a team can take responsibility for the whole, and the sooner you realize that, you can find forgiveness for yourself, instead of looking for it from people like me."

Logan looks like he's been slapped. He even rubs at his cheek, though Bea's arms haven't moved from her sides. "You – You're right," he stammers.

"And speaking of your dad," Bea says. "It wouldn't hurt for you to go visit him once in a while."

"You keep in touch with my dad?" Logan asks.

"Occasionally," Bea says in a calmer tone of voice, all the righteous indignation going out of her, and sudden sympathy shining in her eyes. "When we met, he asked me about stress management techniques, and whether a therapy dog might help, and we got to talking about his illness. You know he may have to retire soon. He could use some encouragement from you."

"I always thought that was the last thing he wanted," Logan says. "What kind of encouragement is he going to get from his screw-up son?"

"He doesn't think of you that way," Bea says. "He's just hoping you find your peace. Then you'll be able to live up to your full potential."

"If I live through tomorrow," Logan mutters.

"What was that?" Bea asks.

"I'll explain somewhere a little more private," I say. I'm convinced – there's no way that Bea is Em. If she's concerned about Logan's welfare, it's better to trust her to help.

The dress shop door opens, and Iris walks in. She's so focused on waving at the shop owner that at first she doesn't even notice us. She says, "I'm looking for a black dress. Something appropriate for a funeral."

As the dress lady starts to show her the section, Iris turns and spots me.

"Felicity!" Iris says. "Are you attending Mitch's funeral too? Enrique said it would be nice for all of us to go." Then she seems to notice that I'm not alone. "Oh, hello everyone." She doesn't seem to recognize anyone in particular. If she was Em, you would think she would at least blink at seeing Logan. Unless, of course, she was following us again and expected to see him here. It's possible – we've already figured out that with an extra day, Em is likely bored. Maybe she is also daring enough to flaunt her presence.

But Iris doesn't seem capable of the intricate planning involved in everything that has happened so far. She's just too flaky and easily bored to put together a revenge plot that spans years. I introduce her to everyone, and Logan moves over to shake her hand. He says, "You look familiar. Weren't you in the Olympics or something? Lisa, right?"

There he goes, being blunt again.

Iris's face goes crimson, and she looks at me and says, "Okay, so my name's not really Iris." Then she tells Logan, "I was almost in the Olympics. Only, a few days before the tryouts, I injured myself. I was trying to sneak out of a window, and I fell and broke my big toe. You'd think that's lucky, that kind of fall and only the smallest injury. But you can't really balance with a broken toe, and landing on it hurts like the dickens. I had to drop out."

"That's horrible," Bea says. "So you're here on the Island trying to re-invent yourself?"

"Something like that. I've tried a couple of different jobs, trying to find what fits – without my father's influence to open doors and make people be nice to me. So far, I'm happiest in the kitchen."

"That sounds a lot like me," I tell her. "I had a completely different career before I became a chocolate maker."

"And let's not forget a detective," Iris says. "Maybe the best thing of all is being able to find justice for people who no longer have the power to help themselves."

"I guess," I say. "I'm not officially a detective. Things just sort of happen around me, and I have to deal with them."

Gently says, "We all have to deal with the unexpected." He looks down at his emotional support cat – only Ruffles has edged around behind Gently, and is basically glued to the back of the guy's leg. This time, the cat seems to be looking to his owner for emotional support.

"Oh, what a sweet kitty," Iris says, scooping Ruffles up unceremoniously from the floor.

"Careful," Gently says. "He might scratch you trying to get down."

Instead, Ruffles hisses and bites down on the edge of Iris's hand, hard. When she drops him, the cat races across the dress shop.

"Or if you really upset him, that happens," Gently says. "I better find him, before I wind up having to pay for scratched up dresses."

Iris says, "He's had his shots, right?"

"Of course," Gently calls back.

The dress lady produces a first aid kit and disinfects Iris's hand. She's giving us all a look like one more thing, and she's going to kick every one of us out of the shop.

We quickly find Bea a dress that suits both her and the rest of the bridesmaid's dresses – with a much smaller tiered skirt. Iris says she'll come back to try on a dress when she's sure she's not going to bleed on it. It looks like she's planning on walking with us to wherever we go next. Which is alarming.

But I don't know what to do without being rude to her. She walks with us over to the galleries, which are about ten blocks down from the dress shop. She and Autumn start talking about jewelry – because Autumn is wearing a stunning necklace, with small emeralds set in pink gold, which leads to discussion about Autumn's shop on Etsy, where she curates a selection of vintage pieces. I hadn't really thought about it, because Autumn always wears stunning jewelry.

When we get to the first gallery, the others go in, but I pull Logan to the side.

"I don't like this," I say. "Did you see the way Gently's cat reacted to Iris? What if she's the one who stole him out of Gently's house?"

Logan says, "You can't arrest someone on the basis of the cat doesn't like them. You saw her back in the shop. She had zero reaction to meeting me. If she's been nurturing a boiling hatred for me, you'd think she'd at least flinch. Or squint. People have tells, and I didn't see any of them."

"That's true," I say softly. Maybe I'm just overreacting, because I've run out of suspects. If Pru didn't do it, and Bea didn't do it, and Iris didn't do it – all I have left is Silas.

I walk into the gallery behind Logan. He heads up to the counter, to stand near Gently and hopefully get information. It feels like too many people may overwhelm the guy they're talking to, so I stay where I am. Bea and Autumn have disappeared. I hear their voices coming from a loft space upstairs.

Iris comes up to me and asks, "Are you okay?"

"I'm fine," I lie. "I just had something in my eye. Logan helped me get it out."

"That's good," she says.

She shadows me as I walk around the gallery. I ask her, "Do you know anything about art?"

"A bit," she says. "You don't grow up a diplomat's daughter without learning an instrument, and to paint, and to ride."

There are some creative pieces in this gallery, with paint layered upon other paint to create 3D ocean effects. And there are realistically rendered images of turtles and octopuses. I like the overall vibe of the space.

"Which one of these is your favorite?" Iris asks.

That's the question everyone seems to ask when it comes to art. "Is there a right answer?" I ask, mostly to myself.

"Not really," Iris says. "Any of these paintings is only worth whatever someone is willing to pay for it. If you like it, and it cost five dollars from some no-name artist, it's worth more than a Rembrandt that you don't actually like." She grimaces. "That's a lesson I had to learn the hard way."

We turn a corner, and I see a wide, panoramic style painting, which basically consists of a beach chair, a palm tree and a fishing boat. But there's something about the use of light, and the playful little details, like the seagull and the hermit crabs in the sand. I could happily step inside that painting. There are a number of pieces on the same wall, obviously by the same artist. It's the same subject matter as a hundred tourist postcards from beaches around the world – turtles and dolphins, beachscapes and ferry boats. But there's something about the style that reaches out to me – and into me.

I say softly, "I think I've found my favorite artist."

"Really?" Iris says. There's something incredulous about the way she says it.

I go closer and read the plaque and I realize why. These paintings are all Mitch's. I get now what Logan said about the way Mitch had rendered Paris in his art – because since moving here, he'd rendered Galveston the same way.

Tears spring to my eyes, though I couldn't say exactly why. There's something about me and Mitch that just matched. And now he's gone – so there won't be any more of this joyful art he has created.

I just stand there, until Iris gives me a hug. "You're going to be okay," she says. "No matter what."

It's a cryptic statement, but all I can do is nod and accept her comfort.

And after a minute, I remember Logan saying Mitch was his favorite painter, too. Does that mean that we have something the same inside us, too?

# Chapter Nineteen

I knock on Silas's door frame, not trusting the flimsy screen door. There's noise inside, and voices coming from the back yard. I look up at Logan, not sure what we should do. I'm also not sure why I didn't tell him about finding Mitch's paintings. Maybe I'm afraid he'll read too much into it. Everything else about the galleries had been a bust. Pru had brought the paintings she meant to deliver to Mitch to one of them instead, and nobody seems willing to say anything else about Mitch or anyone associated with him. Which is weird – considering his paintings are hanging in one of their buildings.

So getting some information from Silas is essential at this point. And his whole family is ignoring us.

We're about to leave when a woman answers the door. She's about Silas's age. She wasn't at the family party Silas had had at NaNa's, so I'm guessing this probably isn't his wife. She peers out at me and Logan. "Can I help you?"

"We're looking for Silas," I say. "Have you seen him?"

"Can't say that I have. What's my miserable brother-in-law been up to this time?"

"Nothing," Logan says quickly. But he clears his throat and steps forward. He doesn't claim to be a cop, but he looks the part and allows her to make her own assumptions. "But it would really help us out of you could tell us where he was Saturday night."

Her eyes widen, like her previous comment had been a joke, and now she's trying to come to grips with the idea that he might actually have been up to something. She stammers, “That’s his night for Toastmasters. Then a big group of them go out to Denny’s and drink coffee until one in the morning. My sister is always telling him it’s bad for his stomach, but at least it gives us time to hang out.” She seems to realize she’s babbling and closes her mouth with a click of her teeth coming together.

Darn. That’s an easily verifiable alibi.

And after we leave her there at the door, it’s easily verified by a phone call to Denny’s, where the waitress specifically remembers Silas, because he always tips five bucks, even though he never orders anything but coffee. We’re still sitting in Logan’s car when Silas crosses the street, coming back from the direction of Wobble House. There’s something in his hair. It looks like cobwebs. He waves at us.

Logan gets out of the car, so I follow. Logan asks, “What have you been up to?”

Silas says, “Taking a walk around the block. I told you, any reason to get out of the house.”

“And the cobwebs?” Logan gestures shaking something out of his own hair.

Silas reaches up and brushes at the cobwebs. “Would you look at that? I did brush up against a low-hanging tree.”

“Right,” Logan says, though it’s obvious he doesn’t believe Silas.

I notice mud on Silas’s shoes. I try to ask him about it, but he keeps walking.

“Well, have a good day,” Silas says. Then he goes into his house.

I follow the tracks of mud back across the street, into the yard of Wobble house. Last night’s heavy rain has left the yard still damp, and there are clear depressions leading towards the side of the house. I say, “I’m not sure what Silas has been up to, but I think he found the hidden side passage Pru was talking about.”

We follow the muddy prints toward the house but they seem to stop at a muddy bare patch nearer to the street than the house. We go up to the house, peering at the foundation, shining the flashlights on our phones at the wall looking for cracks not revealed by afternoon sunlight. There's nothing out of the ordinary.

But we know Silas has gone inside there – probably more than once. Buy why would he do that? I call my dad and ask him, "Is there something about Wobble House itself that is worth something?"

He says, "Hello to you too."

I say, "Sorry. We're outside the place right now, and it seems like someone has been snooping around and may at one point have broken in. I'm trying to figure out what would be worth that."

"Sweetie, that place is full of priceless art. Everything in there would be worth snooping, if you were a thief."

"Exactly," I say. "But this guy is ignoring all that. What else would he be looking for?"

My dad says, "Your guy could be looking for something from before the big hurricane. Eighteenth century china and such can be worth a lot, too. But if it's not money he cares about, it has to be something personal. Could be he has a connection to the house. Or to the murder that happened there in the Roaring Twenties."

I say, "You think Silas has a connection to a hundred-year-old murder? I mean, sure he's old, but not that old."

Dad says, "I don't know. I'm just spit balling possibilities. You asked."

I tell my dad, "Maybe you'd notice something if you were here in person. We're going back through the house in the morning with a couple of police dogs to see what we can find. I can't guarantee it will be safe, but there will be a lot of cops around."

"I'll call Ash." There's the noise of movement on Dad's end of the phone, of his recliner snapping shut as he prepares to take action. "We'll be there first thing."

I hadn't actually meant to invite the blogger, but here we are.

I hang up with my dad, then despite Logan's embargo on phone use, I text Aunt Naomi, *You really want to help out? What can you find out about the murder that happened in Wobble House a century ago.*

She texts back immediately, *On it!*

Then she sends me a picture of Knightley being all cute, nibbling on a flower out of the foraging box. As soon as I make sure there's nothing there identifying the location of Logan's apartment, that one's going on Instagram. Because there's nothing that gets more likes than a cute Knightley pic.

Logan says, "Silas has an alibi, for both the theft of the book and the delivery of the threat to us. So while he was outside at the time of the murder, he couldn't possibly have set the rest of the stuff up. But we know he's doing something weird."

I say, "Pru was inside, but she loved Mitch like a son, and wouldn't have killed him." I can't get it out of my brain. "The only person with no alibi to anything is Iris, but if she has no connection to you or Mitch, then that doesn't matter."

"We have to be missing something." Logan kicks at the wall, but nothing moves. It's just old. And ordinary. Logan makes a frustrated noise. He's running out of time for answers, but I'm not sure where else to look.

We go back to his place. Aunt Naomi is in the kitchen, washing dishes. There's a pot of vegetable soup bubbling on the stove. She looks a little embarrassed as she says, "I got hungry. I hope you don't mind. I raided your fridge for lunch too."

Logan moves over and peers into the pot. "We left you here all day with no phone privileges." He gives her a pointed look, and she looks away. He knows full well she was probably on the phone all day. "What else were you going to do?"

I give Aunt Naomi a recap of our day. As I'm going through it, it feels like there's one thing we missed. I ask Logan why he never got Satchmo to scent on the handkerchief.

Logan looks sheepish and says, “I was thinking at that point that he’d scent straight back to Bea. But after the talking-to she gave me – it didn’t seem appropriate. Speaking of which, I think I should call my dad. Just in case, you know.”

He takes his phone and goes out on the balcony for a long time, and when he comes back in, his eyes are red like he’s been crying.

“Good talk?” I ask.

“Yeah,” he says. “I just wish there was more time.”

There’s a knock on the door, and when I go to answer it, there’s Arlo. He’s holding three bottles of red wine, juggled precariously. He hands one to me and says, “I think we all need a drink.”

“Straight from the bottle?” I quip.

He gives me a, *Really, you think joking’s appropriate* look.

I say, “You’re the one who brought three bottles for four people.”

Arlo says, “I didn’t know Logan’s favorite.” Arlo follows me into the room and puts the bottles on the coffee table. This over-consideration smacks of painful sympathy, like for someone who is really sick and might not make it. I guess that means the police don’t have any more leads on Em’s identity than we do.

Naomi says, “Then we can open one and Logan can save the others for later.”

Logan gives her a grateful smile. I guess he needs a dose of optimism about now.

We open the bottle Logan choses, and Aunt Naomi ladles up everyone some soup. I ask her what she found out about the Roaring Twenties murder.

She takes out her tablet to consult a list of notes and says, “It took a bit of digging, and a call to Drake’s historian friend at the University, but there are a few clear facts. The son of the then-owner of Wobble House was found stabbed to death in the basement bowling alley on April 5, 1922. Young Steven Worhl was just eighteen. They never found the knife, and no one was ever charged. But he had been arrested when he was sixteen, for rum running, and it was assumed that his associates must have had something to do with the death, especially as the neighbor who owned the adjoining property reported seeing six men fleeing the scene."

"What was the neighbor's name?" I ask.

Naomi says, "Vincent Bere."

I give Logan a significant look. "And the current neighbor is Silas Bere. So either he's looking for evidence of rum running . . ."

Logan says, "Or he's looking for that knife."

I think about it for a moment. "On one level it makes sense. If his great grandfather murdered Steven and blamed it on a gang of crooks, it could be alarming to have Mitch suddenly remodeling the house, and unearthing who knows what. But Vincent is probably dead now. So what difference does it make if the murder weapon is found now?"

Arlo says, "That's something you'd have to ask him."

We sit for a moment, all stumped on what else to consider to unmask Em.

"What about the quote?" I finally say. "Is there any clue we're missing there?"

Aunt Naomi says, "It's just Holmes saying, 'I wonder how a battery feels when it pours electricity into a non-conductor?'"

"What are nonconductors?" I ask. I mean, I think I know, but I want to make sure we're on the same page.

Arlo taps his wine glass. "They're substances electricity doesn't travel through well, like glass. Or rubber, or plastic – or my favorite, diamond."

Logan says, "Electricians wear gloves lined with rubber for just that purpose. Because people are actually good conductors. Unfortunately."

Arlo says, "Surely that's not what Em is going for. That would be the most elaborate interpretation of the story."

"But it's the most dramatic one," Logan says.

"Okay," I say. "What about this? What if we confront each of the possible killers, like we've solved this. And we push for them to start monologuing, until the actual killer does?"

Arlo says, "That won't work. You'd have to show at least some evidence you figured out the puzzle to even get Em talking. Plus, people don't really monologue in real life. We need enough evidence to put Em in jail, so you'd have to get a direct confession. Otherwise, Logan is still in danger."

We bat around a few other theories, but nothing concrete gels.

Logan says, "We will just have to hope that we find something when we go back to the house tomorrow. Failing that, I become bait for catching Em, while we're still at the house. Because if I'm protected, and Em wants me, then Em will have to come out in the open to get me."

"Unless it's a long-distance delivery system that we don't see coming," I say morosely.

"That is a possibility we can try to protect against," Logan says. "Just, like I said – don't blame yourself."

Arlo says, "I can get some extra officers to patrol Mitch's house while we're there. Once we're done searching everything, we can get Logan to go out through the side entrance by himself, like he got separated from his detail. But we can have people watching both inside and outside the tunnel. Once we find it."

"You're right," I tell Logan. "Being a bodyguard is a horrible proposition."

I'm a couple of glasses of wine in – enough to take the edge off of my anxiety – when my phone rings. It's Em.

The weird mechanical voice says, "I'm just letting you know – leave Logan alone in the morning. I'd prefer no collateral damage, but I can't guarantee that if I have to pull him away from other people."

I say, "You can't really think any of the people who care about Logan are going to do that. Why would you give me all this warning, challenge me to catch you, and then ask me to get out of the way?"

"You're not in control here. I am." The voice drops low and growly, saying, "Giving you a chance to save Logan is in the spirit of Doyle's story. It's generous, really. Remember the part where there's two pills?"

I quip, "Right? Who knew Doyle was pre-writing the Matrix." This is met with disapproving silence. I guess the killer doesn't have a sense of humor. "Hey, I'm not even that big into movies, and I know that one. One for reality, the other for delusion – and if you think you've been generous, I know which one you took."

The killer asks, "Do you really think you should be toying with me right now?"

"Is anything I say really going to change the plan you already have in mind?" I ask. I've realized that the only way to get ahead of all of this is to stop trying to control what the killer is going to do, worrying about not saying or doing things that would make the killer move up the timetable. That's reactive thinking. Sherlock Holmes certainly never thought that way. He had always put a plan in place that put him in the stronger position. And we have a plan – as shaky as it is. So giving away control is, ironically, the only way to gain the control that matters. I say, "Are you going to miss out on the chance to have your revenge follow the pattern you set, just to spite me?"

Grudgingly, Em admits, "Not really. But Doyle's two pills were different. One poison, one inert. Life and death, as providence, or karma, or just the dance of the spheres in an organized universe. They represented a belief that justice was being done in the guise of revenge, justice that couldn't be attained any other way. And in this case – you know what? Felicity Koerber, you are both pills."

I try to wrap my brain around that. This killer is a person who has no remorse. If I can't stop Em, it becomes a sign that killing Logan – and having already killed Mitch – is the right thing to do. That Em's vengeance burns like clean fire. It's twisted logic that almost makes sense. Except that Logan isn't a bad person, and Mitch had never physically hurt anybody in his life. And chance, in this world, doesn't always favor justice.

Whatever Logan actually did, whether the death was by accident, intent or neglect, the killer is taking it quite personally. It has to be based in grief for either a family member or a lover. I've felt grief that intensely, when I lost my husband – only, I hadn't had anyone to blame. So on an odd level, I can actually empathize with this killer, more than any of the others I've come into contact with. As gently as I can, I ask, "Who was this person to you, the life who was lost? I've lost people too. I understand the pain that goes with it. Sometimes it helps to talk."

"Don't think I'm going to make it that easy," Em says bitterly, then hangs up on me.

I try calling back, but it just rings. And when I try again, the phone is off.

Logan shakes his head. He still wasn't able to trace the call.

After Arlo goes home and Aunt Naomi goes to bed, Logan and I sit on the sofa, watching fluffy Knightley being happy, doing zoomies.

Logan has always said that he had made two great mistakes in his life – the botched operation that had caused him to flee to Europe, and the client he had lost in his subsequent gig as a bodyguard.

"This whole thing about not blaming myself if I can't keep you safe. If you really believe that – you know the situation now is not that different from you and your client. Nobody was responsible for her death, except for the person who pulled the trigger." I put a hand on his arm. "I promise not to blame myself, whatever happens tomorrow, if you promise right now, to forgive yourself for the past."

"I'll try," Logan says. He leans back into the sofa. "You know, it's funny. Em said she was giving me a day to get my house in order. In a way, I've done that today. Emotionally. Financially, it was all already taken care of. So there's no worries of what happens to the shop."

"Don't talk like that," I say. None of this feels right, and none of it is fair. I say, "If Em gave us that much warning, then they must want to be caught, right? Deep down, this killer knows what they're doing is wrong."

"Maybe." Logan reaches down, and Knightley hops over to him. He scratches the bunny's chin. "Or maybe it is a person who can't conceive that they might lose." He moves closer to me, leans against me, almost like last night. He takes my hand in his. "Thank you for being there for me today, trying to figure all of this out. It's been a long time since anyone's looked after me, instead of the other way around."

We sit that way for a long time, and Logan falls asleep with his head on my shoulder – despite what he said yesterday about not being able to trust or relax. I guess I've finally made him feel safe – even if the circumstances would imply that he's anything but. I realize that Logan needs me on a level that Arlo never will. But Arlo is still the safe choice, and the least complicated. It's a decision I shouldn't even be thinking about right now. All that matters is keeping Logan safe.

# Chapter Twenty
## *Tuesday*

The sun is barely up, and here we are, assembled outside the house where Mitch had died. Arlo and the seven officers he'd recruited to come with us are standing in the front yard, facing the street. It doesn't seem like it would be easy to find a hiding space anywhere closer than across the street. Logan is in the middle of the group, but I still don't feel confident about him being here. At least nobody got shot in *The Dying Detective*.

He looks uncomfortable to have so much fuss over him. He has a water bottle in his hand, and he keeps taking nervous sips out of it. He asked me to drive here, because he was too nervous and unfocused, and I realize that without thinking, I've pocketed his keys. We took an obvious route to get here, so Em has to know where we are.

We're waiting for the dogs to arrive before we go into the house, so that our scent doesn't clutter up everything. I'm standing off to the side, waiting for my dad. He and Ash show up together. Dad walks up the sidewalk, holding tightly to one end of a leash. On the other end, there's a dog – I think. From here, it looks like a little cotton ball with legs. It has to be less than a foot tall. True to her word, Mom had sent the foster dog, in case someone should see it and fall in love with it despite its biting and un-home-ability. That seems like a weird thing to do, given the tense situation, but it makes sense if you know my mom.

When Dad gets closer, Logan moves towards the front of group, and the officers move aside as the dog goes straight up to Logan and jumps up against his leg, reaching about knee height. It licks at Logan's jeans, then when he reaches down, it licks at his hand.

I move in closer too and ask Dad, "This is the monster dog?"

Dad says, "I told you, she only bites out of fear. We've really been working on her confidence. She wasn't secure in her last home, and bichon frisés are prone to social anxiety anyway. Her name's Cindy."

"Hi Cindy," Logan says, and Cindy's ears perk up, making her head look less like a round powder puff. He lets her sniff his hand. His expression softens. "I'll take her," Logan says. "If I survive the day, I'll take her home tomorrow. At least for the month, while you need a foster. And we can see how it goes."

I guess he's not worried about Knightley being threatened by this particular dog – even if she does have a history of biting. Cindy is so small, so timid. If the two animals wind up together, Knightley would be more than capable of defending himself.

"We'll all do our best to help make that happen. Won't we Cindy? We like Logan, don't we?" His voice goes up when he's talking to the dog. Her ears perk up again, and she looks between him and Logan, unsure who she wants to lean against. I can see a bit of the anxiety Dad's hinting at. Cindy clings onto Logan. Dad keeps hold of the leash, but offers me a filter mask with his free hand. He says, "Your mom sent this, in case you forgot yours. She's worried about you going into a dangerous situation, but she's even more worried because there's guaranteed to be black mold."

"Yeah," I say. "Mom's always been terrified of that stuff."

Ash says, "That sounds like material for an expose. Or a perspective on you for the podcast. Interviewing your mom would be a trip."

"Please don't," I say.

"Oh, but you know I will," Ash says. "I'm sure the mega murder magnet doesn't fall far from the tree."

I say, "You could be surprised."

Cindy starts barking, then backs around behind Logan, wrapping the leash around Logan's legs. Bea is approaching, with a German Shephard on a leash, and Satchmo heeling leashless beside her.

I hold out my hands towards Satchmo, and Bea releases him. He comes running. Cindy starts whimpering.

"Oh, poor sweetie," Bea says. "We don't mean to scare you." She stops, a fair way away, the big dog at her side looking curiously in our direction, his tail thumping in a friendly wag. Bea gestures towards Satchmo. "You know Sherlock Holmes was compared to a scent dog. And he also sometimes employed a scent dog named Toby. So today, it's only appropriate you get your own four-footed Sherlock."

We wait on the porch, while Arlo unlocks the front door and brings the skein of yarn back into Mitch's study. The German Shepherd scents on it and goes barking through the house. A few minutes later, the dog, Bea and three of the officers come out of the side of the house, through a door that had been disguised as part of the wall. The space is so obvious once it's open – I don't understand the optical illusion that had kept it hidden.

But that's the spot we're planning to send Logan out of, alone and unprotected. I still don't like this plan.

The German Shepherd snuffles around on the grass, picking up scent despite the recent rain, and starts making a slow beeline for Silas's place.

"That's going to take a while," Logan says.

And while the dog has revealed the passage Silas has been using to get in and out of the house, and probably the space where he ran into Pru, that doesn't give us any hints to the identity of the killer. Unless maybe Silas killed Mitch, after all. Maybe he could have used his giant family to commit the other crimes.

Ash says, “Come on, Mr. Marchetti. I want to see this basement.”

Dad picks up Cindy. “If that’s okay?”

Arlo says, “Lead the way. I’d like to get a better understanding of this crime scene.”

I had assumed that Arlo would have gone with the group with the official police dog. But it’s touching that he wants to protect Logan personally.

Dad takes us through the hallway, and into the kitchen, then into the small room off of the main kitchen where Carmen had been making gluten free food on the night of the party. The three officers are sticking to Logan, even inside the house. Dad says, “The flooring in this room is new, but the staircase leading down to the basement is probably still right around here.”

He starts stomping on the floor, until he gets to a spot where the floor sounds hollow beneath his foot. Satchmo is watching the proceedings curiously, especially the enthusiastic reaction Cindy is having to this from her perch in Dad’s arms. She barks every time he stomps.

“I see it,” Arlo says, and reaches down to a nearly invisible gap.

Dad steps back. When Arlo pulls on the gap, the door springs open. It’s obvious that Mitch knew about this place, as the banister on the staircase is brand new, and the steps have been painted, while everything else in the room is musty and damaged.

I put on the filter mask. Mom was right about the mold.

Ash goes down first, taking pictures and video clips with his phone, of the space, and then back up at us. I can just see one of these images becoming the main shot for promoing his podcast. I do not look good in shots taken from below, so it is bound to be hideous. But if anything that happens here today helps save Logan, then that’s a small price to pay.

The original lighting doesn’t seem to work down here, but there are shop lights brought in for the restoration work. Ash switches them on, bathing the room in light, and showing off the two-lane bowling alley in all its ruined majesty. The lanes are warped from repeated water damage. The intricate geometric inlay at the back above the pin deck is mostly intact, though covered in dust.

There are also a couple of octagonal tables roughly in the center of the room – one is on its side – with ruined green fabric tops, and beyond that an elaborate bar that takes up most of the far wall. This space was obviously a Prohibition Era speakeasy – hidden inside a private home. Despite the criminal overtones of that, it must have been a really cool room, when it was in usable condition.

There are paintings on the wall in here too, geometric compositions surrounding women wearing cloche hats and long necklaces. They're tattered beyond restoration.

I find Arlo standing next to me as I stop at the bottom of the stairs. His hand lingers close to mine, brushing at my fingers like he wants to take my hand.

I ask him, "Do you have a favorite painter?"

Arlo says, "Van Gogh. I know that's cliché, but my favorite painting ever is his Café Terrace at Midnight. Someday I'd like to spend some time in France."

I find his answer surprising. Maybe it is unfair, but I tend to think of him as tied to this island. He had wandered for a while and then returned, just like me. I love travel – but Arlo hasn't expressed the same interest. "That is a really nice painting." And it suits his sense of style. I could be at ease in a room centered on its colors.

Dad puts Cindy down, so he can snap a couple of pictures of his own. Cindy suddenly finds herself five feet away from Satchmo, who, to be fair, is minding his own business. Still she lets out a whimper and makes a run for it, straight towards the bowling lanes.

Satchmo decides it is a game, and goes after her. The two dogs go running straight down one of the lanes and disappear from sight past the pin deck.

"Cindy!" Dad shouts, running after her. I follow him. We both bend down towards the opening and try to coax the dogs back, though they have disappeared from sight in the gap behind the pins, where someone might go to do maintenance. There's a door off to the side, which must lead back there. I go through – I can see my dad's feet through the opening in the wall – and find the cotton ball dog cowering down past the second lane, and Satchmo sitting near her.

Between the two lanes, there's a lever set in the wall. "Hey what's this?" I reach out to touch it, and the lever moves more easily than I would have imagined. The space around me starts to shift as the wall with the lever opens up, swinging away from me, and the wall behind the pin deck swings back. Cindy sees a new escape exit, and bolts down the hidden tunnel I've just opened up. I follow her, shouting, "Wait! Cindy!"

I make a lunge for the end of the leash and miss it by inches. As I enter the tunnel, motion activated lights come on. Those don't fit with the 1920's vibe. While the bowling alley had been left more or less untouched, Mitch had remodeled this tunnel. The cement walls are probably old, but they have been sandblasted clean, and some sections of them are a different color – likely due to repair work, since this space must have faced the same repeated flooding and ground shift as the basement. There's a glossy coat on everything, as if Mitch has had it all waterproofed.

I can't catch up with Cindy. I stop trying. But as soon as she realizes she's running into darkness, she returns and huddles against my ankle. I take her leash.

The others have followed me into the tunnel. One of the officers says, "This must have been used by rum runners to supply booze to all the party-goers down here in ye old Free State of Galveston."

Logan says, "Probably. But I think Mitch was using it to transport artworks."

Arlo says, "This is really cool, but I fail to see how this is supposed to help us catch Mitch's killer."

"I'm not really sure," I say. "Since it seems like his killer probably used the side door." Merely saying that sends a spike of dread through me. I really don't like this plan.

But Satchmo is sniffing at the floor, the same way the German Shepherd had been sniffing at the grass outside. And near where he's exploring, I see a reddish-brown stain on the floor. I point this out saying, "Of course, I could be wrong."

Satchmo used to be a cadaver dog, before he retired and started training with Bea to be a therapy dog. I really hope we aren't going to find another body down here. But the trail Satchmo is making, past intermittent red-brown streaks, is unsettling.

We follow Satchmo until he stops outside a small anteroom leading off to the side of the main tunnel. It's a modern-looking space, with glass doors surrounded by seals set into black metal facings, in contrast to the bare cement walls of the tunnel. The glass looks thick, and the seals on it are wide and sturdy.

Arlo moves over and tugs on one of the handles, but the doors are firmly locked.

Logan lets out a long, low whistle. "Whatever's in there is climate controlled. Most people would use a space like that for an expensive wine collection, or for a collection of musical instruments."

I finish the thought. "But Mitch used it to keep the island's humidity from getting to the forged artwork." I know all about island humidity – I had to install a special climate control system in my chocolate shop to keep humidity from destroying the quality of the chocolate produced in my tiny on-site factory. I look through the glass. There's a table, strewn with paints, easily visible. "But this area is prone to flooding, even when there's not a hurricane in the forecast. Most homes on the island don't even have basements."

"For those that do, the flood insurance must be astronomical," Logan says.

"You're not wrong," Arlo says. He takes a closer look at the doors. "With those kind of seals, this chamber is probably watertight. That's a lot of construction for Eberhart to have gotten completed so quickly. And without anyone noticing."

I say, "If this tunnel really is a hold-over from rum running, that room could have been there already, for storing alcohol. And Mitch would just have needed to upgrade the waterproofing."

One of the guys shadowing Logan, Officer Fox says, "Hey. I'm not sure you should be doing that."

I'm startled, thinking he's talking to me, but Logan says, "Doing what?" Though obviously he's tinkering with a keypad set into the tunnel wall.

There's a hissing noise as the doors open.

Logan goes inside, followed closely by Arlo and two of the officers. Satchmo looks up at me.

I say, "Come on, boy," and he follows me in.

Officer Fox says, "I'll wait out here. I'm claustrophobic enough, just being in the tunnel. I don't want to go inside something that can actively seal out the air."

That gives me pause. But I forget my hesitation as soon as I see what's on a workstation farther inside the room. Mitch must have already started work on his chocolate paintings. There's a massive block of chocolate, easily three feet tall and ten inches thick, set up on a worktable. And on it, there's a half-finished portrait of a woman wearing a white chocolate wedding dress. She's posed on a Victorian sofa, her sepia-toned hand reaching for a bouquet of white roses, which are just out of reach, causing her to lean forward in a rather revealing way, given the neckline of the dress. The girl's face isn't finished, just a rough outline, with haunting dark chocolate eyes. And she's holding a white lace handkerchief.

"I recognize that dress," I say.

"From where?" Logan asks.

I say, "Rupert Hertz's Facebook account. That's the dress his fiancé was wearing, in the engagement photos."

Logan asks, "The girl who wouldn't look at the camera?"

I nod, but find myself unable to look away from the image, trying to extrapolate the face from the lines Mitch has painted. "Maybe there was a reason for that. If this is Mitch's killer, then we know she's a gifted thief. If she was also Rupert's fiancé – then she might not want her face all over the Internet."

"Want to catch me up on this one?" Arlo says.

I realize I hadn't bothered to share the information with him, since Rupert was dead, so obviously couldn't be Em. I say, "There was a courier who may have died as fallout from Logan getting Mitch arrested, in Paris. Social media suggested that said courier was engaged at the time, with photos from an engagement party as one of the last things he posted. There wasn't a single photo where his fiancé's face was clearly visible. If she was a thief, marrying someone whose family didn't know he was a criminal, she might have been at the party, keeping up appearances – but not wanted her face on the Internet."

"Detective Romero, look at this." One of the officers, the taller one, is pointing to a much larger red-brown stain on the floor on the other side of the table, where blood had pooled. It's obvious that this is where Mitch was really killed.

Arlo says, "I think we've found our primary crime scene."

There's also a piece of cloth left on the floor under the table, white and shimmery, with embroidery work that is a perfect match for the handkerchief that is still in the trunk of Logan's car. It looks torn, with raw threads all on one edge and specks of red-brown stains. It must be from the bodice of the wedding dress pictures in the chocolate portrait, and Mitch's killer may well have been wearing it while committing the murder.

I think about how Ash had used Autumn's social media to place me at the tea party. Rupert's fiancé might not have wanted her face seen – but how could there have been an engagement party where not a single person had caught her in the background of a photo? What I need to do is check who Rupert followed, and look at their photo albums from that date.

I bet it is going to turn out to be Eunice. How had I not seriously considered her a suspect in all of this? She had been right there in my shop, dropping off the book that had launched all of this. And she is a single mom, who might well have seen marriage as a way out of a precarious financial situation. Already frazzled and overworked, I can see how she might have just snapped.

Only, when I check my phone, there's no Wi-Fi here in the tunnel. I tell Arlo, "I'm going to head towards the end of the tunnel, to see if I can get a signal."

Satchmo pads along beside me, heeling without being told. For once, I'm glad the beagle couldn't control his impulsive nature when it comes to playing with other animals. Otherwise, we never would have discovered this space, which is the key to Mitch's murder. Em obviously didn't think we'd find it. Otherwise the killer would have spent yesterday destroying the chocolate slab instead of attempting to follow me and Logan. Em must plan to come back later, to remove the evidence, once the rest of the plan is complete. Which is careless, again. Em seems to be both extremely intelligent and extremely sloppy.

As I get closer to the end of the tunnel, I can see tilted doors in the distance. This part of the tunnel isn't completely repaired yet, and there are thick lines of orange paint marking gaps in the wall where sections need to be replaced, or gaps filled in and then waterproofed over.

In one of those sections, I find a knife, stabbed into the tunnel wall. The workers obviously realized it was there. Someone painted an orange circle around it. But nobody bothered to remove it. Obviously, it doesn't match Mitch's wounds – since he actually was killed with at least one of the two knitting needles. Aunt Naomi had said that the weapon used to stab Steven Whorl in the murder in this house had never been found. And this tarnished silver knife could well be what everyone had looked for and never found.

I pull it out of the wall and examine the blade, which is relatively shiny compared with the handle, which is adorned with a simple floral pattern.

There's a soft sound from behind me, and then doors whooshing shut. When I turn, there's a masked figure in the hallway, while all of my friends – including the claustrophobic officer – are banging on the other side of the doors, sealed into a watertight space that I can only hope keeps pumping air. I guess the sound must have been this guy shoving the officer into the room before closing the doors on him. He's wearing a ski mask – which nobody ever has a legitimate reason to do in Texas.

He walks towards me and says, "I should thank you for finally finding the entrance to this place."

I recognize the voice, and the glinting blue eyes. I cannot believe that this is Em, after all. What about the bridal dress and the bloodstains? Another red herring?

"Silas," I say, sounding brave despite my fear. "Who do you think the mask is fooling?"

"Hopefully all of them," he says, gesturing towards the glassed-in folks behind us. "Then we can just handle this without anybody getting arrested, if you're willing to cooperate. How much to hand over the knife?"

It takes my brain a second to process that. "Wait. You're not here to kill Logan? And the rest of us as witnesses?"

Silas looks at me like I'm crazy. "Why would I want to do that?"

"You're not Em?" I prompt.

"Who's Em?" Silas asks. "I just want what really belongs to me anyway, then I'll be on my way."

"So you didn't kill Mitch?" I verify. "You're just here because of your great grandfather or whatever? Why is it so important now?"

Silas looks at me like I've lost a few marbles. Really. When he's the one shambling around in tunnels wearing ski masks. "I don't have time to tell you stories," he says as he comes up to me and tries to grab the knife.

"Stay back!" I say, doing my best not to let go of the weapon. Satchmo's growling.

Silas cries out. He's got a pretty deep cut on his shoulder from where he misjudged leaning in while trying to take the blade. His hand goes to the wound. My first instinct is to help him. I drop the knife and grab the ski mask off his head, using it to staunch the bleeding.

Satchmo looks confused. His tail is still down in attack-at-any-minute mode, but he sees me trying to help the person who was trying to hurt me, so his head is cocked to the side as he tries to decide if it is safe to stand down.

"It's okay, little guy," I tell him. Then I turn to Silas. "You want to tell me how this doesn't relate to Mitch?"

"It does, in a way," Silas says, in a pained voice. "That knife was supposed to stay buried forever, but once I heard that Mitch was remodeling this place, I knew I had a limited time to find it. But I swear I did not kill him over it."

"But why would it be so important, after all this time? That is the murder weapon from the 1920s killing, right?"

Silas takes the knife's sheath out of his pocket and says, "My great grandfather lost the plot of land that has become that whole next block of houses to Steven Whorl in an illegal poker game going on in that room, right back there. He then killed Steven and blamed the rest of the guys who had been involved in the poker game to avoid having to hand over the deed. Later, he sold off most of the land for a mint. The family legend is that my great grandpa filed a patent that revolutionized cars and made a ton of money. The patent part is true, but it didn't make much cash. It was just a way to explain where the sudden influx of money came from. I don't want my family to know that their whole fortune is based on a lie."

"How do you know about it, then?"

"Because my grandfather told me, shortly before he passed. For some reason, he decided I was the one in the family who should carry the history – good and bad." Silas looks down at the ski mask, appraising the wound. "I really think I should go to the hospital now, get some stitches."

"I'm not going to stop you. But you probably don't want to show up carrying a century old murder weapon."

"Good point," Silas says. He hands me the knife sheath. "Consider not telling the cops? And maybe giving me the knife later?"

"I'll think about it," I say. After all the craziness that's happened in the past few days, I need a moment to think about the implications. I really don't want Silas to miss his grandbaby's arrival because he might be in jail for pushing a police officer. But is it justice to keep a murder – even an old one – from coming to light?

I sheath the knife and put it in my pocket. Silas makes his way out of the double doors at the end of the tunnel. Hopefully it won't be too much trouble for him to get help.

I go back and try to release my friends from the enclosed room.

Only – Logan isn't there.

## Chapter Twenty-One

Through the glass, Arlo gestures up the hall, back towards the basement. Logan and the two officers who had still been shadowing him must have gone back for some reason, before Silas showed up.

I run back up the stairs and find the two officers standing in the hall, outside a door.

One of them sees the panicked look on my face and says, "Don't worry. Restroom break."

I try to calm my pounding pulse. It's a reasonable explanation. But I have to be sure no one is taking advantage of our group being split like this. Especially if Logan is alone – even in the bathroom.

I knock on the door. "Logan, you okay?"

There's no answer. I knock louder. When there's still no answer, the officers look alarmed. We all know that someone has threatened to kill Logan today. The two officers look at each other, then the taller of the two shoulders the door open. The bathroom is empty, a window open, and curtains fluttering in the breeze. We're on the ground floor. The window barely looks big enough for Logan to fit through, but Em must have managed it, somehow.

The shorter officer pulls a walkie-talkie off his belt and starts saying things into it with code numbers and urgent phrases. After a few moments, I hear the German Shepherd barking outside.

I explain about the locked doors to the officers, and they both race back down into the basement to make sure everyone still has air. Satchmo takes off after them, sensing the urgency.

I don't waste time joining the group outside in searching for Logan, or downstairs in trying to free Arlo, my dad and Ash. I have to trust the people already working on that. And I have to trust Em's word about not wanting collateral damage, that the others will be safe, if I just focus on Logan.

I have to let all of it go – to fight my desperate need to cling onto control and manage everything – and focus on just one thing. Searching Rupert's follows to find Em's identity.

Someone shouts up the stairs that the air is still flowing to the room in the tunnel, and tension goes out of me so hard I find myself on the verge of tears.

It takes exactly eight minutes of searching – I can't stop myself from repeatedly checking the time – but I finally find a photo posted by Rupert's cousin Jillian. And you can clearly see the face of Rupert's bride-to-be. It isn't Eunice. It's Iris.

I had *known* there was something suspicious about her, but I'd kept discounting it because part of me just couldn't believe she was smart enough to be Em. The way she talked, the way she seemed so scattered, the desperation of following a guy and starting a double life. I'd kept forgetting the fact that she's a diplomat's daughter, trained for public speaking. And that her bio had said that as a child, she found solace from a difficult life in books and gymnastics. Which would make for an excellent background for a thief. Which would make her likely to have connections to a forger.

Slowly, it dawns on me that the guy she'd followed here had been Mitch. Of course it hadn't worked out. Whatever she had planned to get from confronting him over Rupert's death hadn't been forthcoming, no matter how long she'd waited, and so she'd stabbed him. She must have talked him into doing a chocolate portrait of her, claiming it was for an upcoming wedding – asking him to paint her wearing the dress purchased for a wedding that never was. I'm guessing Mitch didn't even recognize her, despite her sitting for him however many times it had taken to make progress on the portrait. And that had lit the candle on her slow burn towards revenge.

Once I realize how Iris fits into this, the other puzzle pieces start falling into place around her. If she's that good of a thief, and she knows her way around a kitchen, she could have blended in with the wait staff and brought the threatening tray in through the kitchen. I've seen Enrique's pop-ups. He does the whole white-shirt and black slacks combo for his staff too, to add elegance to his parties on the sand. So Iris would have had the clothes.

And speaking of clothes – if she left after killing Mitch while she was wearing something that would have let her pass as a guest at Silas's party, she must have done something with the rest of the wedding dress. The police hadn't found it. Maybe she burned it. I think satin dresses can be made of nylon blends. It would explain the weird smell and unusual ash in the fireplace in Mitch's study.

I want to turn to Logan and gloat that my vibe about Iris was actually right. Only – he's not here. And he might never be here again if I can't figure out what to do.

My phone dings with a voice message that must have come in while I was underground and without signal. I don't know why there's a delay – but this is a horrible time for it.

The message is from Em. I can almost hear Iris's voice underneath the mechanical adaptation. "I'm starting the countdown now, Felicity. I was going to say half an hour, but I can see that you're a little busy with an unexpected friend so I'll give you an extra twenty minutes. But I'm sure Logan will spend the whole time he has left watching the clock."

As I take in this threat, Adrenaline courses through me, leaving me shaking and scrambling to focus my thoughts. It's a handicap I can't afford right now.

Where would Iris have taken Logan? And will it be too late when I get there? I try to think what clocks are important to

Galveston. There is a small clock tower on the A&M campus. But that's assuming Iris would even know it's there.

She could mean time in a metaphorical sense. But I don't know how to use that to narrow things down.

Satchmo whines at my side. I'd been so much in panic mode that I hadn't even realized he'd followed me up here. But he's a therapy dog, so he probably realizes my threat response system has gone into overdrive, and my blood pressure just spiked. I lean down to pet him with a still trembling hand, and it forces me to take a breath, a moment to clear my head so I can think.

I know who Iris is and what happened to her. Maybe that's enough.

I call the number I've saved for the killer. And the mechanical voice answers. Despite the distortion, I still hear a note of gloating in the opening words. "Felicity. Bargaining for more time?"

"Hello, Iris," I say, as calmly as I can. "I want to give you many condolences for the loss of your fiancé. I mean that. Sincerely."

There's a long silence, during which Iris drops the voice changer and answers as herself. "Thank you, Felicity."

I say, "I figured out the who and the why. Done the detective's motive, means and opportunity. Isn't that enough? Please. Let Logan live."

"I'm sorry," Iris says. "The rules are that you have to stop me. Not just identify me. Sherlock knew who Moriarty was well before he could do anything about it. It's only fair."

"At least let me talk to him. A little reward for having figured out the clues."

Another silence, during which she seems to be considering it. "Fine."

I hear her moving, hear the rattle of metal on metal and Logan says something.

Iris tells him, "If you try to tell her where you are, I will shoot you now and be done with it. Understood?"

Logan comes on the line. "Hi, Fee."

"Hey yourself," I say, like this is a normal conversation. "It sounds like all you can give me is proof of life."

"Well, I can tell you that you have the key to my heart. I had hoped I'd be able to fall asleep again like I did last night, right next to you. Of course, when I woke up, you'd gone in the other room. But it was still the best sleep I've had in a long time."

"I think I understand," I say. I hope I'm not reading too much into what he's saying, because even though what he's saying is literally true – he has to be referring to the key to the annex, right? He'd almost given it to me at the restaurant, but he'd decided to keep it, representing his goal of unlocking my heart. Which is a flip from what he's just said, but close enough. And being right next to him – he has to be talking about me holding the lease on the space next door. "I'm glad you finally found a bit of peace. I'm going to do my best to make sure it's not too much peace, though, okay?"

"Much appreciated," he says.

In the background, I hear Iris say, "Enough. Just say I love you and hang up."

Logan's voice breaks when he says, "I love you."

I manage to say, "I love you too," before the phone connection goes silent.

Where could Iris have taken Logan in the time since she'd left here, and then called me? And also gotten Logan secured wherever she's holding him? The background noise in both calls had been the same. So it has to be close. Which means I'm probably right about the shop. Though I have no idea what the metal-on-metal sound was.

I have Logan's keys, which means I have both his car and his go bag. I have no idea what all is in there, but something is bound to be useful. I call Bea as I head for the front of the house and then the spot on the street where we parked, telling her where

I'm going. This gives me a head start, since it's a lot more likely that Logan will be coming out alive if I show up on my own.

I open the trunk and grab the backpack that serves as Logan's go bag. I place it on the front seat next to me and, even though I am normally a rule follower to the extreme, I run a couple of stop signs on the way back to Greetings and Felicitations. I park a block down and a block over.

The first useful thing I find in Logan's bag is a pair of binoculars. I use it to peer through the annex window while standing in the alley that runs behind the opposite set of buildings. Unfortunately, Gently's tarps are still up, so all I can see is the table where he had been painting me. The chair I had been sitting in is gone. It had been wrought iron, with decorative threads of copper making a floral pattern over the entire surface. Could that chair be part of the metal on metal that I had heard?

I have a horrible feeling that Logan was right. Her comments about conductors, and the sound of metal – she's thinking electrocution. Which means the most effective thing I can do is shut off the power. In my side of the building, the electric box is in the chocolate finishing room, and as far as I can tell from the wires I've seen in the alley I walk down every day, my shop is the main point where power comes into the whole strip of stores. If I'm lucky, flipping the master switch on my box will shut down power to everyone.

I dig through Logan's bag and grab a can of mace and slip it into my pocket. I grab some zip ties – in case I can manage to subdue Iris. I take the duct tape – not sure why, just in case – and drape it over my wrist. I can't see a use for any of the camping gear, and I am highly opposed to weapons, so I leave it at that, lock up the car and go. I walk the long way around the block to the back of the buildings. There are no windows on the alley side of either Greetings and Felicitations or the annex, so Iris shouldn't be able to see me. I use my key to unlock the door to the kitchen at Felicitations, and I quietly slip inside. Without turning on the lights, I go through to the chocolate finishing room.

I'm roughly ten feet away from that beautiful electrical box, a spot of white contrasting the blues and golds of the mural, even in the near darkness. The room is lit only by the slivers of light coming in the cracks from the door where we take deliveries.

I take a moment, fumbling to turn on the flashlight on my phone. I'm a lot shakier than I realized, so it's hard to get the screen to cooperate. I hear a sigh in the darkness and freeze.

"Hello, Felicity," Iris says, just as I get the flashlight working, and the light illuminates her face – and the barrel of a gun pointed in my direction. She gestures with her chin in the general direction of the annex. "Why don't you come over where the lights are on? I didn't want you here – but you just couldn't stay away, could you?"

The gun she is holding is Logan's. Live by the gun, die by the gun indeed.

We walk through the bean room, with its rich scents of recently roasted cacao. It's one of my favorite places in the world, and here I am at one of the worst moments of my life. I look for some way to escape, but there's no getting around that gun.

We make it the entrance to the annex, and Iris gestures me through the plastic sheeting, then stops me before I can go very far into the room. I'm not sure what Iris has been doing in here, but there's dust in the air, along with a haze like smoke. Immediately, I feel a cough coming on. I turn towards the table where Gently had left his materials. I had dropped my filter mask there too, earlier on my way out of the room, intending to clean everything up when I got back. Thankfully, I had been so flustered over everything going on that I completely forgot.

Iris watches closely as I pick up the mask and put it on. The thick fabric makes it both easier and harder to breathe. I take in the room.

Logan is sitting in the middle of it, cuffed to a chair and that chair is sitting on something metal. It takes me a second to figure out that Iris has taken down that stupid rusted bedspring light fixture – with all its exposed wires – and just set it on the floor.

Logan looks calmer than you would expect for a man in his predicament. He says, “Fee, I had hoped you’d bring reinforcements.”

“That didn’t seem like a good idea for negotiations,” I say. Though I can’t help but second-guess my decision to come inside on my own. Was that bad tactics?

“There’s not a lot of time for negotiating,” Logan says, gesturing towards a pool timer that has been attached to one of the cubicles. As it ticks, a lever attached to it moves a plastic tub full of water infinitesimally closer to tipping over. It had taken me a while to get her message, to get my clue, then time to get over here, and to carefully sneak around the building. From the way everything is labeled, it looks like Logan only has eight minutes left. Which hardly seems fair.

## Chapter Twenty-Two

I stare at that tub of water, feeling unrelenting dread. I tell Iris, "You're going to burn the whole place down."

"Maybe," Iris says. "I already burned my wedding dress. Which I never really got to wear."

I just knew that's what had wound up in the fireplace. I feel a moment of vindication that my guess had been correct. Of course, I guess she doesn't count wearing it to pose for the portrait. Or wearing it while killing Mitch. I say, "You said you wanted to avoid collateral damage. This shop is my dream, and not only do you want to take Logan from me, you want to take my livelihood as well."

"Your insurance will cover it," Iris says. "You'll be fine."

I give her an incredulous look. "Do you have any idea how many small businesses go under when they're shut down for just a short time? Insurance processing takes a while, you know."

"Is that really important?" Logan asks.

"Stay out of this," Iris snaps at him.

"I have to know," I ask Iris. "I put together most of what happened to Mitch. Pru vacuuming things up, while Silas peered in the windows and you made your way to the car with that copy of the Scream – that you wound up having to leave behind after your stop in at Silas's party. But what was that scraping sound?"

Iris grimaces. "Gently's cat just would not stay put. After I tossed it out of the study twice, I wound up chasing it around the house and sticking it in the pantry. Boy, was it angry about it. I hadn't counted on what cat claws could sound like against tin louvers, as echoed through the duct system. It scared *me*, and I was already heading out the back door." She leans closer to me, still holding the gun on me. "Anything else you want to know?"

She's willing to talk – because every exchange we have is that that much longer for the water to tip towards Logan. She's keeping me over here by the doorway, out of the splash zone. Maybe she really does intend to let me walk out of here, while she disappears into another new identity. I don't know how I feel about that.

I say, "When you hugged me yesterday – you were telling me that even if you kill Logan, I'm going to be okay without him. You were trying to make yourself feel better."

"No," Iris protests. "That hug was for you. I meant it. You will be okay."

"Really?" I try to process her sincerity. "Wait. That's why you called last night. You wanted to warn me and my friends away because you had a good time wandering the galleries with us, and you didn't want to see us hurt. You weren't just being fickle. You liked us. And so you felt bad that by challenging me you'd put me in danger."

"Am I that transparent?" Iris asks.

"I'm afraid so." I try to figure out a way past her. I don't think I can outrun her gun to get back to the power box in my building. So I guess what I need is to get to Logan. If I can get her talking, maybe I can distract her. I say, "I guess you knew Pru when you worked for Mitch."

Iris smirks. "Hardly. I never met any of his forgers. I would fake the theft of a painting, and they would sell multiple copies of it. No need for contact. I introduced Rupert to some influential people, to get him the courier job. That put him in touch with Mitch. Otherwise, there's no need for a thief and a courier to meet, either."

"Not just meet, but fall in love. Only to have that love taken away because Mitch didn't deliver what he promised before he got arrested. I get why you're angry."

Iris winces. “Do you know what happens to couriers when people think they’ve stolen the merchandise?”

I take advantage of her moment of emotion to try and sidle around her, but she recovers and the gun is even more solidly in my face.

“Don’t even try it.” She gestures me back closer to the doorway. “I will kill you if I have to.”

I swallow back dry fear and clear my throat. I keep her talking while I try to think. She wants me to know and appreciate her plan. “So how did you get all the cooks sick?” I ask. “I can understand the one caterer, but all of Enrique’s freelancers?”

“It was simple.” She grins. The planning is obviously the part of this she actually likes. “I stole Enrique’s list and sent them all free tickets to a late-night food festival. Which happened to have a not-so-accidental outbreak.”

“You’ve put a lot of work into this plan” I say. “But why now?” I genuinely want to understand. “After eight years, why go halfway across the world to track these two men down and kill them?”

“Because they haven’t stopped,” Iris says plaintively. “They got my Rupert killed, and they split up, and I thought that was the end of it. Mitch at least went to jail. But something didn’t add up, when I found out Mitch was in Texas. He shouldn’t have gotten out of jail after just a few years, unless his initial arrest was a scam. And then a few weeks ago, I stumbled across Ash’s podcast and realized that Logan – the guy who claimed to be working with the cops – was right here too. It couldn’t be a coincidence. My fiancé died, but the men responsible were just going to start over, like nothing happened, after walking away with who knows how much art that was supposedly seized by the police.

Logan rattles at his cuffs. He says, “It wasn’t a coincidence. Mitch followed me here. He was angry at me, too, for getting him sent to jail. I got a letter after he died, where he challenged me. You actually saved me from him.”

Lot of good that does him, if she just kills him now.

"Liar!" Iris practically spits the word in his direction, though she doesn't break eye contact with me. Nor does the gun waver.

Logan says, "For what it's worth, I'm sorry about Rupert. He was probably the nicest guy connected to the whole mess. I didn't know who his buyer was, or that they'd kill him over showing up empty handed."

"You're lying again," Iris says.

"Why would I lie?" Logan insists. "It doesn't change what happened. It probably doesn't even change how badly you want me dead. I could have called in favors and gotten Rupert police protection, but I didn't. Because I didn't even think about what might happen to him. For that, I'm deeply sorry."

A single tear slips down Iris's cheek. "You think I don't blame myself a little too? Rupert was an electronics salesman before he got involved with me. He never would have been a courier, if I hadn't been a thief. That's why I had to do all this – to show my own remorse by the extremes I'd go to set the moral balance right. That's why I took *The Scream.* It seemed appropriate that the scream of the eternal void was the first thing I saw after stabbing Mitch. It seemed like everything was falling together perfectly, poetically. She turns her attention back to me. "That's why I can't let you stop this now. The plan is too perfect."

I say, "You've already changed something, though, didn't you? Because me loving Logan makes things less than perfect. The second death in *A Study in Scarlet* was supposed to be by poison. But when I pushed for a real chance to save him, you came up with all of this, on the spot. The switch to another Holmes story – that was your attempt to give me a fighting chance. I don't think you really want to do this."

"I still have to," Iris says.

I can't get past her, and there's no way to make it to that electrical box. So what's in the doorway that I can use? There's the table, the shards of chocolate, a few paintbrushes. I still have the mace, and the knife. There's an outlet at waist height, with no faceplate, obviously something that the former tenant had installed. There a light fixture attached to the wall above it, with exposed wires leading from the gap surrounding the outlet.

A desperate plan comes into my mind. It has to do with what Gently said about plugging in a microwave. Which I don't happen to have. I do still have the knife I'd found in the tunnel, though.

I look over at Logan's clock. It's already down to three minutes. And who knows if that bucket will tip exactly when expected.

I tell Iris, "Nothing's perfect. It can't be. You can change the plan. All this modeling things off Sherlock Holmes – even the stories Doyle wrote had inconsistencies. Watson's war wound seemed to travel between his leg and his shoulder. And Moriarty had two different first names. And potentially either one or two brothers who also had the same name. People were able to overlook a few inconsistencies and enjoy the stories just because they were entertaining."

"Those were different times," Iris snaps. And I get the idea she would have preferred to live in those times. Or at least live out of the spotlight.

I start coughing. I'm not faking it. I've done too much running, inhaled a bit too much mold and smoke and whatever the weird smell is in the air. My inhaler is in my purse – in the car.

"Fee," Logan says. "I'm out of time. Do something. Please."

Ignoring him, Iris leans towards me, looking concerned. "Your inhaler?"

I act like I'm pulling an inhaler out of my pocket, but instead I pull out the mace and spray her in the face, knocking her aim with the gun away from me as I turn and take that silver knife out of my pocket. She cries out, and as much as she can see, I think she believes I'm going to attack her. But I'm not about to give into committing violence. Even if I did, that wouldn't help Logan.

I do throw the roll of duct tape at her to keep her off balance, while I unsheathe the knife.

I grab one of the silicon molds and wrap it around the handle of the knife, hoping beyond hope that this is going to work. Silicone is related to glass, right? Which means it should be a nonconductor. The exposed wires sticking out of the back of the plug is a perfect place to cause the circuit to blow. So I keep a tight grip on the silicon as I jam the knife in the exposed wires.

I jump away as sparks fly, and there are two pops, then the building is bathed in darkness.

Moments after that I hear the sound of water hitting the floor and splashing across it.

Logan cries out with fear. It doesn't sound like with pain. There should have been almost two minutes left on his clock, so I'd cut it closer than I realized.

Iris, on the other hand, is not only hurting, but she's still waving the gun, in the dark while she can't really see.

There's movement behind me as Arlo rushes in from the book nook of my shop, with the officers who had been with him at Wobble House. Obviously, they had been waiting for a moment where rushing in wouldn't get anyone shot.

One of the officers manages to grab the gun from Iris, while another grabs her hands and cuffs her.

Logan calls out, "She has the key to these cuffs in her pocket."

The key is quickly produced, and soon, Logan is over here with me, out of danger.

It takes mere minutes for them to read Iris her rights and then march her away. But it feels like much longer than that, because I'm in the middle of an asthma attack.

"Your inhaler," Logan says. When I tell him it's in his car – and give directions to where I've parked – he holds out his hand for the keys, then sprints off to retrieve it, despite the ordeal he's just undergone.

Arlo stays with me, taking my hand in his, trying to help me stay calm. He helps me go into the kitchen in the Felicitations side, so I can take off my mask and try to breathe better near the open back door. Somehow, he's gotten me a bottle of water, which he opens one handed then gives to me to sip. Between that and him modeling slow, deep box breathing, I've recovered a little by the time Logan gets back with my inhaler. I take it gratefully, though I resent the fact that I still need it in my life, when I keep thinking I'm cured. I mean, I've been able to do more and more physically as time has gone on since the treatments. So hopefully this won't happen again.

When I'm feeling a bit calmer, I ask Logan, "How did Iris get you in here, anyway? You're twice her size. And you're usually aware of your surroundings."

Logan scowls. "She drugged me. She bragged about it on the way here. A diuretic to make me have to pee, and something else to make me groggy and compliant. Which means she could have poisoned me, if she had wanted to. And then she would have won."

"I'm glad she didn't," I say, trying to lighten the mood. "I would have missed you."

I don't remind him that it was supposed to be poison, if Iris had been following the original script from *A Study in Scarlet*. My being there with him really had saved his life.

Logan gives me a wan smile. "What I'm saying is there's something at least noble about her playing by her own rules, and giving you an honest chance to save me. And I can understand her being driven by love and grief – I get that so much more than the motives of the other killers we've dealt with."

"I do too," I say softly. Logan and I have both lost people we loved. And there is a point in there somewhere where grief becomes anger. I don't like to think about it, but I had felt it.

Logan says, "If I can, I'll try to testify at her trial, shed some light on the extenuating circumstances. Maybe they'll show her some mercy."

"You'd do that?" Arlo asks. "Right after she tried to kill you? You know that wasn't a bluff, right, and that a few more seconds and you'd have been electrocuted?"

Logan looks back towards the annex, where that rusted bedspring is still on the floor. "Well, maybe not right after. Trials take a while, you know?" He mock-scowls at Arlo. "You could have done something too. How long were you out there, waiting for the right moment?"

"A while," Arlo admits. "Almost too long. I don't know if I would have been able to live with myself if Felicity hadn't been able to save you."

"But you didn't want to get anyone else hurt. Not your men and especially not Felicity. I get it." Logan claps a hand on Arlo's shoulder. "It was the right call."

Ironically, I think Logan is more okay right now than he's been since I met him. Which makes this a win, even if the floor in the other room is a total loss, and we're going to have to shut the whole shop until we can get the lights back on safely.

## Epilogue

It's taken a few weeks to get things finished in the expansion, and we're finally up to code to let people into it. So far, the opportunities for customers to watch each stage of chocolate making through the glass has been limited to once a week – when we have enough staff to show someone working on each stage. I just finished roasting a batch of beans, to a smattering of applause. I come out from behind the glass partition to greet the couples who just finished the tour – my mom and dad and Ben and Pru.

Mom wraps me in a hug. "I am so proud of you, honey. This place has come together beautifully."

"In part thanks to y'all," I say. I point at the chocolate fountain my dad designed and Logan's crew quick-built, according to Dad's specifications. It features white and dark chocolate, flowing through tubes that have been divided to create a striped effect, then breaking off to move through a series of mini-pools. You wouldn't want to eat that chocolate – there's additives to keep it from clumping – but it may be the coolest thing my dad has ever built.

I think my mom may be grudgingly proud of the fact that I saved Logan's life here not so long ago, but she still refuses to talk about it. And I'm okay with that.

Logan is standing at the next station, ready to show off cracking the beans into nibs and winnowing the shells away. He waves. He's had a hand in planning today too. He couldn't bring his dog into the chocolate processing area, but he knew my dad wanted to see her before leaving for Europe, so he's got Cindy crated in the classroom. He also pulled a table outside, so Dad can sit with Cindy and enjoy Carmen's newest cake recipe, while Cindy gets a cup of whipped cream. And then we're all going over to visit my grandmother, along with Aunt Naomi, for a family dinner.

While we watch Logan work, Mom asks Pru, "Are you keeping the house?"

It's common knowledge now that Pru and Ben are going to inherit it.

"I think so," Pru says. "This area has a vibrant art scene, and Wobble House has that beautiful gallery space. I'm thinking of retiring completely, and just opening the space for tours on the weekends."

Mom blinks. "I thought you were already retired."

Pru and I share a look and I almost bust out laughing. I'm not planning to tell anyone she's an art forger. Changing the subject, Pru says, "At least we've gotten to be on better terms with Silas."

I still can't believe he managed to convince them at the hospital that he was involved in a freak lawn mower accident. I'm pretty sure Arlo figured out Silas was the one who locked everyone in that room in the tunnel, but as he's a homicide detective, and nobody got hurt, he decided not to pursue it. Silas got to be at the hospital for his daughter's baby, and his mood has greatly improved since. He's become a regular at the shop, trying everything one item at a time, and chatting with me about the flavor notes, one foodie to another. A few days ago, I finally gave him back the knife. Maybe someday he will use it to tell the truth. Who knows?

Enrique is here today, since Carmen promised him samples for desserts she'd like us to offer for his next pop-up. Ash is chatting with them. He's probably here for samples, too, though he's photographing everything, like he's really working.

Carmen is wearing a polka dotted dress today – a departure from her usual jeans. She has her hair down too and is wearing a significant amount of makeup. I hear Ash ask her, "Why so dressed up? Hoping to make the blog?"

She says, "Actually, I'm about to sit for a portrait. Gently is using me for one of his sample chocolate paintings. I'll be holding the cat. You can stop by the classroom if you want to watch."

We're advertising the class by showing off a completed chocolate portrait of Knightley – always the animal nearest and dearest to my heart – both in a case and on the advertising, but I created a new limited-edition bar in honor of Ruffles. After all, the big tuxedo cat had helped clue me in on Iris being less than trustworthy.

I wave Gently out of the classroom and tell him, "I have something to show you and Ruffles."

Gently picks up the cat and brings him into the area where we just had the tour.

"Everybody," I say. "I want to share something special with you. This is my limited edition white and dark bar, with just a touch of lime. You should all try a sample. Or two."

I hold up a wrapped bar, with Ruffles' picture on the cover. I give it to Gently to unwrap. It has a layer of white chocolate, with a thinner layer of dark poured on top and then delicately feathering, giving an artistic look to the way the two colors are blended. On the back, there's flecks of pink volcanic salt, to balance the sweetness. Gently asks, "How did you know white chocolate was my favorite?"

I actually had no idea about that one. I say, "I took a guess."

Arlo comes in and heads directly over to the sample tray. He seems a little more subdued lately, and I think it is because Autumn's wedding is so soon, and he knows I'm going to have to give him an answer, one way or the other. I'm letting the emotions die down, after the intense experience Logan and I just went through together, before I make any final decisions. But I think, after all of this, I'm finally capable of making important decisions about my life, without freezing up or waffling. Which feels oh so freeing.

Autumn is here with her writers' group. She waves from their usual table back in the main shop, which you can see from the open double-wide doorway of the expansion. I've finally had time to read Autumn's book. Which was awesome, obviously. We've had several conversations about pulling art from life, and how books are somehow personal to the writer, even if writing about people different than themselves. I've never felt so literary. I've also never felt so seen, as the parts of the book Autumn adapted from my life, and the almost-me character's reactions to them, show that Autumn really understands me as a person. The fact that I have so many people here now who really get me makes me so happy today.

I don't even mind the people clustered around the Murder Book case in the other room, some of whom have been here before, back to get a glance at the newest addition. After all, Drake convinced the library to let me keep the copy of *A Study in Scarlet*.

Logan finishes his part of the demo and heads over to the front of the annex, peering out of the window, onto the street, where there's a big sculpture of a sea turtle, part of a town-wide art exhibit. I catch Logan playing with that stabbed heart charm again, worrying it between his fingers. I walk over and ask him, "Are you really okay?"

"I think so." He looks down at the charm and takes the cover off the chocolate fountain. "Do you mind?" When I gesture that it's okay, he throws it the charm into the churning chocolate, where it whirls its way through the tubes and presumably settles at the bottom. "Whoever said revenge is sweet obviously didn't know what they were talking about."

I study the expanded store. It feels like I've expanded my life at the same time. It's going to be impossible to encompass all of this in one selfie. So I step to the corner by the shop window and I focus the camera on me, next to the reproduction of The Girl with the Pearl Earring that now hangs on the wall above the coffee station, getting the counter and as many of the people here as possible in the pic. And you can just see the corner of one of Mitch's paintings, there in the expansion, bringing life and light to the space. The picture is a bit chaotic, but that doesn't mean it's not perfect, because after all, good art is whatever you like.

# AUTHOR NOTES

While Wobble House is entirely fictional, there are nods to several actual historic homes on Galveston Island. If you are ever on Galveston, I encourage you to take the time to visit them and learn a bit about the island's history.

# ACKNOWLEDGEMENTS

Special thanks to Jael Rattigan of French Broad Chocolates in South Carolina, who has consulted extensively on this series. And to Sander Wolf of DallasChocolate.org, who put me in touch with so many experts in the chocolate field.

I'd also like to thank Bud Humble and the Writers in the Field folks, who always put on a great conference. It gave me a chance to ask all of my hands-on questions about horses.

I have to thank Jake, as usual, for reading the manuscript umpteen times, being my biggest fan and cheerleader, and doing all the formatting things to make this thing happen. He always keeps me going, even when things are stressful.

And thanks to my agent, Jennie, for her input on this series, and her encouragement to keep moving forward.

And for this series especially, I'd like to thank my family for giving me a love of the ocean and a curiosity about history. The Cajun side of both mine and Jake's families comes through in Felicity's family in the books. This has given me an excuse to reach out to family members for recipes and inspiration, many of which you can find on the Bean to Bar Bonuses section of my website. Thanks y'all!

Thanks to James and Rachel Knowles for continuing to sharing their knowledge of bunny behavior, despite the loss of the ever-adorable Yuki.

I'd also like to thank Cassie, Monica and Tessa, who are my support network in general. I don't know how I would have gotten through these years of social isolation without you three.

Thank you all, dear readers, for spending time in Felicity's world. I hope you enjoyed getting to know her. Her sixth adventure will be available for you soon.

# Did Felicity's story make you hungry?

Visit the Bean to Bar Mysteries Bonus Recipes page on Amber's website to find out how to make some of the food mentioned in the book.

AMBER ROYER writes the CHOCOVERSE comic telenovela-style foodie-inspired space opera series (available from Angry Robot Books and Golden Tip Press). She is also co-author of the cookbook There are Herbs in My Chocolate, which combines culinary herbs and chocolate in over 60 sweet and savory recipes, and had a long-running column for Dave's Garden, where she covered gardening and crafting. She blogs about creative writing technique and all things chocolate related over at www.amberroyer.com. She also teaches creative writing in person in North Texas for both UT Arlington Continuing Education and Writing Workshops Dallas. If you are very nice to her, she might make you cupcakes.

www.amberroyer.com Instagram: amberroyerauthor

Lightning Source UK Ltd.
Milton Keynes UK
UKHW020756230123
415815UK00015B/573

9 781952 854163